FEARLESS

Visit us at www.boldstrokesbooks.com

By the Author

Venus In Love

In Every Cloud

Stealing Sunshine

Between Sand and Stardust

Fearless

FEARLESS

by

Tina Michele

2019

FEARLESS

ISBN 13: 978-1-63555-495-3

This Trade Paperback Original Is Published By
Bold Strokes Books, Inc.
P.O. Box 249
Valley Falls, NY 12185

First Edition: November 2019

Credits
Editor: Cindy Cresap
Production Design: Susan Ramundo
Cover Design By Tina Michele

Acknowledgments

I wasn't sure I could do it, but thanks to some great friends and all-around amazing people, I did.

Thank you to my fabulous beta readers—Sue, Angela, Gia, Nancy, Teresa, Steph, and Ameliah for your precious time and insight. An extra BIG thanks to Dawn for your invaluable knowledge and connections in absolutely everything SCUBA! All my love to my little sister, Jennifer, for *suffering* through countless trips to see all the fishes.

Thank you to my friend and DC trainer, Katie, who patiently spent nine long hours walking, talking, and swimming me through a day in the life of a marine mammal trainer. And of course to Capricorn, Akai, and all of Pod B for giving me a day I will never forget.

To my editor, Cindy, everything you've taught me has all come together to create this book. You are priceless. Rad, Sandy, thank you for still believing in me.

For anyone battling depression, anxiety, or PTSD, remember that none of us are alone in our fight against mental illness. There is no shame in fear or asking for help. Don't be afraid to start over, try again, push forward, or take a break. Every day is another chance at the life you've always dreamed of. You've got this.

This book couldn't have happened without every single one of you. Thank you for supporting me, believing in me, and getting me through the dark times. You make me FEARLESS!

Dedication

More. Most. Bonanza.

CHAPTER ONE

Jillian Marshall stretched out her body and smiled in pleasurable pain as her bones snapped and crackled from head to toe. She rolled over and waited until the last minute for the alarm clock on her nightstand to catch up to her internal one. It was a rare occasion that the alarm ever went off before she'd woken up, but she didn't dare not set it. After eighteen years of the same routine, her body ran on its own, and she couldn't change it even if she'd wanted to. And why would she want to?

Jillian was doing what she loved every single day of her life, and there wasn't a reason on earth that would change that. At four thirty a.m., her alarm rang out, the exact moment her coffee maker began to brew her favorite morning blend. As the scent of freshly brewing coffee made its way to her, she got in one more perfect stretch and tossed back the covers. She swung her legs out of bed onto the cool, hardwood floor and padded off to the bathroom grabbing her swimsuit from the drawer on the way.

Jillian pulled her work shirt over her head and tucked it loosely into her shorts. She picked out a pair of socks and grabbed her sneakers on the way out of her bedroom. Once her socks and shoes were on, Jillian was ready for another day. She sat in the quiet of her kitchen sipping her coffee and scrolling through the early morning news on her tablet.

Through the peaceful silence came a shriek that set the hairs of her neck on end. While the sound itself wasn't unusual, the timing most definitely was. She glanced at her watch. Indi, the hyacinth macaw, was a creature of habit just like Jillian, and it wasn't like him to be causing such a ruckus at five in the morning. He was a rigorous keeper of order for himself and his caretakers. The next deafening cry sent chills down Jillian's spine; there was nothing at all normal about that sound.

Jillian jumped up from her seat, toppling the chair over behind her. Within seconds, she'd grabbed her two-way radio and was out the door running toward the aviary. A dense fog hovered in the air and obscured everything mere inches from her nose. The scent of night-blooming jasmine filled the air with a sickening sweetness. It had never been a scent she was fond of.

Indi and his mate, Anna, were now sounding the alarm that cut through the thick air. Their enclosure was a couple hundred yards away, and Jillian was relying on stress, muscle memory, and their cries to guide her. Her heart pounded with each footfall. She could see Indi clinging to the side of the enclosure with his feathers puffed and ruffled in agitation. It took him just a couple of seconds to recognize Jillian as she approached through the haze. She stroked his feathers through the cage and shushed at both of them.

She spoke softly while inspecting the area for any signs of what could have set them off on such an unusual tirade. Any possible threat could have gotten them riled such as a snake or raccoon, and it was at that moment both she and Indi caught a glimpse of what it was. A figure emerged from the fog behind the enclosure, and Indi and Anna once again sounded the alarm. Jillian's breath caught in her throat and her heart stopped in her chest. The blast of screeching from the birds startled not only her, but also the shadowy figure.

In her rush to get to the aviary Jillian hadn't seen anyone lurking in the area, not that she could've seen through such a thick mist. "Hey," Jillian hollered at the figure, half hoping it was just a figment of her imagination. In a flash, they'd taken off down the path, and Jillian instinctively took off after them. "Shit!"

The haze was beginning to rise off the ground, yet it was still almost impossible to see where she was going. The moisture in the air was thick and soaked her hair and face as she ran blindly after the intruder.

Her heart hammered in her chest, and she remembered her radio. Keeping her pace, she called out for Ricardo, or any of the other guards or staff on duty. "Code, uh, shit. Code? What's the code?" Jillian had used the code for trespassers just one other time in all her years at the park. "Screw it," she said before yelling into the radio. "We've got some punk in here headed toward the lagoon. Ricardo? Anybody?"

She refused to think about what could happen if they made it to the lagoons before she could stop them. With no railing, thick fog and water that was more than a hundred feet deep in some places, the results could be tragic. Although, they might choose that fate instead of the one she was going to give when she caught them. Her radio crackled, and Ricardo called back. "Jillian, we're on our way."

She was gaining on them, and now she was close enough to smell the heavy scent of alcohol they were leaving in their wake. When she was within striking distance, Jillian leapt for it. With her arms outstretched, she hit them from behind like a linebacker. The impact sent them both tumbling to the ground. He struggled under her grip, cursing and thrashing against her. She pressed her weight into him and mashed his face into the concrete path. He jerked against her like a wild bronco in an attempt to buck her off, but she held fast.

She heard Ricardo call out his location on the radio. He was within moments of arriving. In her relief she adjusted her hold, which allowed her captive to slip his arm free and swing his fist into her face. The crack of impact stunned her and rung the bells that now sang in her skull. A warm flow of liquid dripped into her eye. Jillian could smell the fresh blood as its scent mixed with the jasmine and booze in the air, and it made her queasy.

Thankfully, Ricardo, Alan, and several other guards descended on the area and took control of the perpetrator. She sat back on her heels and took several deep breaths before Ricardo came over to check on her. "Oh, damn, Jillian," he said, lifting her chin to get a better look at her face with his flashlight. "You need to get that taken care of. We've got this under control now."

She knew they did, but she just needed a minute or two to settle herself before she lost her breakfast all over the sidewalk. When she looked at her shirt her stomach turned over. Jillian pulled her shirt over her head and pressed it to her face to slow the bleeding. She took several deep breaths and tried to work her heart rate back to normal. Once the guards had the intruder restrained, they pulled him off the ground and started to lead him away, but Jillian called them back as she pushed herself to her feet.

Everyone looked at Ricardo, then Jillian, and the trespasser, and then back again. "Jillian?" Ricardo said.

"He's fine." She wasn't going to attack him. She just needed to know a few things before they carted him off. Turns out that the "man" was more like a kid who couldn't have been more than eighteen years old. "What were you doing in here?" she asked.

"Nothing, man. I swear. I was just chillin' with my bros having some beers, and they dared me to hop the fence back there."

"Back where exactly?"

He shrugged in the direction where they'd begun their chase at the aviary. "By those loud ass birds. Probably would've gotten away with it too had they not started screaming." He stumbled around as he talked.

Jillian was relieved that his drunken daredevil adventure had been short and sweet. She didn't want to imagine he'd spent all night ransacking the park and harassing her animals. Ricardo once again pointed out that Jillian's face was split open and bleeding. She didn't need a reminder; she could feel as much. As her heart rate slowed and the adrenaline began to wear off, she could feel her eye beginning to swell. So much for starting her day the same way she always had. While Ricardo was right that it needed looking at, Jillian had more important things to do. She needed to check on her pod; stitches, and everything else could wait.

❖

Dr. Shaw popped his head out into the lobby and smiled. "Hey there, Laura. Come on back."

Laura returned his smile and followed behind him. In her imagination, Dr. Shaw always seemed much shorter than he was. At every appointment, she was reminded that, if anything, they were just about equal in height. As he had done at each session, he held out his arm and offered her the guest chair opposite his. His office never changed. Not even when he relocated his practice across town did he alter the simple setup of his space. There was no comfy couch or chaise lounge stacked with pillows, and no inspirational quotes on tissue boxes or placards cluttering the space. His desk, two mismatched recliners, a fish tank, and a framed print of his time on Broadway as King Mongkut from *The King and I*, were all that made up the room. Yet despite its seemingly uninviting nature, Laura felt her most comfortable in this room with him.

That hadn't always been the case, of course. During the first two years of her treatment, the fish tank terrified her. As she had begun to progress, Laura began to use her ability to cope with the sights and sounds of the water as a barometer for her healing. All these years later, she no longer imagined herself stuck at the bottom of the tank tangled in amongst the coral and plants as the light flickered and reflected from the surface. She took a deep breath and settled in her seat.

Dr. Shaw turned to her and raised his eyebrow. "Are you holding your breath?" he asked before giving her time to naturally exhale. He sat and crossed his legs, resting her open file on his lap. He clipped his reading glasses together at the bridge and set them onto his nose.

Laura exhaled with a chuckle. "Nope. Just breathing."

It was a legitimate question for her therapist to ask since it had long ago become her go-to coping mechanism following her accident. She still turned to it in times of stress when she needed to gain control over herself and her surroundings. When she had first begun seeing Dr. Shaw for PTSD she had read somewhere, the internet most likely, that professional swimmers and divers could hold their breath twice as long underwater than they could on land. It was then that she convinced herself to put the theory into practice for herself.

Over time, Laura had become able to hold her breath for an average of two minutes and thirty-two seconds. If the time ever came where she would need it, the odds guaranteed that she had at least three whole minutes under water. Thankfully, it was a theory that she had yet to test, and today wasn't a holding-her-breath kind of day. Laura was trembling with anticipation and had been since she woke up that morning.

"So, Laura. How've you been?"

"Amazing, and today's my admissions interview at the Tampa Marine Research Institute!" She happy-danced in her chair. For the first time in a decade, her life was finally on track.

"That's right. And how are you feeling about that?" he asked, making scribbles in the folder on his lap.

"I feel..." There were about a thousand different emotions zipping around through her head. "Scared, excited, nervous, hopeful. You name it, I probably feel it."

"That's normal. This is a huge step for you, Laura." He uncrossed his legs and leaned forward. "It may not be as easy as you're hoping it—"

She cut him off mid-sentence. "I feel good about it." As much as she trusted and respected him, sometimes she wished he didn't always try to put doubts in her head. Not that he did it on purpose, surely. It was just his head-shrinking way to prepare her for the worst. "I'm not having any nightmares or panic attacks. I'm not holding my breath. I've got this."

Although, as she listed her accomplishments, she was doing more than just trying to convince him. Laura was terrified. She was afraid that this was her last chance to become the person she always dreamed of being. The person she'd wanted to be before she swung off that rope into the cold water below. The crystal-clear water flowing up from deep in the aquifer that had stunned all of her most primal senses. A shiver ran through her as she recalled just how the spring water had shocked her body that day.

"Laura? Where'd you go?" Dr. Shaw asked.

She blinked away the memory. "I'm here. And I'm ready. I've let what happened that day control me for too long. Maybe I'll fail or maybe I won't, ya know? But this is my last chance. I've gotta do it."

"This has been a long time coming. I think you're ready for this step if you do. But—"

She cut him off again. "No buts." Laura wasn't naïve enough to think that something might not go to plan. She learned all about that ten years earlier, but she'd spent all these years since doing whatever she had to in order to reduce those risks. He wasn't the only one who could prepare her for the worst.

They wrapped up their session, and Laura headed off to the institute. She pulled up to the guard shack and stopped at the bright yellow bar that hung across the road. Rolling down her window, she smiled at the large and imposing woman who stepped out of the small building. The greeting returned was one of indifference as the guard held out her hand and asked for Laura's credentials.

Laura continued to smile as she handed over her license and the temporary parking pass the school had sent along with her interview confirmation. Her heart raced in excitement as the guard scanned her documents and searched for her name on the list. Laura's smile began to wane as time crept by. She tried to peer over the edge of the clipboard. "It's C-A-arrrrokay..." her voice failed when the woman glared down at her before handing back her paperwork. "Sorry," Laura said as she slunk back into her seat.

When the barricade rose, Laura offered another apology and pulled into the parking lot. She picked the first vacant spot she came across. She was ready to be done driving and out of the car, but now that she was there her hands trembled. She wiped the excess moisture on her palms along the tops of her thighs, rubbing them back and forth over her slacks even after her hands were dry.

Laura flipped down her visor to give her hair and makeup a final once-over. She practiced a welcoming smile that came across a bit more frightening than she'd intended. Her second attempt wasn't any better unless her goal was to mimic a constipated lunatic, which she most definitely was not. She shook her head at herself and then ran a finger over each of her already smooth eyebrows. She closed the visor with a slap and sighed. It was now or never, both literally and figuratively.

Each click of her low heels on the blacktop brought her closer to her future, the one she'd wanted for so long. All she had to do was make one hell of an impression in her interview and become one of the nine lucky applicants chosen for this year. She took a deep breath and grabbed the handle on the thick glass door. "No problem," she said, pulling her shoulders back and opening the door with a confident tug.

When Laura stepped into the room, at least half a dozen people popped their heads up and gave her a quick gander before dropping their eyes back into their laps. It appeared there wasn't a single person in the room who wasn't fascinated by their own crotch. "Ah, smartphones," she murmured. "Helping people avoid other people since 2001."

Laura approached the receptionist who greeted her far more warmly than the security guard had. "Laura Carter," she said.

The woman flipped through a manila folder stuffed with pages. "Here you are," she said, handing Laura the temporary name badge that had been paper-clipped to her file. "Go ahead and have a seat or help yourself to a beverage." She motioned to a well-stocked coffee bar at the far end of the room, and Laura knew right where she was headed.

She clipped the badge to her lapel and made a beeline toward the coffee. By the looks of the setup, Laura half expected the station to be manned by a professional barista. She grabbed a mug, and then stared blankly at the contraption. An electronic screen listed every coffee beverage possible—with milk or without, foam, no foam—and even offered chocolate or vanilla flavorings. "Master's degree and can't make coffee," Laura said under her breath.

Laura was just about to return her mug to the tray when someone said, "It's probably not one of the interview questions."

As she turned, she said, "I hope not." The last word caught in her throat when her eyes met the woman's next to her. Blue eyes the color of glacial ice looked back at her, and even despite the wicked black eye, the butterflies took flight deep in Laura's belly.

CHAPTER TWO

O h, Christ!" The words flew from Laura's mouth before she had a chance to stop them. She slapped her hand up over her mouth to keep any more obscenities from escaping.

The woman standing before her laughed, and Laura felt her face flush. Her stunning eyes were enough to capture Laura's attention, but the brilliant smile that spread across her face was what held her captive. Dark, midnight hair framed her angular face, and Laura imagined how the smooth bronze skin might feel beneath her fingertips. She gripped her mug tighter to prevent herself from reaching out to caress the unfortunate injury that marred the otherwise perfect complexion.

A flesh-colored bandage hid the epicenter of a fresh bruise that had begun to spread its way across her face. There was no way the injury could have been more than a few hours old. She wanted to ask what sort of monster could've done such a thing to her, but it was none of her business. She wondered why she even cared beyond simple curiosity, but hoped it was nothing more than just an unlucky accident that caused it.

The woman pressed a few buttons on the machine and set her mug under the dispenser. Long, lean fingers selected the options on the screen, and within seconds, the machine whirred to life and hot, fresh coffee filled her cup.

Despite watching intently, Laura couldn't have repeated the actions. "So, yeah," Laura said, tapping at her lip and then pointing to the coffee maker. "I missed how you did that."

Another gorgeous smile, and Laura's knees trembled. *Good Lord. What is with me?* The goddess slowly took Laura's mug from her hands and replaced hers with it.

"How do you like it, Miss...?"

Laura leaned her hip against the counter, no longer trusting her legs to hold her up. "Laura. Black. Not Laura Black, Laura Carter. My coffee is black." *Black? Why did I say that? I hate black coffee.* Only sociopaths drank their coffee black or so she had read somewhere on the internet.

"Me too."

Of course, she does. "Oh yeah? Well, that's quite a *fluke*." *Jesus Christ, Laura, stop talking.* No. No, she did not just say that aloud. *What's wrong with me?* Laura closed her eyes and shook her head.

"Did you just make a dolphin joke?"

Laura covered her face and peaked out through the crack she made with her fingers. Her face was on fire, and she was afraid to open her mouth again.

"Was it on *porpoise*?"

Laura dropped her hand from her face and laughed. "No! You didn't."

"Why not? It's not like you're the only one who has terrible jokes."

"I swear I'm not nearly this awkward in real life. I'm just crazy nervous about my interview."

"Eh, don't be nervous. I'm certain that you'll do just fine." She poured what must've been four teaspoons of sugar in to her coffee, along with a healthy shot of half and half and gave it a long stir.

"I thought you said you liked it black?"

"Oh no. I just said that to be nice. Only sociopaths drink their coffee black." She flashed another beautiful smile and took a sip.

Laura just stared at her for several silent seconds unsure of what she could or should say next. Had this been a bar, and six or seven years earlier, Laura would've pulled this woman into the nearest bathroom stall and jumped her bones. She'd never before wished to be the rim of a coffee mug, until she saw those soft lips press against it. How the hell was she going to keep herself focused with this woman alongside her? Part of her hoped that maybe she wouldn't get selected by the board, but the other part prayed they ended up roommates.

"So, thanks for showing me how this contraption works. I didn't get your name," she said, holding her hand out in greeting and wishing she would've wiped it on her pants first in case it was sweaty.

"Jillian," she said as she took Laura's hand. A rush of energy coursed through her body. Jillian's grip was strong, yet her hands were soft. Once again, the heat rose within Laura, and her ears burned. Without letting her go, Jillian turned her wrist and looked at her watch. "I apologize, but I've got to excuse myself. It was a pleasure meeting you, Laura."

The sound of her name on Jillian's lips echoed in her mind as she walked away. She spoke for a second to the receptionist before heading off down the hall that presumably led to the restrooms. Laura poured her coffee down the sink and set the empty mug on the tray table. Her heart had been racing all morning, first from anticipation and now arousal; the last thing she needed was to add caffeine to the mix. Laura couldn't recall the last time anyone had caused such an instant and visceral reaction throughout her entire body. She could feel the energy of Jillian standing next to her, but even more disturbing was the feeling of her absence now that she'd gone.

Laura chose a seat with a clear view of the hallway in case Jillian was looking for a familiar face when she returned. *Sure.*

That was the reason. While she waited, she took out the copy of her application and thesis submission to review until she was called back. Yet, no matter how hard she tried to focus on the issue at hand, Laura's mind was filled with visions of Jillian. The sway in her hips and swagger in her step replayed on loop in Laura's mind. Her tight black pants hugged the curves of her hips and muscular ass. She couldn't help but wonder if the sun had kissed every inch of her bronzed skin or if there were hidden parts left secret for the chosen few. Laura looked forward to the idea of spending the next few months getting to know her in and out of those fine, tailored slacks.

The sound of an opening door drew her out of her spiraling fantasy. For that, she was grateful, although a pang of disappointment hit Laura when it didn't announce Jillian's return. However, Laura knew it was for the best; the last thing she needed was to be derailed and distracted by a gorgeous woman while she was at the crossroad of her future. Just as it had been when she was five years old, becoming a marine mammal trainer would always be her number one priority.

Jillian stopped a few feet from the doorway once she was out of sight and could no longer feel Laura's penetrating gaze watching her walk away. Even if she hadn't felt those jade eyes on her ass, the receptionist, Katie, had been kind enough to point it out. She peered at the mug she gripped in her fist. Jillian didn't even like the coffee from the lobby machine, yet here she was holding a cup of it. She pressed the tips of her fingers between her brows, closed her eyes, and shook her head at herself.

Jillian couldn't explain what had come over her. As soon as she'd laid eyes on Laura she was drawn to her, and before she knew it, Jillian was standing making small talk and awful jokes about cetaceans. She'd caught a glimpse of Laura as she'd chatted with Katie when she arrived. In those brief moments, she had been mesmerized at being on the receiving end of such a bright and genuine smile.

Laura was as awkward as she was attractive. Her dirty blond hair was fine and light, cut around her shoulders. It brushed against her neck every time she moved, and her neck was pink the whole time they stood there. Laura wore her emotion on her sleeve, but also over her entire body. From the trembling of her voice and the moisture on her palms, to the darkening of her eyes into a deep verdigris shade when Jillian moved in closer. She wondered if Laura was aware of just how easy her body language was to read.

Jillian's pulse quickened as she recalled how responsive Laura was to her. She fed off the intense energy that had pulsed between them, an energy that became tangible the moment her fingers swept across Laura's to take her hand. It was that same jolt that brought Jillian out of the moment and back into reality. Looking back, it was still so hard for her to believe that she'd fallen so easily and willingly into that rabbit hole. She couldn't remember the last time she'd found herself so intrigued by someone.

Every minute she stood in the hallway, she fought against her desire to return to the lobby to pick up where they'd left off and carry on the rest of the day in Laura's presence. The problem was that they both had someplace to be, and flirting like teenagers by a coffee maker wasn't that place. As if on cue, Diana stuck her head out into the hall and looked around. When she spotted Jillian, she stepped out of the doorway. "Hey, there you are. You coming?"

"Yeah," Jillian said. She looked at her cup, and then all around her for a place to get rid of it. But seeing no mature way to dispose of it, she just took it with her.

Nothing about this day was normal. She could now describe it as the weirdest one she'd had in her most recent memory. Jillian could say with absolute certainty that she'd never once started a day off with a heart-pounding foot pursuit or a busted eye and fourteen stitches. Maybe the impact to her face knocked her brain loose, and she had a mini stroke, because yesterday's Jillian probably wouldn't have been such an easy target of an overcharged libido. Hers, not Laura's, of course. But now was the time to get things back on track.

Jillian took her seat at the center of the table, flanked on each side by her two most senior training instructors. Diana and Fletcher were both experienced animal behaviorists, each heading their own division of the program. Fletcher was Jillian's right hand and manager of care and interaction, while Diana handled areas regarding research and education. Jillian was the program director, but unlike her staffers and department heads, she rarely taught courses at the institute. It was no secret to anyone that she relied heavily on her exceptional team so that she could spend as much time as possible in the water, working one-on-one with the animals.

One of the few exceptions to that was the annual acceptance interviews, and today was that day. They would perform the hard task of selecting nine of the most talented and qualified applicants to be admitted into their marine mammal training program. Every year, fifty or more eager individuals put their hearts, souls, and hopes on the line to be one of those lucky ones just as she had twenty years earlier.

The Tampa Marine Research Institute was the leading dolphin education and conservation center in the Western Hemisphere. Jillian had trained there prior to accepting an internship, and this eventually turned into her permanent home. She began the long years of exhaustion and lonely nights, but it was the most rewarding career she could ever want. She was living her dream, and there wasn't anything on earth she would trade for it.

As long as Jillian could remember, her dream had been to work with dolphins. When she was in kindergarten, she answered four questions about her favorite things for a school time capsule. What is your favorite color? What is your favorite food? Who is your best friend? And what do you want to be when you grow up?

Her favorite color was no longer pink. She couldn't remember when she last had chocolate milk, and she had no earthly idea who Betty Lu was, but she did know what she wanted to be, and that hadn't changed. Jillian had always wanted to be a dolphin trainer.

It hadn't been an easy road, but it was her life's mission to protect and preserve marine mammals, and as she had physically demonstrated earlier that morning, she would do so with her life. Jillian took great pride in her work, and she was dedicated to instilling that passion in each trainer, student, or visitor she encountered. She was excited to introduce nine more to this world she loved so much.

Jillian flipped through the pages of documents set before her. Twenty-two amazing candidates boiled down to a few pieces of paper each. She wasn't looking for Laura's packet, but she smiled uncontrollably when she found it. Jillian rarely, if ever, reviewed the applicant files before the day of the interviews. She trusted her team enough to allow them the responsibility of narrowing the list to those they felt deserved to be at this stage of the process. Jillian preferred to see the heart of the individual and look beyond the words and résumés. There was so much more than grades that went into working with these animals, and looking at Laura's information, she most certainly had the grades.

Jillian was a bit surprised to learn just how advanced Laura already was in her career. So much so that she could easily be among her top employees like Diana and Fletcher. It wasn't every day that she came across someone more qualified than ninety percent of her existing team. If it were possible, Jillian was now even more anxious to speak with Laura again. She looked out across the three rows of empty chairs waiting to be filled by twenty-two new hopefuls. Jillian slapped her hands on the desk and looked back and forth between Fletcher and Diana. "Let's get this party started, shall we?" She called Katie and told her they were ready.

Jillian and the others welcomed the group as they filed into the room and to their seats. She kept her eye out for one face in particular. When Laura came through the door, a rush of heat burned through her, and she didn't even try to prevent the smile that everyone was sure to notice. However, Laura's reaction, seemed quite the opposite. There was no smile or blush of color. Instead the friendly smile of greeting disappeared, along with all the color in her bright cheeks. Her face was stark and pale. Laura looked at the floor for several minutes as she followed along behind those in front of her and took her seat. Laura gently slipped a few stray strands of hair behind her ear.

Jillian never took her eyes off Laura, willing for her to look back up. When they'd all found their seats and Diana thanked them for coming, Laura finally raised her head and looked at her. Jillian was pleased that the painful look of anguish had vanished from her beautiful face. Her cheeks were once again pink and vibrant, and the smile Jillian liked so much had returned. She was impressed by her quick ability to recover. She began to think that she'd underestimated Laura and maybe she wasn't as easy to read as originally thought, an idea that further intrigued Jillian.

As she did every year with each new group, Jillian welcomed them all to the institute and congratulated them on making it this far. "It's an honor to just be nominated." She paused for laughter. "In all seriousness, ladies and gentlemen, if you aren't selected this time around don't be discouraged. If you're dedicated to pursuing this career you will need as much perseverance as you have passion." It was never her intention to discourage anyone, but in this competitive field they could struggle for years before landing even a part-time position. "You will be painfully exhausted and painfully broke. Your families, friends, and partners may forget your name. You will smell like fish every day for the rest of your life. Maybe longer." As expected, her last statement elicited laughter from around the room. "Our days are long, and since our animals don't take weekends or holidays, we don't either. I know you're all aware of these things, so you also know that there's nothing like it in the whole world. I can't imagine any job better than the one I have."

As she wrapped up her spiel, she scanned the room studying each face for the telltale signs of boredom, indifference, or worse, arrogance. In her experience, the latter was the most dangerous and destructive, and Jillian would have none of it. She was pleased that everyone was alert and not one person showed signs of falling asleep in their chair. They all passed the easiest test they would encounter on their journey, and it was time for the next one.

"Each of you will have the opportunity for a one-on-one interview with the panel, followed by a CPR certification course, and a routine physical exam all of which will be broken up over the next two days. Keep in mind that we've all seen your applications and we know how you got here. That's not what we want to know. We are interested in the why." She could see the engines revving to life in their heads. "It'll be a long couple of days, but for now, who wants to go first?"

Once again, human behavior proved itself predictable as they began to look around at each other waiting for someone else to speak up. All except Laura, whose hand went up within seconds of her asking the question. Laura's eyes shone with confidence. Was there any end to her surprises? Jillian smiled and nodded, pleased by her courage despite having admitted her nervousness earlier. Laura passed her second test with flying colors.

"Thank you," Diana said, acknowledging Laura's initiative.

Jillian was hopelessly turned around by everything that had happened that day, and meeting Laura was almost becoming more significant than getting her face smashed in by some drunken hoodlum. Her attraction to Laura was more intense than it had even been with her former girlfriend. Their relationship had been built more on proximity rather than physical attraction. Which had been the fuel for both the development and the demise of that relationship. At least the ending was mutual, and both she and

Diana had managed to put all that well behind them long before she became the director.

Jillian dismissed the group and gave Laura a few minutes to prepare herself for the meeting. Once they'd all gone, Diana and Fletcher wasted little time expressing their initial reactions and working out the rest of the interview schedule. To Jillian's dismay, Diana focused on Laura in particular.

"No."

"What?" Diana said, feigning innocence.

"I know that look. And no."

"But she's..." Diana waggled her eyebrows.

"Yes, she is. But no," Jillian said.

"You're the boss, you can't claim dibs on this one." Diana asked.

"Neither of us can." Jillian said. She hoped her denial was convincing to both herself and Diana. "Of all people, *we* should know better."

CHAPTER THREE

Laura paced around in the parking lot where she now found herself after rushing out of the building as fast as she could. "You hit on the director. Way to go, Laura. Talk about a first impression." She cringed at how she had blatantly coveted Jillian's tight ass as she strode away from her. But God, what an ass it was. Laura grunted at herself in disgust. "What's wrong with you?" She slapped her hands onto the top of her head and spun around in place. Laura screeched in surprise when she came face-to-face with the gate guard from earlier.

"Is something wrong, ma'am?"

"Nothing. Everything."

"Do you need help with something?"

"Can you turn back time to the moment in my life when I became so awkward, and I don't know, kill me?" Laura asked, clasping her hands beneath her chin like a criminal begging for mercy.

"Um, what?"

"Nothing," Laura scanned the guard's lapel for a name badge, "Officer Williams."

"All right. As long as everything is—"

Laura cut her off. "Have you ever been so close to getting everything you've ever wanted in life and then..." She finished that sentence by scrunching up her face, ringing her hands together, and making a sickening and dramatic crackling-squish sound with her mouth.

Officer Williams laughed. "No. Can't say that I have."

"Lucky you," Laura said, wiping the spit off her lips.

"Okay, then. Well, you have a good day, ma'am." Officer Williams rolled her eyes this time.

"I mean it was an honest mistake, you know. I didn't know who she was. Plus, it's not like I slapped her on that unbelievable ass. She flirted with me, too." *Exactly.* Jillian did flirt with her, and blatantly she might add to anyone who was asking. *She most definitely flirted.* "She's the director. You think she of all people would know better."

Officer Williams's eyes flew open. "You didn't."

Laura slapped her hand onto her chest with an echoing thud. "I didn't. *She* did."

"You hit on Jillian Marshall, the program director?" Williams hooted and laughed.

Laura's face burned like hot coals. "She...I...but I didn't..." Laura gave up. "Yeah, I did."

"Damn, girl."

"I know," Laura cried out.

When Williams stopped chuckling she looked at Laura. The humor gone from her face. "Don't even worry about it. Trust me. She's not even gonna hold it against you. She ain't like that. Now, if you did something to mess with her dolphins all bets are off. Hell, after the morning she had I'm just glad that she can still recognize a beautiful woman when she sees one."

Laura blushed and blinked in disbelief. Did she just call her beautiful? What was this place? The lesbian Atlantis? "So, what did happen this morning?" Her question was both a means of changing the subject and finding out how Jillian's beautiful face incurred such damage.

"Let's just say that somebody messed with her dolphins." When Officer Williams had finished retelling the story about how

Jillian single-handedly tackled a perp for picking the wrong park to trespass in, Laura's heart was racing. She took a deep breath and held it for several seconds listening to the pounding in her chest and the rushing cadence of blood in her ears. She tried to imagine what those intense moments had been like for Jillian. Was she scared? Had she been prepared for the worst? What if she'd gotten more than a black eye? It wasn't until Officer Williams grabbed Laura by the arm that she gasped for air.

"Hey, there. Are you okay?"

Laura nodded as she controlled her exhale. "Yes. I'm fine." Laura was taken aback by her unexpected reaction to Jillian's experience. It was only ever her own anxieties and stressors that triggered her coping mechanisms.

"Well, you look a bit warm. Maybe you should get back inside."

Laura glanced at her watch. Williams was right about one of those things, she needed to get back inside. She had ten minutes until her interview, and the last thing she needed to be was late.

When Katie called her name, Laura's stomach somersaulted. She smiled as she stood to meet Katie again and followed her back to the conference room. The space had been rearranged and the chairs had been placed around the head table. Jillian was at the end of the table with her assistants on each side leaving the far end open for the candidate. She could have been Belle sitting opposite the Beast, except that Jillian was far better looking.

Despite the large space, this seating arrangement felt much more intimate. Laura found comfort in the presence of the others as she sat across from Jillian. When Laura smiled at her it was with an increased level of respect knowing how she had come to acquire her battle wounds. She was more than a bit surprised at just how much more attractive the truth made Jillian appear. As if she needed any additional help in that department. Jillian was a dark-haired goddess.

The smile that greeted Laura in return was warm and inviting. When she welcomed her to the table the atmosphere in the whole room changed. Not in a bad way. It made her feel calm and relaxed. Her confidence had been wavering all morning, yet as she sat here with Jillian and her most trusted colleagues, Laura felt a deep sense of belonging. It was as if she was right where she was meant to be. She sat up straight and pulled her shoulders back. This opportunity was hers to lose.

Jillian reintroduced herself, as well as the others, and then leapt right into the questions. "So, I can't help but ask, why are you wasting your time here? Ninety-nine percent of our applicants are new college freshman, not postgraduates ten years out of high school."

Both Diana's and Fletcher's heads snapped toward Jillian in obvious surprise, and Laura grinned. She had expected the question, even if the others hadn't. She was in her late twenties, whereas most, if not all, other applicants for this program were barely out of high school and pushing nineteen if she was giving them a year or so. She was guaranteed to be the oldest, and therefore most experienced in psychology and behavior. Unfortunately, in a career this competitive, youth and vigor gave you the greatest advantage. While ten years of experience couldn't seem like a bad thing, losing a decade pursuing an education that wasn't even necessary could do more harm than good.

"Right out of the gate. I like it." Laura was thankful that Jillian had chosen this as her lead off. The sooner they got it out of the way the easier this would be. "Well, it's been my dream to work with dolphins pretty much since I can remember. Of course, as you can see, it's taken me a bit longer than I'd hoped to get here."

"I think we can all understand that," Fletcher said as Diana and Jillian both nodded.

"I'd had a pretty good plan going into my senior year of high school, but life had a different idea. I'd been accepted to the University of California in San Diego, but about a month before graduation I had an accident, and despite my best efforts to overcome it, it got the best of me for a while. I made it about five weeks at UC before I was forced to drop out and reevaluate some things."

"It didn't keep you down for long though," Jillian said, holding up a piece of paper that Laura recognized as her curriculum vitae.

"About two years, which seemed long at the time. After that, I enrolled in community college, and then kept on through until my master's. Seems like a hundred lifetimes ago now."

"You've already had a busy education and successful career as a behaviorist. What makes you want to step away from all that and go all the way back to the beginning?" Diana asked.

"I suppose you're looking for something more profound than, 'I love dolphins.' But really, it's as simple as that. To me anyway. I remember the first time my parents took me to SeaWorld. I was around five years old." Laura paused and smiled as she recalled the memories of that day.

Jillian leaned back into her chair with the fingers of her right hand stroking her lips where a soft smile had formed. "Go on," she said.

Good Lord in heaven, she's gorgeous. Laura pushed the invading thought from her mind and continued. "I was five or so. Do you remember when they still had those fiberglass strollers shaped like orcas and dolphins?" Everyone around the table chuckled and nodded at that nostalgic blast. "They also still called it the whale and dolphin theater with the pilots and Pseudorca in the same exhibit. During the show they always picked a kid from the audience to have a special up-close interaction with the animals. I was so jealous of that little boy that I just started bawling my eyes out."

"I used to think that system was rigged," Fletcher said.

"Right? Well, I was still crying at the end of the show when one of the trainers came out to the front and waved right at me. I was wiping away the tears when she took me by the hand and led me down to the glass." Laura could remember the salty scent of the seawater and the cool chill of the glass beneath her hands as she pressed them and her face against the tank. She stared into the crystal blue water that seemed so vast and infinitely deep in her young mind.

"And?" Jillian asked.

"And then there she was. The most beautiful creature I had ever seen, with her dark, soulful eyes staring right into mine. She saw me, and I saw her. It was in that moment, in front of thousands of people, that I fell in love."

She had. It was from that day forward that Laura lived and breathed dolphins. As she grew older and learned more, that love evolved to include just about every marine mammal there was. Yet, there was always that special place in her heart for the Atlantic bottlenose dolphin.

"And let's just say that had they not phased out those awkward cetacean strollers, I'd have been that chubby, thirteen-year-old forcing her parents to push her around the park in a creepy plastic dolphin."

❖

It had been two weeks since the interviews, and Jillian was overjoyed that move in day had arrived. The week before she could hardly wait to begin making her congratulatory acceptance calls to the chosen few. They had finalized the list and the alternates that Friday, and it ate away at her to wait until Monday to call Laura with the great news. There was never a doubt that they would accept her into the program after hearing her heartfelt memory. Those moments are what set her apart from the others. There was a passion in her eyes and fervor in her voice. Whatever accident she had when she was a teenager might have derailed her for a time, but she never lost that drive inside her.

It was a fire that Jillian could feel burning on the other end of a line when she called to tell Laura that she'd been selected as one of the nine. The conversation had started out professional enough when Laura had answered the phone. There had been a moment of silent tension when Laura had taken an audible breath before she said, "I'm ready."

❖

Jillian was surprised that Laura had thought even for a second that she was calling with bad news. "So, Ms. Carter, are you ready to finish what you started when you were five?"

"Seriously? No. Really?"

Jillian had always loved this part but even more that it was Laura on the receiving end. She gave a quiet laugh and said, "Yes. Seriously.

"Fuck me!" Laura shouted and gasped. "I'm so sorry. Oh my God."

Jillian laughed out loud this time. "It's okay. I've heard worse."

"Really?" Laura's voice was hopeful.

"No. You seem to be the only person who makes a habit out of yelling profanities at me."

"Oh, God, you're right. I'm usually far more reserved than this crazy person you've seen."

"I have no doubt, but I look forward to the excitement you'll bring to the team. We'll see you next week, Laura." Before Jillian hung up, she heard Laura let out a howl of undeniable elation. She was very much looking forward to finding out just what Laura was going to bring into her life.

❖

Jillian sat at her desk finishing up her morning logs and charts while passing time before the trainees began to arrive at nine a.m.

As she signed and initialed the last page in the stack, she heard low rumbles of activity outside. She turned around to the window behind her and smiled. It was two minutes after nine, and already a convoy of trucks and packed cars lined the curb in front of the residence hall. She liked to see that it was barely past the hour, and most, if not all of them, were there and raring to go. Although the true test would be if they could have the same vigor at six a.m. after a grueling eighteen-hour day.

As she scanned the crowd, she was drawn almost immediately to a red Ford Escort at the front of the line. She recognized Laura as soon as she laid eyes on her. She was dressed in a pair of ragged denim capris and a coral tank with matching sneakers. The sinuous muscles of her arms were defined as she lifted a tote from her trunk. Jillian held her breath when Laura bent over to set it on the ground.

"Holy crap."

"Jillian?"

The voice from behind her gave her a start, and she spun around as if caught with her hand in the cookie jar. "Yes?"

"Hey," Katie said from the doorway. "Um, they're here, but it appears you already know that." She chuckled at Jillian and walked away.

Jillian thanked her anyway and picked up the clipboard from the corner of her desk before heading out to greet the arrivals. She gathered everyone into a circle and congratulated them once again on making it into the program. Proud smiles and hefty pats on the back went around the group. There were nine new trainees that day, but with the addition of family and friends that had been wrangled into helping them move, the number had tripled.

"Let's get moved in, shall we," Jillian said.

A round of cheers and hoots echoed through the group as they gleefully followed Jillian to the dorms.

Jillian was pleased when they entered the building, as it smelled fresh and clean. She made a mental note to thank the maintenance staff for their hard work. The lobby was a large open space that was set up more as a living and gathering room than a true lobby. Large overstuffed sofas formed a u-shape around the square coffee table that aligned with the flat screen television mounted on the opposite wall. On either side of the living space were the rooms, five on each wing.

The hall was coed, while the bedrooms were private, each with their own microwave and mini refrigerators. The bathrooms and showers were located on the end of each hallway. Any other luxuries they would want or need during their stay were their responsibility. Despite Jillian's repeated reminders that they wouldn't have time for such needs, everyone always over packed.

She started at one end of the hall, calling out names as she passed each room. When she got to Laura, Jillian was a little surprised that she was alone. Unlike everyone else, she didn't have a single person with her that day. She couldn't recall in all her years that a newbie hadn't brought at least a friend along with them. She left the group alone to move in their belongings and gave them just under an hour before they were to meet her back in the living room to collect their uniforms and change.

Off to the side of the room, Katie had set up the tables. Each trainee would receive a mound of clothing to last them through the program—six shirts, a tank, two pairs of sweatpants, shorts, and work pants, plus a full wet suit and a hoodie all emblazoned with the TMRI dolphin logo and their trainee status. They were about to forget what it was like to wear anything but two shades of blue for the next nine months. The fashionistas often complained in the beginning, but if they made it past the first three weeks of training, what they were wearing was the last thing on their mind.

With uniforms assigned and the trainees off to change, Jillian mingled with family and friends while they waited. As each of them returned in their new uniform, they were bombarded with cheers and camera flashes as proud parents snapped commemorative photos. All of them except Laura who stood off to the side watching the excitement and even offering to take pictures of the others for them. Jillian wanted to feel sorry for her, but something about Laura told her it would be pointless. Jillian made her way over and smiled.

"Is it everything you expected?" Laura handed back the phone she was holding and looked at Jillian. Her heart skipped. The sky blue uniform brought out the color of her eyes which glistened in the light. Jillian could have bet money that she was going to or had already cried.

"I don't know what I expected, to be honest. Until last week I never thought I'd get this far."

"You're kidding. Right?"

"Let's just say I've learned not to take things for granted. I hoped to get here but never could've imagined what it would be like if, well, *when* I did. "

"Well, you deserve it." Jillian and Laura stood there for several moments, neither one speaking or moving until Jillian said, "Would you like me to take a picture of you on your first day?"

"I...yes. I'd like that very much," Laura said, handing Jillian her cell phone.

"Say cheese," Jillian said. When Laura smiled at the camera it felt like she was smiling at her, and the butterflies in Jillian's belly swarmed to life.

CHAPTER FOUR

Laura's fingers curled around Jillian's as she took her phone. She paused a few moments longer than necessary and felt the wave of heat spread up her arm and neck and then flood her cheeks. Jillian slid her tongue slowly over her lips, and Laura's pulse pounded in her burning ears. Jillian had her under a spell. What was it about her that had Laura so off kilter? How could someone have such an intense and overpowering effect on every inch of her mind and body?

Jillian tugged gently under her grip and realized that she still had hold of her hand. "Oh Christ," Laura said, loosening her fingers and letting Jillian pull her hand free.

"There you go again with the profanity, Miss Carter." Jillian smiled and winked. The flirtatious wink nearly buckled Laura's legs right on the spot.

"Oh, Chr—"

"Eh," Jillian cut her off and wagged a teasing finger.

Laura managed to grunt out a thanks and her throat tightened up. This was getting out of hand, and by the look on Jillian's face she was enjoying every moment of it. Laura fumbled over her side trying to slip her phone into her pocket. Laura kept sliding her phone against her leg, farther and farther down. *Where the fuck's the pockets in these things?* Jillian caught the commotion and glanced to her side. The break in eye contact allowed Laura to see that she was nowhere near any of the pockets and had just been rubbing her phone all over the front of her thigh. Jillian hooked a finger into the pocket and pulled it open for her.

Laura dropped the phone into the deep opening in her navy cargo shorts. "Thanks."

"Glad to help," Jillian said.

What kind of person can't find her own pockets? Good grief, Laura. She felt like this was her first day on Earth not just her first day wearing big girl pants. What an idiot Jillian must think she was. Clearly, her graduate degree in animal behavior didn't translate into normal human interactions. At least not in the company of Jillian Marshall, that was for sure.

Yes, she was attractive, but she wasn't the only good-looking woman Laura had ever encountered before. And fine, she had an enjoyable and quirky sense of humor, but that wasn't a surprise. Animal people, by nature, were a curious *breed*. She laughed inwardly knowing that such a statement would be just the kind of thing Jillian would find funny. Laura found the irony of it humorous as well.

"I know you finally got the phone into your pocket, but don't forget to send those pictures to your family. Or friends. Or whoever."

"Oh yeah. Right. My parents will be pleased to see them I'm sure. You know, I didn't even realize it was a thing. The whole family experience." Laura supposed she should have known. She'd very much been one of those kids on her first "first day."

"I reckon it's a first timer thing."

"True. I've had my fair share of first times," Laura said, but then added, "in college." However, that didn't exactly eliminate any innuendo.

"I knew what you meant."

Of course she did, because unlike Laura, Jillian didn't have a horny teenager trapped in her head. "I did the obligatory first day photos when I moved into UC San Diego. I was there a month, so those pictures are pretty much all the memories I have of that college experience. There was less pomp and circumstance each time after that."

After her epic fail at UC San Diego, Laura put far more importance on the end rather than the beginnings. "Don't get me wrong. Had I invited them they would've been here." Laura now almost wished they were if only to have kept her from making an ass of herself. Otherwise she was okay with doing today on her own. She was at least ten years older than any of her fellow trainees. Had any of these kids been her age they'd be running the place with Jillian's team. She didn't see the need in emphasizing her situation. The fewer eyes she had on her during the next nine months the better. Not that she was off to the best start, and it would help if she could stop finding herself within such proximity to the director every time she turned around. Now she was also becoming more and more afraid that Jillian was going to keep standing right in front of her for the rest of the day.

"Well, I'll be expecting them for graduation then."

Katie caught her eye from the other side of the room and pointed to Jillian. "I think you're being summoned," Laura said, pointing toward Katie.

Without turning around, Jillian excused herself, and Laura tipped back toward the wall for support. "That woman is the worst kind of distraction," Laura mumbled under her breath as Jillian strode away.

Jillian stood at the center of the group, and as if she had flipped a switch, Director Marshall appeared before them. Laura was impressed by her ability to transform before her eyes. The woman who just minutes before had entertained Laura with flirtatious banter and eye contact was now commanding and professional as she addressed the room. Laura wasn't sure if she was aroused or frightened by Jillian's metamorphosis. Who was the real Jillian Marshall? As curious as she was, Laura had to remember what she was here for, and bedding the director was absolutely not it.

"Ladies and gentlemen, thank you," Jillian said after having gotten everyone's attention. She thanked all the family and friends for their help and welcomed them to the TMRI family before giving them just a few more minutes to say their farewells.

The moms and dads held back tears as they kissed their children good-bye and filed out the door, leaving their babies behind. She remembered how emotional it was when her parents left her alone for her first night on her own in San Diego, and her heart panged a little for these kids. The moment was over as soon as Jillian addressed the group.

"This isn't overnight camp, and it's not a popularity contest. From now until the end of this program you will be working your tail off to be better, smarter, and stronger than you were the day before."

Laura was surprised by the unexpected turn of the emotion in Jillian's voice, but she'd be lying if she said it didn't make Jillian that much hotter.

"You aren't here to compete with each other. There's one way you will get through this and that's to work as a team. Everyone at this park is here for one reason. It's not you. It's not me. It's the animals. If you're here for any other reason, we made the wrong choice in bringing you on."

Laura couldn't help but feel like Jillian was speaking to her alone when her gaze cut through the crowd and right at her. Laura looked around nervously. She was looking straight at her there was no doubt. But why? Laura was very much here for the animals. It had been her dream for as long as she could remember, and she had even said as much during her interview. So why did it seem as though Jillian just accused her of anything but? Sure, maybe there was that small part of her that was doing this to prove to herself that her accident was behind her, but that was far from the only reason. Besides, her past was her secret and no one except her therapist could know that. Unless Jillian could read her mind there was no way in hell she would know, nor would she ever.

As Jillian wrapped up her speech, she handed the reins over to Diana who would take over and finish out the day with a park orientation. The group of trainees lined up like mallard ducklings, and Katie handed each of them a blue binder that must have weighed as much as a newborn baby. Laura was surprised to get a friendly smile and wink from Jillian as she filed out the door behind Diana. *Ugh.* Leave it to Laura to have a crush on the director of all people. She looked back to see if Jillian was following them, but she and Katie were already headed in the opposite direction.

A wave of pride washed away the brief coolness of Jillian's absence when Diana herded them through a hidden entrance marked Staff Only. She was there. She had made it. She had overcome tragedy, sadness, failure, and defeat and now here she was. She was living the next part of her life. The one that was almost stolen from her ten years ago. The tears stung as they welled in her eyes and she swallowed around the large lump of emotion that formed in her throat. The scent of the sea and salt water hit her face. Laura closed her eyes and wiped away the tears that pooled in the corner of them.

Diana stopped the group once everyone was through the gate and latched it behind them. Just as Jillian had, Diana welcomed them to the next thirty-six weeks of their lives. Laura had counted about seven times that they'd mentioned the length of the program. She couldn't imagine that any of them were unaware of how long they would be there. It seemed like an odd thing to keep mentioning. They got it. It's thirty-six weeks, or nine months, or two-hundred and seventy days. For Laura, it was a very short time in the grand scheme of things.

Diana introduced herself again. She was an animal behaviorist, specializing in the care and conservation of California sea lions. "While many people think of us as merely a dolphinarium, it's important to understand that we aren't anything of the sort."

Everyone at the institute was passionate about setting the record straight when it came to who they were and why they were there. Laura was drawn in by her dynamic personality, as well as her devotion to the mission of the institution.

The institute was closed to the public Tuesday, Wednesday, and Thursday so they had open access to every habitat without worrying about the guests. In spite of this, the grounds were far from a ghost town. Full-time trainers, technicians, veterinarian staff, and maintenance workers hustled around throughout the park. Laura found it rather surreal to see everyone hard at work in plain sight. The veil of magic had been lifted, and the important inner workings of the park were exposed for her to see. It felt like being gifted a power few others would ever experience, and she had been invited to join another realm.

Diana led the group along a well-manicured path and around the large circular aviary that housed a variety of tropical birds. As pretty as they were, large birds made Laura nervous. Ever since she learned the power they had in those beaks, she always imagined one of them mistaking her thumb for a Brazil nut and snapping it off. She clenched her fists tight, tucking her thumbs safely inside.

Beyond the aviary was the otter habitat. They stopped by the glass to watch a pair of small-clawed otters jump and slide into the water. A small school of fish darted back and forth fleeing from the otters hunting for their afternoon snack. While they were occupied, two trainers sprayed down the rocks and boulders that made up the rest of their environment. The furry inhabitants showed their appreciation by feasting on their fresh catch on the nice, clean surface.

The group pushed forward pressing Laura against the glass in the alcove. The playful otters flipped and twisted beneath the surface of the water. Branches, rocks, and roots created an underwater playground for them as they squeezed beneath a sunken ledge to then pop up on the other side. The water was as clear as crystal as the midday sun filtered down to the bottom of the tank with its long rays. Laura's heart rate kicked up. She could feel her chest begin to tighten and her breaths grew shorter and faster with every quickening beat. Beads of sweat formed on her upper lip, and she wiped them away. She pressed her fingers against her neck and felt the rapid pumping of blood through the pulsing vein. Laura took a deep breath, filling every inch of her lungs with as much air as she could, and began to count.

One, she stepped back, trying to find an open space in the area. Two, she listened to the sound of the blood rushing through her ears. Three, she reminded herself that she was above water. Four, she tapped her fingers on the side of her leg in a slow, steady rhythm. Twenty more seconds passed, then thirty. Her lungs burned and sweat dripped from her hairline down to her eyebrows. Forty-five seconds now. She had pushed herself to the back of the group, away from the glass. A light breeze blew through. The air was free flowing and cool over her moist skin. Fifty-three, she needed to breathe.

Breathe, Laura.

Fifty-eight. It had been almost a minute, and she needed to take a breath. At fifty-nine, she coughed and gasped, drawing the attention of everyone around her. "Sorry," she said, her voice hoarse. She bent forward with both hands on her knees to keep herself from falling over as the rush of oxygen hit her brain. Diana had rushed to her side and pushed everyone back to give her space. Laura coughed and offered another weak sorry as she waved her arms.

"What happened?" Diana asked as she helped Laura stand upright.

Think of something, Laura. She grabbed her throat with her left hand and grunted. "Ugh. I...choked." Her voice was raspy. "I choked on a peppermint," she said as she pulled a wrapped candy from her pocket. Of course, she hadn't choked on anything, but there was no way in hell she could admit to that.

CHAPTER FIVE

L aura paced back and forth, wearing a rut into the floor between the toilet and the changing table on the wall. Every minute or so she would sit on the toilet for just a moment, except the stillness of her body increased the activity in her mind. Even as her heart rate and body temperature began to return to normal, she could still feel the tension in her muscles. It was an internal struggle between forging on or hiding away. She knew that retreating to the blanketed fortress of her bed wasn't the way to win this battle. She'd spent ten years hidden away, trapped by fear.

It was the fear that she found the hardest to face. She could breathe through the panic. She could talk herself back into reality. But the fear of dying, of losing control, of being lost in the darkness, cold and alone, those things were the most agonizing. Fear didn't go away when the physical symptoms subsided. It always stayed longer, like an uninvited guest who stuck around long after the others had gone but made no attempt to help with the aftermath. Fear was never alone, however; it always brought doubt.

Laura sat on the toilet once again. She rested her elbows on her knees and hung her shaky hands between them. She stared at them as they trembled with the effects of the adrenaline still coursing through her veins. Her head floated somewhere above her shoulders, and her brain was clouded with foggy thoughts.

Her right leg began to tap on its own accord, vibrating her entire body. She sat up straight, pulling her shoulders back and craning her neck all around producing sounds reminiscent of crispy rice cereal being drowned in milk.

You know where you went wrong. You lost focus.

She stood once again and resumed her pacing. The tension in her legs had eased enough during her sit that they wobbled beneath her when she took her first few steps. Here she was on her first day, a day that had started out full of hope and excitement, and she was locked in a bathroom trying not to curl up into a ball and sob in the corner.

Snap out of it, Laura. For fuck's sake.

She stopped and stood at the sink. Resting both hands on the basin, she stared at her reflection in the mirror. She pulled out the band that held back her ponytail. She shook out her hair and scrubbed her fingers through it.

"Look. You're fine. There wasn't any reason to be afraid," she said. "You lost focus, that's all."

Laura knew the very instant it had happened. However, it was the recognition of that very moment where she lost her grip on reality and tumbled headfirst into the abyss. She had let her mind relax and allowed it to wander off on its own.

Laura had been so overwhelmed with the excitement of the day she had allowed herself to live in the moment. It had been so long since anything had been able to overshadow the memories of her past, she hadn't realized it until it was too late. For those few minutes—or were they hours?—she had lived a normal life. Until fear reminded her that she was anything but normal.

"What if it happens again? It's going to happen again."

The thought that she was right made her stomach turn. The pink from her face washed out into a pasty white. Her own mind was against her, willing her to fail. She turned on the water and splashed her face a few times until the color began to return. She needed to rejoin the group. If she spent any more time in the bathroom arguing with herself, she was going to go mad. Although anyone who argued with themselves probably already was mad to begin with.

She tied her hair back up and pinched some color back into her cheeks. "You've got this shit, Laura," she said to herself before leaving the bathroom.

When Laura opened the door, she came face-to-face with one of the other trainees from her group. She jumped back with a start thinking she had almost walloped him with the door. "Hey, so sorry about that."

"Oh, no worries. You didn't get me. Hey, are you okay?" he asked.

Laura looked around, curious to see if someone had sent him over to check on her. Maybe even to spy on her? She was sure the latter was just a result of her paranoia, as she had been in the bathroom well over twenty minutes. Perhaps Diana had sent him to see if she'd fallen in.

"I'm okay, thanks. Have you been sent to round up the stragglers?"

"Nope. They're all still over there chatting away. I've just been waiting to use the bathroom."

"Oh shit, I'm sorry. I didn't realize the others weren't working," Laura said, stepping out of the way, and he reached for the handle of the door.

"They are. I think. I'm just…particular about the facilities I use."

"I understand. I just needed a few minutes alone to recover from—"

"Your near death experience?"

"What?" Laura's heart slammed to a stop in her chest.

"Your peppermint incident," he said, cocking his head to the side and raising an eyebrow.

"Yes, right." Laura chuckled nervously trying to brush off her awkwardness.

"I also may have overheard you talking to yourself in there, and I'm pretty certain you had nothing to be afraid of surrounded by a dozen CPR certifications."

What had he heard? What had she said aloud to make him say that? There were so many voices in her head she wasn't sure which were out loud. "Oh."

"Listen, I get it. We all have secrets, and I know a panic attack when I see one."

Laura's mouth dropped open to protest, but the honest eyes looking back into hers assured her that there was no point in trying to hide it. "I just got overwhelmed, you know? Please don't tell anyone."

"Trust me, I'm the last person you need to worry about blabbing other people's shit."

"Thank you, um?"

"BJ. And you're welcome…"

"Laura."

BJ smiled and disappeared into the bathroom. Save for her, he must have been the second oldest in their group. Even so, that didn't put him any older than twenty-one she guessed. Laura wondered when she'd gotten old enough to think everyone else seemed so much younger. While the interaction was a bit strange, it hadn't been uncomfortable. She should've been more upset that he'd been lurking outside the door, for who knows how long, spying on her. Yet, she could see in his eyes that he was concerned about her, and it was a relief not to feel judged by him when he called her out. She liked him. He was cute, and no doubt already had a couple of young girls swooning over him. Although she might still have a talk with him about loitering outside the toilets, but otherwise she liked him.

Laura rejoined the group and slipped into an empty seat at the end of the long table. The smell of corn chips and coffee made her stomach roll. Even more unsettling was watching the girl across from her enjoy the mix of flavors. She couldn't be certain because she had quickly looked away, but Laura swore she'd dipped a Frito into her pudding, or was it yogurt? Either way she reminded herself to avoid sitting near this person in the future.

After they left the otter exhibit, Diana called for a break. Laura had no idea if it had been a planned intermission, but she was thankful either way. She brought them to the dining hall, which was also the public restaurant during visitor hours and pointed them in opposite directions. One end for snacks and beverages, and the other end for the restrooms. Laura had zero interest in food then, and after watching the snack abomination she was certain her disinterest would stick around for the rest of the day.

Diana approached the head of the table where Laura was sitting and leaned beside her. "How are you feeling? Better?"

"Much. Thank you."

"All right, kids," Diana said to the group. "We've just had a longer break than the staff gets for lunch. Don't get used to it."

Laura couldn't help but feel that Diana had directed that last statement to her when she tapped her fingers on the table in front of her. Although she made no eye contact or other obvious motion toward her. Her nagging joyriders, fear and doubt, taunted her from their perch on her shoulders. Laura looked up at Diana trying to discern any meaning or intent she might have had behind her statement, but she was met with a smile and a pat on the shoulder.

"Let's go."

The Florida sun was high in the cloudless sky when they stepped back outside to continue their orientation. BJ appeared next to Laura and pinched at his shirt, flapping it against his chest.

"How are you not dying out here in this?" he asked.

"I was born here."

"What does that mean? You have gills?"

"Basically." During her childhood, you could have believed that.

"Seriously though, we're surrounded by water and can't get into any of it." Laura laughed. He was right, although she hoped they would soon be spending countless hours in the water, and he'd look forward to the few dry days they would have.

As much as Laura loved the water, the one thing this state had more of than sun was rain, and she'd learned to appreciate the hot, beautiful days as well. When the warm breeze carried with it the strong scent of fish, she almost changed her mind. There wasn't anyone, save for Diana, who didn't react to the odor. Laura had smelled worse things, but at two p.m. in June on a hot day with a queasy stomach, this ranked up there.

She was a little taken aback to see the sea lion habitat void of any actual sea lions. In their place were a handful of humans scattered about the enclosure with an arsenal of buckets, brooms, and brushes. On top of the artificial stone mountain was a woman, soaking wet and wielding an industrial pressure washer. Laura's mind flashed to Jillian and how ruggedly attractive and delectable she would look standing on top of those rocks with her clothes clinging to each of her countless curves. The gust of wind blew the overspray into her face and snapped her out of a most inappropriate fantasy. Especially as there was nothing sexy about scrubbing down an animal enclosure. Even less so after Diana explained what the white streaks and splats covering just about every surface were. It seems that the unofficial residents of the park left behind quite a mess while they spent their days swiping free meals from guests with bad aim. Laura was certain that cleaning up bird shit was going to rocket to the top of her list of "Worst things to do." Right up there with dead fish in the hot sun.

However, she wasn't complaining about the light misting they were getting while they stood at the railing. Regardless of her Florida roots, she could appreciate a cool down as much as the next guy. She took the vision of a dripping wet Jillian with her when Diana moved them along. They stopped for a few minutes here and there until they reached a tall wooden gate wide enough for two-way motor traffic. Mounted in the gate was a door marked, "No unescorted visitors beyond this point."

As Laura stepped through, the lush and tropical landscape disappeared and was replaced by a much more industrial, post-apocalyptic setting. Enormous tanks towered like skyscrapers in downtown Tampa. Pipes of various colors and sizes snaked through the lot. Rows of them traveled along in parallel before one or two shot off in their own directions where they joined up with others or disappeared deep into concrete tunnels underground. The whir and hum of pumps and generators filled the air. The noise was amplified as the sounds echoed off every solid surface around them. Laura and the others stared in awe at the infrastructure behind the scenes. It was like standing at the heart of a living, breathing machine. Beyond the buildings that housed the intricate computer systems and servers was the metaphorical belly of the operation.

"Welcome to your new home," Diana announced. "You will spend more time here than you will in your bed." She pulled the door open and let out a gust of frigid air ripe with the scent of a Seattle fish market. The smell was strong, levels above what they had experienced earlier, but didn't elicit any reaction from Laura's belly. *Thank God.* Maybe eating a meal was in her future after all.

"Now we're talking." BJ nudged at Laura's ribs with his pointy elbow.

"I know, right?"

Laura was glad to see that the others were just as excited to get into the fun stuff. Around the room, trainers shuffled, sorted, weighed, and handled every manner and species of seafood. There were boxes of squid, totes of capelin, and buckets upon buckets of clams, mussels, and crab. The clanking of steel, the chopping, and the chatter all added to the symphony of meal time.

"Is it weird that I want to grab a fistful of that fish to see what it feels like?" BJ asked, not so rhetorically.

"Yes, but then that makes us both kind of weird." It was true. She had an overwhelming desire to smash her fingers into the cold buckets of slimy seafood just to complete the whole sensory experience. Looking around, it seemed that they weren't the only weirdos; everyone in the group pumped and bounced on their toes like racehorses at a starting line. Before any of them could do anything they would regret for the rest of the day, Fletcher appeared.

As if he knew what they were all thinking, he said, "You will get plenty of opportunities to play in the fish guts. And when the day comes, and it will come, where you can't bring yourself to touch another mackerel, remember this moment." Diana bid the group adieu and left them in the fish house with Fletcher.

"Are you thinking what I'm thinking?" BJ leaned in close and muttered against Laura's shoulder.

She wasn't sure who was more excited as she thrummed her fingers against her thighs. All but three of the staff had gone, leaving just the nine of them and two dozen pails of fish ready to go.

"You, me, and the seven of them." Laura laughed and flicked her head in their direction.

As soon as Fletcher told them to grab a bucket in each hand, the squeals erupted. Laura lunged forward like all the others and snatched the handles of the two buckets closest to her. Her new partner in crime, BJ, did the same and then flashed a goofy, exaggerated smile at her as he clutched the pails close to his chest. Laura was so happy to be surrounded by so many others just as excited as she was for the same silly reasons. They got her, and she got them.

When they each had their pails, Fletcher herded them outside. The humid air slapped her in the face like a soggy mop. But she'd be damned if that was going to dampen her mood. The group lined up on the sidewalk, and Fletcher had them each hold their buckets out at arm's length in front of them. It was then that Laura noticed the colored tape around each one. He called everyone forward with red markings and sent them off with Kristina. He held back the remaining five with the buckets marked in blue.

Laura's heart sunk just a little at the idea that she had chosen the wrong color. She hadn't even thought of the possibility that she wouldn't be feeding dolphins when Fletcher had told them to take their two pails. However, when Jillian came jogging up to them from out of nowhere, Laura forgot all about fish and dolphins.

"Oh Christ," Laura said a little louder then she'd hoped, but not loud enough for anyone except BJ to hear.

It was almost as if Jillian had jumped right out of her earlier fantasy. Her short black hair was slicked back and pulled into a small, tight ponytail. She wore a light blue, long-sleeve rash guard that accented her feminine curves. A thin whistle hung from her neck and rested between her breasts. The shape of her hidden bikini top stood out in contrast to the lighter and dryer areas of her fitted top. But it was the barely-there bottoms that exposed her long, muscular legs that stopped Laura's heart. Her mouth watered as she tracked a drop of water down the inside of Jillian's thigh. She licked her lips and could almost taste the salty droplet on her tongue. How in the hell was she going to be able to function within a hundred yards of this woman knowing at any moment she could appear out of nowhere dripping wet and dressed like that?

While her legs wobbled beneath her, Laura's arms felt like lead, weighed down by the ten pounds of dead fish she was carrying in each hand as she followed behind Jillian. She had an ass that made Laura's head spin, so she was glad for the extra weight to keep the rest of her body firmly planted on the ground.

CHAPTER SIX

It was about ninety degrees outside, but no one would know by the state of Jillian's nipples. The way Laura's eyes had raked over her had set off a chain reaction within her body starting deep in her core and manifesting her arousal sharply against her tight suit. She avoided making any eye contact with Laura as she raked her predatory gaze over Jillian's body eliciting reactions she couldn't control. She had no recollection of ever feeling so exposed, at least not when clothed. Granted, she was wearing less now than she had the other times they had interacted, but not even Diana had ever looked at her this way. For the first time since she'd met Laura, she was concerned about the irresistible draw she had toward her.

As they approached the dolphin lagoons, several of her full-time trainers milled about waiting for her and the group. In the pool behind them a dozen playful and hungry dolphins splashed and leaped about seemingly practicing pieces and parts of previous lessons. Jillian directed everyone along the wooden boardwalk that led out over the water where it split and divided their own slice of the bay into five deep pools.

Jillian stopped under a covered awning and gave them a few minutes to process the moment. Mouths dropped open, and everyone bounced with excitement, including Laura who looked as awestruck as Jillian felt the first time she had stood in the very same spot. As much as she wanted to stack the deck and assign trainers so that Jillian just so happened to get Laura in the deal, she didn't. Each trainer got a new trainee, and she started with pairing Laura and Kaylea in order to remove the temptation. She had a feeling that doing that for the next nine months was going to be her saving grace. Thankfully, she was only scheduled to teach one course this time around, and by then this childish infatuation would have run its course.

Jillian walked along the boardwalk, pausing at each pair to observe and assess everyone's initial interactions with each other as well as with the animals. There wasn't a single person who didn't have a smile plastered across their face. It was one of the many make-or-break moments they would face during their time at the institute. Jillian didn't like to think about the statistics of choosing this as a career. Even if all nine made it through the program with flying colors, which was unlikely in itself, at least three of them would struggle for years to land their first job. It was her job to help keep that spark alive inside them, to feed that fire with everything that they'd need to succeed.

She stood on the platform above Peter and BJ who were interacting with Kaipo. He was one of the youngest members in the pod and had a joyful and curious personality. He found BJ a worthy playmate as he interacted with his youthful energy. Jillian was pleased with the pairing. Across the corner of the pool, Jillian could see Kaylea and Laura. Jillian made her notes and observations while Kaylea took over working with her two favorite girls, Pepper and Luna.

Kaylea sat back on her legs on the edge of the floating dock with a bucket set between her and Laura. She watched intently as Kaylea ran through the process with Laura. Unlike the others, Laura seemed hesitant and uncertain. While Peter was barely keeping an excited BJ from diving face-first into the water, Kaylea had to almost coax Laura closer to the edge. Luna seemed intrigued by Laura's aloofness, spyhopping and turning onto her side to focus on her. Pepper on the other hand wasn't as fazed.

As always, she was more interested in that ten-pound bucket of food. She pushed herself up onto the dock and caused it to dip into the water under her weight. Laura gasped and gripped at the side of the dock to keep from falling forward, although in reality it hadn't tipped far enough to toss anyone in. Jillian laughed and when Laura realized her overreaction she did too.

"Stare any harder and your eyes are going to fall out of your head."

"What the hell are you talking about?" Jillian said as she turned to face Diana who must've spent more than a few minutes watching her.

"You told me no. So I'm just returning the favor is all."

"Thanks, but I don't need any favors. I'm simply trying out pairs and making initial observations."

"You don't even observe holidays that seriously," Diana said.

"Funny," Jillian said, but didn't laugh. She was well aware that she had taken a special interest in Laura, but the idea that Diana thought she'd somehow caught her red-handed irritated her. Mostly because it felt like she had done it on purpose and made a calculated move. Jillian got it. Like she'd told Diana, they of all people should know better than to start a workplace fling. However, Jillian was human and what harm could there be in seeing and being seen? It was flattering to have such a smart and beautiful woman react to her the way Laura did. It was nice to feel that part of herself was still alive and kicking.

"Just think twice about it, okay? If she has any chance of finishing this program having you as a distraction won't do her any favors."

As irritated as she was with Diana for ruining her fun, she wasn't wrong. There was a reason they were ranked one of the top accredited certification programs in the country. "You're right." And with that acknowledgement, Diana walked away.

She said it, and she knew she should have meant it, but what harm was there in an innocent and unspoken attraction?

Especially since it had been so long since someone had made her feel so visible. She knew how much potential Laura had. With her experience and education, there was no doubt that her career would skyrocket with this certification behind her. Who was Jillian to put that at risk to feel better about herself? And she'd be an idiot to think that anyone would approve of the director dating a trainee. "Ugh," she grunted. It had been nice being caught up in the playful back-and-forth, but Diana was right; it was time to get back to business.

Day one was nearly over, and Jillian's role in the action was as well. It was time for her to step back and let Diana, Fletcher, and the rest of her instructors do what they did best. Except for a course on performance skills, she had scheduled in the third term, Jillian would be spending her days stuck in an office or enjoying a few brief moments in the water with her pod.

She couldn't help herself when she let her gaze settle once again on Laura. Jillian was pleased to see that she seemed more at ease at the edge of the dock leaning over to give a few soft kisses to Pepper. She was a bit surprised that Pepper had let someone new get so close in such a short time, as she had been her usual disinterested self just an hour earlier. Pepper opened her mouth wide, and Laura splashed a handful of water into her mouth. Jillian knew exactly what was coming next, but Laura had no idea. She wanted to shout out a kind warning, but her devilish side decided it would be funnier not to. Laura laughed and splashed as Pepper clicked and tossed her head around playfully.

The joy on Laura's face was undeniable, and Pepper was loving every moment of the interaction because she knew what was coming. When she closed her mouth and dropped her head into the water, Jillian cringed. Oblivious, Laura leaned forward laughing as Pepper raised up and spit a gallon of lagoon water right in her face.

Jillian howled with laughter, not even trying to hide her delight. Laura responded with a wide-mouthed surprise and a short-lived scream that died when she inhaled Pepper's mouthful of water. What hadn't made it into her mouth had drenched just about every inch of her chest.

Still afflicted with the giggles, Jillian headed over to the dock where Kaylea had climbed up onto the boardwalk to wait for a soaking wet Laura to make her way up the ladder. When she paused and looked up from the top rung, Jillian lost herself once again in laughter. Laura looked just like a toddler who'd sprayed herself in the face with the garden hose.

The loose wisps of hair that had blown free from her ponytail throughout the day were now plastered to her rosy cheeks. Jillian looked over at Kaylea, who was doing her best to suppress her own amusement. When Kaylea shrugged it was clear that she had also known what was going to happen. Jillian gave Kaylea a light fist bump, chuckled, and then looked back at Laura to see that they had been caught in their little joke.

Laura's mouth dropped open in surprise as she glanced back and forth between them. "Did you make her do that?"

"Oh man, I wish," Jillian said.

Laura looked at Kaylea and raised her eyebrow. She raised her hands in front of her and shrugged.

"She didn't stop her either." Jillian snorted and wiped the tears of joy from her eyes. "It's kind of her thing. She does it to me all the time. Unless, I catch her first, of course."

"I was surprised," Kaylea said. "She doesn't do that to just anyone, and certainly not to a newb."

"I know," Jillian said, reaching to give Laura a hand up onto the boardwalk. "I saw it coming as soon as she started tossing her head around."

"And neither of you said a thing?" Laura said as she wrung out her shirt.

The water splashed and pooled onto the deck, and she chuckled. "Nope. Where's the fun in that?" There was so much about this moment that she was enjoying she wouldn't have known where to begin.

Laura flopped her wet shirt in the air. "Well, I'm sorry to disappoint, but that was awesome! I mean I could have done without the gallon of fish water in my mouth, but everything else was amazing!" Laura's voice was in a pitch so high Jillian thought the dolphins were going to respond.

Laura danced around in utter elation, and Jillian felt a sharp pang in her chest followed by a slow warmth that spread throughout her body. There was so much joy and light in Laura that Jillian was blind to the world around them. This was going to prove to be the longest program of Jillian's life.

❖

Bright fluorescent lighting flooded the empty lot outside of the fish house, and illuminated every nook and cranny of the area. Anything beyond the range of a couple of feet was lost in the pitch-black darkness. By Laura's guess it was a little after eight, although it could have been well past midnight and she couldn't have told the difference. She was too exhausted to make small talk with her companions as they used what remaining energy they had to scrub, scour, and spray down every last bucket, cart, and cooler within a forty-mile radius. At least that's what it had seemed like judging by her sore and pruned fingers.

She sat back on her legs to give her knees a rest and stretch out the stiff muscles in her back. Laura surveyed her progress, comparing the remaining dirty equipment to the clean still waiting for BJ to rinse before racking it up to dry. BJ, Brooke, and Laura had established their own assembly line method the first week when they drew the lucky stick and were assigned scrub duty right out of the gate. Laura hadn't thought much about it then, but as the days passed she came to realize why Fletcher told them to hold on to their enthusiasm.

"Switch," Laura said, having had enough scrubbing duty.

Neither BJ nor Brooke heard her as it seemed they were too busy flirting shamelessly over control of the hose. It was cute, but

Laura's energy and patience were waning. There was a hot shower and a rock-hard mattress calling her name. "Hey, lovebirds, how about we put a pin in that and finish this first?"

BJ froze like a deer in headlights and his face washed of color. After a few seconds of awkward silence, he forced a thin smile before dropping the hose on the ground. He reached for Laura's scrub brush, though he didn't make eye contact with her.

"Hey," she said as she leaned to force him to look at her. "I didn't mean anything. I'm exhausted, and I don't want to be out here all night."

"It's fine," he said, grabbing the brush from her and blinking away from her stare. She let him have it, but before he walked away, he said, "We aren't lovebirds."

Ah. He wasn't mad or scared, he was embarrassed. Laura wanted to apologize for calling him out like that. It hadn't been her intention at all. There was no denying the obvious attraction between the two of them. Maybe he hadn't yet gotten up the courage to let her know. She knew all too well about not so secretly crushing on someone. Unfortunately, unlike BJ and Brooke, Jillian seemed to have made herself scarce over the last couple of weeks. Laura could count on one hand the few times she had gotten to see her. Each time it was always from a distance and just for a few fleeting moments. Part of her couldn't help but feel the avoidance was intentional.

Even at the end of the day, when she was bone tired and stumbling back to the dorms at night, the idea of running into Jillian along the way excited her. Although she had yet to do so she was always hopeful. BJ didn't say a thing to Laura as they finished up for the night and prepped the stations for the next morning. Brooke had said good night to them both and headed off to the dining hall for a late dinner with the others. Laura was too tired to eat anything heavy, and even though BJ most often accompanied Brooke, tonight he didn't. Clearly, she had upset him. He was walking several paces ahead, and while he never slowed or looked back, he knew she was behind him.

She called his name, but he kept on. He was her friend, and she would force him to talk to her if she had to. She increased her pace and had just about caught him when, as luck would have it, Jillian appeared at the intersection of the paths. Her belly flip-flopped when Jillian called out for her. She glanced between Jillian's smiling face and BJ's back. She knew she should follow him and clear the air, but for the first time in weeks fate had placed Jillian on her path home.

"Hey," Laura said.

"Hey there. I didn't mean to stop you. You look like you were on a mission." Jillian pointed after BJ.

"No. Well, yes sort of. I was trying to apologize for something I might have done wrong."

"Might have? You don't know?" Jillian asked.

"Yeah. I think I embarrassed him in front of a girl."

"A girl? Really, who?" Jillian asked.

"Brooke. They were flirting and giggling over the hose, and I kind of called them out. I was just exhausted and not in the mood."

"Interesting," Jillian said.

"Interesting? Which part? Because none of that was what I'd call interesting." Did she find it so because she'd lost her cool and snapped at the kids? In all likelihood it was not.

"BJ and Brooke. Interesting."

"Oh." Laura wouldn't have called that interesting either. This woman needed to get out more. "Not really. They're both young, smart, attractive kids. Makes complete sense, but not especially interesting as you keep saying."

"Well, BJ—" Jillian stopped herself short. "You're his friend, right?"

"If he forgives me." Jillian's expression turned serious. Laura's heart skipped a beat when Jillian took a step closer and set her hand on Laura's shoulder.

"Watch out for him, okay?" she asked, looking deep into Laura's eyes.

Laura was taken aback by the intensity in her question, which despite sounding like one, it wasn't. It was a command, sort of a call to action it seemed. Laura covered Jillian's hand with her own, and she answered without question. "Absolutely."

Before letting go, Jillian squeezed her hand. "Thank you."

She released Laura's hand and walked off the path into the dark. Laura stood cemented to the spot wondering what the hell had just happened. She was aroused, intrigued, and inspired all at once. Laura might have a degree in animal behavior, but that didn't keep her from responding to Jillian in the most carnal ways. Maybe that was the problem. When Jillian disappeared, the coolness of her absence settled over her. She shivered in spite of the balmy evening air and then rushed along after BJ.

He was doing so well in the program that Laura found it odd that Jillian would want her to keep an eye on him. He was young but hardly innocent. He was pretty much what she'd expect from a kid his age. Although it wasn't like she spent a lot of time with people that much younger than her, at least not before coming here.

He didn't seem to be in danger, or struggling, and he got along with everyone she would say. So, the one thing Laura could think of was that maybe he was gay, and Jillian was invoking the unspoken family bond of their community. She supposed it made sense, although they'd never discussed their sexuality with each other. It had been a non-issue when they connected that first day. If he was gay it could explain why he'd been so uncomfortable being teased by her in front of another person. She sped up her pace to a light jog; she didn't want her apology to wait any longer than it needed to. She felt awful and couldn't even imagine what BJ felt like.

Laura saw his silhouette in the light that spilled out through the glass doors of the residence hall. She called his name, but either he didn't hear her, or he was ignoring her. She went with the latter. Her jog puttered out with a few exasperated footfalls. When she reached the building, she headed straight to his room.

Laura knocked on his door and waited for him to answer. After a few moments without a response, she knocked again. "BJ, it's Laura. Can I talk to you for a sec?" Several more seconds passed until he finally opened the door.

It was obvious that he had been crying and tried in vain to hide it. He stared at the floor when he spoke. "Yeah?"

"I'm sorry," she said.

"For what? I'm fine," he said, yet still not looking up at her.

"Obviously, what I said upset you. I didn't mean to embarrass you or—" When he looked up at her she stopped talking.

"You didn't embarrass me, Laura."

"Then what?"

He stepped back and opened the door. "I want to tell you something."

Her heart leapt into her throat. Very few good things ever came from stringing those words together. "Okay," she said as she stepped into his room and closed the door behind her. She spun around quickly and blurted out, "Please tell me you're not dying."

His smile was small, but Laura was relieved by it anyway. "No. I'm not dying. Although—"

Laura cut him off. "Well, if you're not dying, then whatever it is can't be all that bad. Just tell me." She had begun to ramble.

"If you'd shut up a fucking minute, I would."

"Okay," Laura said before sinking onto the bed properly scolded.

He took a deep breath and ran his hands back through his hair. "Look. I like Brooke. But it's...well, it's complicated, and she doesn't know."

Laura chuckled. "Oh, she knows. I didn't call you two lovebirds for no reason. It's a bit obvious, I would say."

"Maybe so, but that doesn't change anything."

"I mean sure it might be distracting dating someone you work with, but I wouldn't call it complicated. It happens all the time." Laura knew that for sure.

"Well, it is for me. I'm not…I'm trans. I was born a biological female, but I live and identify as male."

Laura wasn't certain how to respond. She wasn't surprised; she just wasn't sure what to say. "I've never had anyone come out to me before." All of a sudden, she understood Jillian's requests loud and clear. He was family.

"Does it bother you?" he asked.

"Bother me? Fuck no, not at all." Laura tried to recall how many times she had asked that same question. It wasn't every time she came out, but it was close.

"Really?"

"Yes, really. Thank you for trusting me enough to tell me. I know it's never easy," Laura said. "You know I'm a lesbian, right?"

"Yes. Well, I mean, I assumed. Mostly because of the way you covet Jillian Marshall's body every time she walks by."

"No, I don't. Okay, yes, I do." He was right, and there was no sense in denying it. "So, listen, I'm not going to bombard you with a million questions or anything, but if you wanna talk I'm here."

"Thank you. Any other time I'd totally take you up on the offer, but I'm freaking exhausted," he said as he slumped onto the bed beside her.

"Oh, thank God." Between the physical and emotional workout, she wanted to fall over dead. "But first we need to shower, because one of us smells like a sea lion's butthole."

Jillian wondered how long it would take for Laura to figure out what she had been talking about. Her warning might have sounded a bit more dire than she had intended it to, but seeing as she was running after an upset BJ, she felt the timing was apropos. It was just a matter of time that those close to him would find out, and while it was Jillian's professional job to protect him from any backlash, it was also her moral obligation. As much as she wished for such things to be a non-issue, they weren't yet. When you lived and worked with others 24/7, 365 days a year, there wasn't much you could get away with. There were bound to be attractions, revelations, and even disagreements. However, there was one thing Jillian wouldn't tolerate and that was discrimination.

Thankfully, BJ and Laura had connected early in the program and had eased most of Jillian's initial concerns. Now that she had Laura on the official watch, any worries that she still had were gone.

Laura's unquestioning acceptance to protect someone she barely knew was inspiring. So many others would have needed more detail, more information, and spent several selfish minutes determining what was in it for them. But not Laura. She had looked Jillian in the eye and gripped her hand in her own as she accepted her request without hesitation. The confidence in her response sent a wave of warmth throughout Jillian's body. She could have stood in the dim light of the pathway finding anything to keep her there talking all night. Yet as much as Jillian had wanted it, it was obvious that Laura wanted and needed to be with BJ.

She adored Laura's inability to hide her emotions whether it was passion, desire, elation, or anxiety. And in that moment, she could see the battle to stay or go that mirrored her very own struggle to hold on or let her go. As long as they held each other's hand, neither was going anywhere. Reluctantly, Jillian had released her and Laura ran off after him. As she headed home along the path, she wondered what it would be like to have Laura chase after her that way, and to be on the receiving end of such care and affection.

CHAPTER SEVEN

After they'd finished lunch BJ, Brooke, and Laura wandered down to the lagoon to catch the last few minutes of the afternoon dolphin interactions. The crowd was decent for a Friday afternoon, although it seemed made up mostly of high school students. Laura guessed it was one of the many career and college field trips that the area schools used to light fires under the kids who hadn't yet chosen a path. It was trips like these that kept the fire burning inside her during her school days.

As the session ended, the three of them made their way backstage. Jillian was there praising and treating the girls for their job well done. When they were finished, she and her team sent the pod off to enjoy a few hours of free swim in the deep pools. With the entire pod out to enjoy the day, it was time to clean.

There was never any shortage of areas that needed to be cleaned. Sometimes Laura and the others wondered if the program was just some elaborate scheme to get free labor. If they weren't in class, they were scrubbing shit off something, and today they were swabbing the decks, literally.

Each pool was separated by thousands of feet of underwater fencing. There were two remote-operated gates between each to allow animals in and out as needed. At the surface there was artificial stonework that ran the length and width of each pool, as well as boardwalks and pathways that allowed trainers and staff access to all sides of the enclosures.

Two of the five pools were larger than a football field each, and Laura calculated that there were over two miles of recycled decking and concrete waiting to be scrubbed. If it weren't for the damn freeloading birds that shat on everything in sight, they might not have had to clean as much.

"If I didn't know better, I'd think those assholes threw a party out here last night," BJ said, bumping his chin toward the flock of egrets that perched on the nearby railing.

"I used to think they were such beautiful, majestic birds," Brooke said.

No sooner had she finished her statement than one of them fluffed his feathers and released a great white splat onto the ground and Laura laughed. "I swear he just did that shit on purpose." They laughed.

"What's wrong, Beej? Gonna lose your lunch over a little bit of bird shit?" Steven said as he sauntered up to them.

"No," he said but didn't engage.

Laura didn't understand why there always had to be one in every crowd, and Steven was that one. He was an attention-seeking jokester whose terrible sense of humor was always made worse by his poor timing. Steven shooed away the birds before bending and swiping his hand through the fresh splat. Laura was mortified that anyone would do that, and her stomach turned. A devious grin spread across his face, and he locked eyes with BJ.

"Don't you dare, Steven," Laura said as he took a slow step toward BJ, but he didn't listen.

"Not funny. Cut it out," BJ said, stepping back and holding up his hand.

"Aww. Is lil Beej afraid of some poopy?"

"Steven, knock it off. You're not funny." Laura warned him again, but he ignored her.

Before she could reach out to stop him, he lunged at BJ with his nasty hand. Instinctively, BJ jumped back out of his reach, but there was nowhere to go except for into the water. His feet kicked wildly at the edge of the deck before he fell backward off the boardwalk. Steven howled with laughter as BJ landed flat on his back against the water. Laura could see the wind knocked from his lungs before he went under engulfed by a huge splash.

The others stood in silence staring at a proud Steven, his chest puffed as he wiped off any remaining bird shit down the thigh of his sweatpants. Laura's heart raced with rage and anxiety. She wanted to lunge at him and scratch his face like a mountain lion, but she was more worried about BJ. He'd hit hard and sunk quickly. Instead of jumping on Steven, she leapt into the water where BJ had gone under.

The water was cloudy where the commotion had kicked up sand from the bottom. She fumbled around, feeling with her hands for any sign of him. She opened her eyes to get a quick look for where he might be but saw nothing. The salt water stung her eyes. Clouded shadows and flickering rays of light that streaked into the water all around her. She began to second-guess her decision to jump in. She tried to focus on finding BJ, but she couldn't see him. All she could see were millions of tiny bubbles racing to the surface as she looked up toward the light.

The blue sky beckoned her to the surface much like it had that day. But she couldn't reach it no matter how hard she tried. She kicked her legs, but they felt weighted as she sunk deeper. Her boots. She still had on her rubber muck boots, and now they were filled with water. The realization that she was sinking to the bottom of the lagoon terrified her. She struggled with each boot until she was free. She kicked her legs and flailed her arms, but she wasn't moving. Her lungs burned for air. Something grabbed hold of her ankle, and she transported back to those last few seconds before everything in her world turned black.

There she was once again ten feet beneath the water's surface with her foot tangled in the cypress roots. But this time the roots released her and pushed her toward the surface where she found herself gasping for air as she broke through. The sound of blood rushing through her ears muffled the chaos around her as everyone's hands and arms grasped at her, pulling her out of the water.

Sitting next to her was BJ. She hacked up the salty water she'd swallowed. Through the crowd, she spotted Jillian. Her face was fire engine red, and she towered over a very submissive Steven. Laura couldn't hear what she was yelling, but the anger on her face spoke volumes. A hand gripped her arm, and she turned to face BJ. She was filled with relief to know that he was okay. No thanks to her.

"I'm sorry," Laura said.

"Sorry? You jumped in to rescue me. Don't apologize."

"But I didn't. It's clear that I made the situation worse by trying to help."

"Don't be stupid. It was Steven's fault, and nobody else's. Big dumbass."

Laura looked up to see a concerned Jillian staring at her. "Is everyone all right?"

BJ and Laura answered at the same time, "Yes."

"What happened down there, Laura? BJ came up long before you did, and then went back for you."

Laura's head snapped to BJ. "You did?" BJ shrugged and nodded.

Of course, he had. Laura hadn't any idea where she was or how long she'd been underwater. From the moment she'd gone under, all her ability to rescue BJ had vanished. She'd been worse than worthless and she had made herself a liability. She wasn't even in a clear mind when she jumped in after him, instead of going after Steven. Now here she was soaking wet, amidst curious onlookers reliving the memories that haunted her nightmares.

The difference now was Jillian, who stood among the group yet said nothing. The disappointment on her face was clear, and Laura began to cry. This was it. This was the true end of her dream.

Laura pushed herself up from the ground and opened her mouth to speak, but no words came out. She could feel everyone's eyes on her. They were judging her, shaming her. Her last chance slipped away from her like it was her very last breath. She had failed. Laura pushed through the crowd and ran. She was so out of control. She wanted to scream, cry, and throw up, but she couldn't even focus enough to choose a physical reaction.

Her adrenaline was in overdrive. She could run a hundred miles without ever stopping. Maybe if she did, she could outrun this haunting shadow that was smothering her. This phantom of death that had followed her every day for ten years. She had no command over the debilitating fear that it would one day come for her again and succeed at holding her under until her last breath was pressed from her lungs. Laura knew that feeling all too well, yet somehow, she had narrowly escaped that fate. She was certain, however, that the reaper would keep trying every time she got into the water.

She found herself standing at the edge of the property where the last pool bordered the teal blue waters of the Bay. She might have kept running if she'd had on shoes and the barbed wire fences around the perimeter of the park had not been there. Her body and soul were torn between the peaceful view and her fear of the water that stretched out before her. She allowed herself to cry freely here out of sight of anyone. She sobbed without restraint, so much so that she'd not heard anyone approach behind her.

"Laura?"

Laura gasped, choking on her tears. She swiped at her face with both hands. She didn't need to turn around; she could recognize Jillian's voice in a crowded room. "Yeah?" She continued to stare out at the blurry horizon.

"What's going on with you?" Jillian asked.

"I…I'm sorry. I can't do this."

"Can't do what?" Jillian asked, grabbing Laura by the shoulder and turning her around to face her.

"Any of it. I thought I could. I thought I was better. And he warned me, but I wouldn't listen."

"Laura, look at me." Jillian cupped Laura's chin and tipped her face up to hers.

"Who warned you? Steven? I'm taking care of him. I will not tolerate that sort of behavior in my program."

"No. Dr. Shaw. He told me I might not be ready. But I didn't want to hear it."

"What aren't you telling me? Because this all seems a bit of an overreaction to what just happened."

The urge to be sick rose into her throat, and Laura's mouth watered. She took a few deep breaths through her nose and blew them out slowly.

❖

The anguish on Laura's face was clear. Whatever she was about to say went much deeper than the incident with Steven and BJ. Laura looked her in the eyes, and Jillian's heart sank. The sparkle of happiness they once had was masked by the tears. "Please tell me what is going on."

"I have PTSD."

The words took her aback. They weren't what she expected her to say. Jillian hadn't seen anything about the military or being overseas in her file, and there was certainly no mention of post-traumatic stress disorder.

"Well, that along with the other things that go along with it like depression, anxiety, and panic attacks." Jillian knew the latter were par for the course with a PTSD diagnosis. Plenty of her friends and relatives were happily medicated for their own synaptic battles, but PTSD wasn't a common mental illness and no doubt should have been mentioned in her medical disclosure. Jillian's head was spinning. She needed to grab hold of this situation before it, and Laura, continued to spiral out of control.

"Come here," she said, running her hand down Laura's arm and taking her hand. She pulled her to a nearby bench and sat her down. "I need to know everything, Laura. If your illness puts yourself and others in danger, I need to know about it."

"I thought I was better. I wanted to be better, but I guess I never will be." Laura was rambling and mumbling, and Jillian was growing more frustrated with every second that passed.

"Laura, spill," she said, squeezing Laura's hand.

"I drowned. Well, almost drowned. Ten years ago."

Jillian's stomach somersaulted. "What?"

"It was a senior field trip to Crystal Springs. A biology thing. We'd spent the morning collecting samples and specimens from the river for a class project. After lunch we got free time to spend down at the springs for a swim until it was time to head back."

Jillian had visited Crystal Springs on several occasions for manatee rescues. So, she knew where Laura was talking about. "That sounds like an interesting trip," she said, hoping she would continue.

"It was. At first. The water was abnormally high after one of our Florida monsoons. It had rained for three days straight or something, and the water level was well over the banks. Not that us kids thought anything of it, of course."

Jillian could feel Laura's hand trembling beneath hers. "As kids we were all invincible. Or so we thought, right?"

"Right, and I learned the truth the hard way. My friends were taking turns swinging out into the river from a rope. They were doing flips and tricks one after the other as I sat back and tried to find my courage. Everyone was giving me shit, and I knew they weren't going to stop until I did it." Laura looked up and into Jillian's eyes. "I wanted to do it, so it wasn't like they pressured me. More like built me up until I got up the courage."

"I understand that limbo between fear and excitement." Jillian felt something similar every time she got into the water, even after all of these years.

"So, I did it. I grabbed the rope, got a running start, and swung out over the water just like everyone else had before me.

I suppose I went a bit farther out than they did or let go a few seconds later than everyone else." Laura was wringing her hands as her leg tapped.

Jillian rested her hand gently on Laura's knee hoping to provide some sort of comfort. "And then what happened?"

Laura took a deep breath and sighed. "Well, that's where things get a little fuzzy. I remember hitting the water because it was freezing cold. I also remember feeling my legs scrape against a root or branch of some sort. But then everything else is a bit of a blur. I see most of it in flashes, like photographs. Things like streaks of light from the surface, my hair sort of loose and weightless, dark shadows in the distance."

Jillian's pulse was racing as she listened to Laura's haunting memory. "Oh, Laura."

"The worst part was the urgent need to breathe but knowing that I couldn't. My body was on fire as I struggled against whatever was holding me down. I could feel my heart rate begin to slow, and I knew I was dying. I wanted to scream out for help, but no one would have heard me."

Jillian spent half of her life underwater and had never experienced something so terrifying. She wanted to hold Laura, to protect her. She wanted to save her from this never-ending nightmare.

Laura pulled up her pant leg to expose a long scar that ran from her calf to her ankle. "I don't remember anything else until I woke up in the hospital with this."

Jillian ran her fingers down the rigid imperfection on her otherwise perfect skin. The suture marks were still visible after all these years and looked like a zipper. "Why didn't you tell me? You should have said something."

"Would you have honestly still accepted me into this program if you had known?"

"Maybe. Well—"

"We both know the answer to that, Jillian. I'm a liability. To you, my teammates, and to the institute. I wanted this all my life, and I thought that if I pushed myself into it that maybe it would all work out." Laura hung her head. "But I guess I was wrong."

Jillian sat quietly as she contemplated what to say next. She wanted to shower Laura with words of confidence and understanding, but she wanted to chastise her for putting lives in danger including her own by keeping this a secret. She didn't want to rage at her the way she did with Steven. She wanted to pull her into a tight embrace and tell her she was safe in her arms.

She understood why Laura chose to hide her past. There was no way TMRI, or any other reputable program, would take a chance on someone like Laura when the competition was so intense. She had lied her way into the institute and denied another student this rare opportunity. She had done so out of drive and passion to succeed, which Jillian wanted to commend. "I don't know what to say."

"There isn't anything to say. I'll pack my things and be out by the morning. I'd like to say good-bye to BJ, but if I can sneak out early without a big, err, bigger scene, that would be great."

Jillian knew that was the best option for everyone. Quick, relatively painless, and then on with the show. Without Steven and Laura, she could clean up this mess in one easy swoop. However, there was one problem; she didn't want Laura to go.

"Just...just wait a minute. I need to think about this for a minute." Jillian stood and paced back and forth. *You need to expel her. Do I? No, you could let her quit like she said. But she'll never get another chance. I don't want to be the person to shatter her dreams like that. It's not your fault. You can't possibly take on that burden.*

Laura stood in front of Jillian to stop her from pacing. She rested her hands on Jillian's biceps and rubbed her thumbs against her skin. The sweet gesture sent chills over Jillian's body. Here in this moment of personal anguish, Laura was comforting her instead.

"Look, this isn't a surprise, Jillian. Hell, I should have hightailed it out of here on the first day after my meltdown at the otter exhibit."

"What meltdown?" Jillian hadn't heard a thing about it.

"Nothing. It's not important now. I long ago convinced myself that becoming a dolphin trainer would never happen. That way when I turned forty and looked back, I wouldn't be too heartbroken."

"No expectations. No disappointments. I get it."

Laura's tears were gone, and her face was soft and composed. She had accepted her fate and was ready to move on. Or at least that's what she wanted Jillian to think. The woman who wore her heart on her sleeve was gone. Laura had extinguished the light that shone in her eyes, and it was Jillian who stood there brokenhearted for her.

"Thanks for everything, Jillian. I won't soon forget it. Or you." Laura pulled her in for a hug and pressed herself into Jillian. The moisture from Laura's shirt was warm as it soaked into hers. Jillian could feel Laura's soft body meld against her own, her full breasts and curves fitting perfectly. An unexpected heat burned in her core. Afraid that Laura could feel her sudden desire, Jillian pulled back from their embrace. Laura's eyes were no longer void of emotion; now they were filled with heat, desire.

Her dark eyes locked on to Jillian's as she licked her lips. Jillian's body hummed and her mouth watered as she wrapped her arms around Laura's waist pulling her back in. She wanted to kiss her, to taste her, but she didn't. Instead she let go and pushed away from the heat that fused them together. A rush of cool air chilled her skin where Laura's wet body had been pressed against hers. In that moment, her absence was more than physical.

Jillian adjusted her shirt and smoothed back her hair "I...I need to take care of some things. Don't leave yet, okay?"

"But, Jillian?"

"Just don't go. Not yet. Promise me?" Jillian asked, and Laura opened her mouth to protest. "Promise?"

Laura sighed. "I promise."

CHAPTER EIGHT

Laura stood in front of her bed and stared at the heap of clothing that covered it, nearly every piece of it was some shade of blue. Those she picked out and set off to the side. She wasn't sure if they'd want them back, but she didn't want to assume otherwise. If they didn't, maybe she could put them in a basket and let the others take what they wanted. All of them except maybe the one she had on. Laura was still a bit taken aback by the intimate turn her time with Jillian had taken. Who in their right mind could have predicted that what had begun as a pouring out of her heart would have ended in such a sensual embrace?

She could still feel the warmth of Jillian's belly pressed against hers. And those lips. Her full and luscious lips but a breath away from her own. She could only imagine how sweet she tasted. A fantasy that would forever remain just that.

She dropped to her knees and folded her arms on the edge of the bed. Everything was so fucked up, but that didn't come as a surprise. Laura couldn't help but wonder if she had sabotaged herself on the very first day. That fearless woman who'd stomped confidently out of her therapist's office was nowhere to be found. As a matter of fact, that might have been the last time she'd seen her.

She got up off the floor and stood in front of the full-length mirror that hung on the back of her bedroom door. She pulled her hair out of its ponytail and ran her fingers through it. Laura studied her face, sliding her fingers over the tired bags beneath her eyes. She stretched the skin across her forehead and pulled up on the corners of her mouth to force a smile. She'd been here before. Many years earlier, she stood in her dorm at UC in front of a mirror much like this one. Nothing much had changed since her first college experience except the few added lines and wrinkles.

She had cried more the first time, too. Laura was numb. There was no devastation, but also no overwhelming relief. She was exhausted.

She crossed the room back over to her bed and pulled out her suitcase from underneath. As she flopped open the top, there was a knock at her door. BJ hadn't even waited for her to respond before he came crashing in.

"Where have you been? I had to cut and sort capelin by myself, soaking wet even." He stopped and pointed to the new mess on her bed. "What are you doing?"

"Packing."

"Uh-huh. I see that. What I should have asked was what the fuck are you doing? Where are you going? You aren't leaving."

"I have to. I don't have a choice," she said, blowing a huge breath as she tossed a pile of shirts into her case.

"Don't have a choice? Who isn't giving you a choice? You don't just leave the program, Laura. You die or get expelled."

"Well…"

"No well. Do I look like Bruce fucking Willis talking to dead kids and shit? And there's no possible reason you'd be expelled." He put his hands on his hips.

"In a way, I suppose. Sort of a self-inflicted expulsion."

"That's not a thing. What happened?" BJ picked up her suitcase, tossed it onto the floor, and sat where it had been. The piles of clothes Laura had sorted and stacked toppled over.

"Hey, watch out." Laura grunted at his disregard for her hard work.

"Screw that." He waved off the mess. "What the hell happened, Laura?"

"Christ, you sound like Jillian." Before Laura could go into detail, a loud crash startled them both. It damn near sounded like the walls were coming down around them. Another loud bang echoed from the hallway, and they stared at each other with wide eyes.

"We should lock the door," BJ whispered, and Laura crept over to turn the deadbolt.

Once the lock engaged, she stood with her ear at the crack listening for familiar voices. She could make out some muffled conversation and distant banging. BJ pressed up against her back as he tried to get a better listen.

"That sounds like Brooke," he said, squeezing between her and the door so he could get it open.

"Wait!" Laura called out. But her warning was far too late, and BJ flung himself out into the hallway.

Brooke and two others were huddled together watching the action unfold. The look of surprise on everyone's face piqued Laura's curiosity, and she stuck her head out into the hallway. Two male security guards blocked the men's dorm wing, while Jillian, Fletcher, and Officer Williams stood in Steven's doorway. Between bursts of shouting and profanity, pieces of clothing and garbage flew out into the hall. Jillian stood fast with her arms crossed, unflinching. She only moved to kick the debris into a loose pile off to the side. She looked like a beast, angry and daring anyone to step to her. Laura almost wanted to see Steven try just to watch her lay his ass out on the tile. She was a different woman from the one who just held her in her arms a little more than an hour ago.

Laura and the rest of the gawking crowd gasped when Jillian turned her head toward them. There were no daggers, but there wasn't a smile either, just obvious acknowledgement of their undesirable attention. Laura stepped back into her room and commanded, "In or out." BJ and Brooke scooted in while the others scampered back to their own rooms.

"Now that's how you get expelled. Holy shit." BJ covered his mouth and stifled a mischievous chuckle.

"He had it coming. Childish lug," Laura said. She picked up her suitcase and set it back onto her bed.

"Why's she packing?" Brooke asked BJ before she turned to Laura. "Why are you packing?"

"I'm leaving the program. Some things have come up that I thought I had dealt with. And well…turns out I haven't," Laura said, stacking and restacking the pile of clothes, but not putting any more into her suitcase.

"So, deal with it now," BJ said.

"I wish it was that simple. Believe me."

"Maybe you just need help. How can we help?" Brooke asked.

Laura appreciated their concern, but she just wanted to start putting this all behind her. "All right, look." She sat and slapped her hands on her knees and let out an exasperated breath. "Ten years ago, I was in an accident and almost drowned. I've been in therapy since then, but turns out my issues aren't getting better, and I am putting myself and others in danger."

"Wow. So that's why you went into full panic that day," BJ said.

"Yes. I probably should have walked away then, but I'm a little bit stubborn."

"So today when you went into the water after BJ…"

"Let's just say it brought back a lot of memories that aren't ever going to go away."

"But—"

"No buts, BJ. I lied to get into this program. I don't even deserve to be here."

"That's crap," Brooke said. "Steven didn't deserve to be here. You do."

"Thanks. That means a lot to—" Laura was cut off by a loud knocking at the door that made all of them jump. "Yes?" Laura's voice rattled.

"Laura, it's Jillian," she said through the door.

"What the?" BJ mouthed, leaving his eyes and mouth wide open.

Laura hushed them shaking her hands for them to sit and look normal. "Coming." Laura opened the door wide so Jillian could see that she wasn't alone. Not that she thought Jillian would take advantage of it if she were.

"Hey," she said before peering around Laura to greet the others. "BJ, good. I know it's late, but can I see you both in my office, please?"

"N...now?" he asked.

"Yes, please," she said to him. "Is that all right?" she asked Laura.

"Of course."

Jillian smiled and walked away. That woman had the uncanny ability to make Laura's knees weak whenever she smiled like that at her. Laura closed the door slowly and took a few beats before turning around to Brooke and BJ. When she did, she thought he looked like he was about to be sick all over her area rug.

"What did I do? Oh my God. If she comes at me the way she did Steven, I'll pass out. Did you see her face?"

"Relax. I have a feeling that you must do something terrible to get that side of her. Trust me, she's much softer than that." Laura recalled just how soft when her body was pressed against hers.

"You don't say?" BJ's color was back now. He waggled his eyebrows having caught her unintentional innuendo.

"Shut up. That's not...let's go."

They headed off to Jillian's office, leaving an apprehensive Brooke alone in the now empty hallway. Laura hoped BJ would grant her the gift of silence as they walked, but he didn't. He spoke quietly, just loud enough for their ears alone. He didn't say her name or look in her direction. Laura didn't need to see his tears to know they were there.

"You know, I thought about killing myself more than once before I even turned sixteen." Laura's heart dropped like a weight. "I know it doesn't compare to what happened to you, but here we both are today. We're battered and bruised, but alive. We're right where we need to be. I don't know what it's going to take for you to overcome your fear. But whatever it is, I am here for you."

Laura wiped away the stream of tears that poured down her cheeks. She thought she was all cried out. BJ sniffed and cleared his throat before continuing.

"It's when we want to give up the most that we're about to overcome. That last tired push before we reach the peak."

Laura grabbed him by the arm and pulled him to a stop. "I've tried to climb this mountain so many times before." Her voice cracked.

He turned to her and held her hands in his. "So, try again. We get one life, but it's filled with as many chances as we want to take."

❖

BJ and Laura stood awkwardly in Jillian's open doorway. BJ looked like he was about to be ill, and both appeared to have been crying. Their noses were pink and their eyes glassy with fresh tears. Jillian was worried that they both had very wrong ideas about why she'd called them to her office. Although Laura pretty much had one foot out the door, by the state of her bedroom. Both were still wearing their stale work clothes, and the scent of sea salt, old fish, and river muck wafted into the room with them. They both looked as bad as they smelled.

"Good Lord," Jillian said, covering her nose and mouth. "That smells like death." BJ and Laura looked themselves and each other over before breaking out in laughter. "I'd threaten you both with a hose, but I'm afraid that would just make it worse."

BJ looked at Laura, and then to Jillian, "I'm sorry, was it something we said?"

Jillian was glad that after all this afternoon's chaos, everyone could still laugh. Jillian explained to them both what had happened with Steven. She didn't go into detail, but she wanted them both to be aware of how seriously she took bullying of any kind. She spent a few minutes alone with BJ, to make sure that he understood why she had made the decision and to make sure that he was okay. This kid was wise beyond his years for reasons she couldn't imagine. Maybe she had overreacted with Steven, but she couldn't have cared less.

"Is there anything else you'd like to discuss? Questions? Concerns?" Jillian asked as she wrapped up their short meeting.

"Don't let her go," he said.

Jillian wanted to say that she wouldn't. She wanted to say that she'd hold on for as long as she could, and that she was going to do whatever it took not to. She wanted to say that the one thing she wanted was for her to stay, but she didn't. "Unfortunately, I cannot discuss another trainee's situation with you. However, if Laura or anyone chooses to withdraw from the program we have no authority to keep her from doing so."

BJ sighed and rolled his eyes at Jillian's professionally disguised cop out. Had she been in his place she probably would have too. "Right." He pushed up out of his chair and headed for the door.

"BJ," she said, stopping him in his tracks. "I'm going to do everything in my power to try."

"Thank you."

BJ left the door open, and after a few brief moments, Laura stepped into the room. Her hair was awry, her clothes were threatening to stand on their own, and she looked beaten and weary. But damn it, was she beautiful. Even in her darkest moment, she brought light into Jillian's life. How could she not do whatever she could to help her?

"How are you feeling?" Jillian leaned forward over her desk.

"I don't even know anymore."

"I couldn't help but see that you were packing up your things."

"I was. Sort of. I kept getting interrupted. Is everything okay with BJ? I don't want him dragged into my mess. He didn't know anything."

Their devotion to each other was intense. Each of them more concerned for each other than for themselves. "He's fine."

"Good. He's an amazing person and doesn't need me screwing things up for him," Laura said.

"You're right. About the first part, of course. Although he's more concerned about you."

"Yeah. He gave me one hell of a pep talk on our way over here."

Had he managed to convince her to stay? Was it that easy?

"Yeah, I'll miss him." And just like that Jillian had her answer.

"So, you're still planning on leaving?"

Laura groaned in frustration and slapped her hands on Jillian's desk, holding them there. "Jillian, I could be the best animal behaviorist, nutritionist, public showman, and husbandry technician at this institute, and still—"

"Second best," Jillian interrupted and smiled.

"Fine, second best. But if I can't get in the water, what's the point?" Laura was talking like she couldn't be within a hundred yards of a pool without going into a panic. Jillian knew that wasn't the case. She'd seen her wade into the lagoon without issue, as well as kneel in the shallows to feed the dolphins. There was obviously a trigger. If they could figure out what it was, maybe that would be the key Laura needed to unlock the fear inside her.

"Hear me out, please." She added the please when Laura opened her mouth in obvious protest. "I did some research earlier.

Not much, but a few Google searches and earmarked a few psychology textbooks, and I came up with an idea."

Laura slid one of those large books off the top of the pile, "*The Psychology of Behavior*? This is a developmental text on animal behavior. There's literally a moose on the cover," Laura said, pointing to the image on the front.

"Right. Actually, that's an elk, I believe. But not the point." She took the book from Laura and set it back on top of the pile. "The basis of behavior is psychology. It doesn't matter if we're working with dolphins, humans, or…elk." Jillian held up the book and grinned. "As you know, our cognitive capacities are strikingly similar."

"I already have a therapist. A pretty good one, too."

"Okay, but do they work with you in the water? In your natural environment so to speak? Because that's what I want to do." If she could get Laura in the water with some cognitive reframing and exposure, she truly believed they could make this work. Jillian sat back as the emotions played out across Laura's face. There was so much doubt, but there in her tired eyes was a glimmer of what looked like hope.

"Jillian." Laura sighed.

"Stay. Keep attending your classes and keep your work schedule. Then, during your free time you'll be with me. Give me four weeks. If we don't make any progress by this time next month, you can go."

Jillian held her breath as Laura contemplated her offer. What she was doing was unprecedented, and almost certainly against some institute policy. But she wanted this, and she wanted this for Laura. The scientist in her wanted the challenge, but the woman in her wanted Laura. The seconds ticked by. Laura looked up from her lap, and deep into Jillian's eyes, she could see her searching for something. Whatever she was looking for Jillian would give her.

"I'll give you four weeks."

CHAPTER NINE

Laura was still reeling from both BJ's emotional pep talk and Jillian's unbelievable proposition. She couldn't say if she'd have accepted the offer had BJ not punched her in the gut with such truths. Laura couldn't help but feel like a petulant child when she compared her experiences with someone like BJ's. It was an unfamiliar feeling to have people with such unwavering faith in her. Sure, she had her family and Dr. Shaw, but no one else had such intimate knowledge or understanding of her dreams.

Laura remembered when she had that same faith in herself. That had been before her accident, but she knew a small part of that young girl was still somewhere inside her. The rest of her was locked away in an old wooden box at her parents' house. Laura looked at the clock on her phone. It wasn't quite eight o'clock. She was surprised it was still that early considering the absolute whirlwind the day had been since lunch. She even checked her alarm clock to make sure.

She did the math in her head. If she left now, she could be to her parents' place in Lakeland within an hour and back by eleven p.m. She slipped on a pair of jeans and snatched her keys from the bowl on her desk. On her way to the parking lot she called her mom to let her know that she was heading her way.

"Why? Are you all right?" her mom asked.

"Everything's fine. Mom do you remember my box? The one Daddy made me to put all my keepsakes in?" Laura unlocked the car and slipped into the driver's seat.

"Of course, honey. It's in the garage Why?"

"Good. I'm coming out to get it."

"Laura Christine Carter, if I have to ask you why one more time."

"Mommy, relax. I'm just looking for the fearless little girl I hid away all those years ago. I'm certain she's in that box with all of that crap I squirreled away."

"Oh, sweetheart. I'm almost positive that she's hidden inside of you and not that old thing. But I'm so glad you're looking for her."

Laura gave her mom an ETA and said good-bye. There was so much more than a hopeful future dolphin trainer in that chest. There was an entire eighteen-year-old who had saved her whole childhood. From a set of Lion King trading cards that her first girl crush had stolen for her, to the crushed Coke can filled with pennies from her first junior high pep rally, it was all in there. Her whole young life was packed away in it, and Laura felt more than a bit anxious about opening it up again. Of course, she still wondered if everything in it still smelled like that broken vial of Liz Claiborne cologne.

The drive took less time than she had calculated either because she drove like a bat out of hell or because she had been preoccupied with all the memories waiting for her. When she got inside the house, she saw the sticker-riddled eyesore set out on the kitchen table. It seemed that her mother had gotten her dad to haul it out of the darkest corner of the garage. Thankfully so, as there was no way she could've wrestled it out on her own. Rainbows, dolphins, and NASA stickers were just a few among what could very well have been hundreds of stickers, and she only had to stand in front of it to get a whiff of its trademark scent.

The clasp on the front used to be locked, back when all her deepest secrets were contained within. Now it was so bent and misshapen it didn't even close right. She ran her hands over the top and down the sides remembering the last time she'd seen it. Laura slid her fingers along the black charring that marred the back. Laura was so grateful that her mother had taken the hose to her bonfire before she had destroyed it and all that it held.

It was right after she dropped out of UC San Diego, maybe two weeks after coming home. She was in the worst depression of her life. She did little more than sleep and lose weight. On an exceptionally dark day she built a raging fire in the middle of her front lawn and tossed in books, clothes, photographs, and finally the box. Thanks to her mom, both she and the box were still around today, as it went into the garage and Laura went into therapy. Her heart was racing, and she held her breath. She got to forty-six seconds before a tap on her shoulder made her gasp.

"We're holding it again I see," her mom said.

"Unfortunately, yeah. Things have been sort of intense these last few days." Laura sighed and hugged her mom tight.

"I can imagine since you drove all the way here at nine o'clock at night for this thing."

Laura fingered the clasp with sweaty, shaking hands. She took several deep breaths as she prepared to open the box. She had wanted to be alone for this part, yet now she was kind of glad to have her mom with her.

"What are you looking for in there, kiddo?"

Laura thought about it for a few moments. What was she hoping to find in a box of old dreams and reminders? She looked at her mom and smiled. "Me."

Tears welled in her mother's eyes, and Laura looked away. "Okay, honey. Well, I'll leave you to it."

"No. Wait, please stay," Laura said as she reached for her mom's arm.

Her mother nodded and sat at the table next to Laura. With a swift flick, she clicked open the misshapen latch and flipped back the top. As expected, the strong, stale cloud of old cologne puffed up into her face, and she laughed. She slid out several books and pamphlets, laying them out on the table. The pages and sheets were crispy with age. Growing up, Laura had amassed an impressive collection of books, guides, and info sheets on everything to do with marine mammals and their care, training, and education.

Laura felt an unexpected sense of solace when she saw one in particular. It was worn, yellowed, and distorted from the years she carried it around with her. She flipped to the front where the author had signed it to her. She brushed her thumb over the inscription as she had done a hundred times before. She'd never known another person besides Lyle Littleton who had such passion for the career until she met Jillian. And now BJ, and Brooke, and everyone at the institute, and they all believed in her, even as she struggled to believe in herself. She left the book off to the side and gathered up the rest to put back in the box. She would have loved to spend more time going through it, but she needed to get back.

"Did you find what you were looking for, sweetheart?"

Laura gripped the old paperback to her chest. *How to be a Dolphin Trainer* had been her Bible. She studied it tirelessly, making sure she met each and every requirement and prerequisite for success. Colored flaps and tabs marked nearly every page, sticking out like a ragged paper fan. The book had been her lighthouse and Lyle's words her guide. Yet as she stood there before her collection, clutching her past, she realized that she'd found something at the institute that Lyle never included in any of his lists.

Laura looked at her mother and said, "That and so much more."

❖

It was just after seven a.m. when Jillian entered the fish house. She double-checked her watch as well as the clock on the wall. By this time in the morning the hustle and bustle of clanging buckets should be done. However, BJ, Brooke, and Laura were still elbows deep in smelt. Fletcher stood stone-faced against the counter with his arms crossed.

"What's going on?" Jillian asked.

"It seems one of our trainees needed an extra thirty minutes of sleep this morning and set us all back because of it."

Laura set the last bucket onto the rack and pushed it into the freezer. She came back out and smiled proudly. "Nothing we couldn't handle."

Jillian looked over at BJ and Brooke, who weren't quite as confident. When BJ averted his gaze, she knew who the guilty party was. It was a good sign of solidarity and teamwork that Laura had so confidently stepped up to take the slack, however it did little to excuse the error or eliminate the ripple effect it would have across the park for the remainder of the day.

Working with animals for almost two decades, Jillian was used to frequent and last-minute schedule changes, as they worked around them and not the other way around. It was for a reason that everything that could be controlled was. Being late, delaying schedules, postponing feedings, training sessions, and visitor interactions was unacceptable, not just for Jillian but for the institute.

A line of trainers began threading through the room to collect their first of the day's meals from the refrigerator. Nearly all of them flashed surprised glances at each other and Jillian. Several of them hurried in and out as if knowing what was coming next and wanting to be as far away as possible when it did.

"Spray it down," she directed them in a stern tone. All three of them looked at each other and then to Fletcher.

"It's out of my hands now, kids," he said, holding up his empty hands.

As if just now realizing the seriousness, they each scrambled around the room. Jillian shook her head as a flustered BJ grabbed the same push broom as Brooke.

Laura had witnessed it as well while she unraveled the hose from the wall. "Guys, for real? We do this every day," Laura said as she pulled the other broom from the hook and handed it to him.

Jillian chuckled to herself while they sprayed down every nook and cranny in the room. She was almost afraid that Laura's thoroughness was going to rob her of the fun of the next part. When she thought she was finished, Laura set down the hose and the three of them traded their tools for scrub brushes and a long-handled mop.

Jillian hadn't done this in so long that she vibrated with excitement. "Wait just a sec," she said.

They looked at her curiously as she surveyed the room inspecting its various surfaces, walls, and basins. She stopped near the ice machine and tapped on the cold, wet steel. Next to her finger was a small iridescent fleck. She could see them everywhere now. She'd spent her first semester schlepping fish too, and she sometimes swore that she even saw them in her dreams at night. Sure, their next round of scrubbing would take care of them, but it wouldn't be as much fun. Not for her anyway.

She slipped her hand into her pocket where she had stuck a thick permanent marker. Jillian gave it a little shake between her fingers before uncapping it and drawing a bold, black circle around the sparkling fish scale. She turned back to see all three of their mouths flop open. She moved around the room circling every single scale and shrimp leg that she found. When she was finished, hundreds of them marked every surface in the room. Jillian might've gotten a little bit carried away with it, but it was a guarantee that they'd never forget the day or how they had gotten there.

They stood rooted to the floor with shock on their faces. Jillian looked at her watch; it was just past eight o'clock. She had hoped to be in the water with Laura around now, and while she was disappointed by the turn of events, she'd gotten her consolation. Unfortunately for Laura, she was going to be spending the next three hours scrubbing marker off the walls in the fish house.

"You have until lunch," Jillian said as she walked out the door.

❖

Jillian pranced out of the room. Laura couldn't help but smile at the added swish of her hips as she sauntered out the door. She had been so proud of her little stunt and had no doubt been chomping at the bit for any reason to pull the trigger on it. As much as Laura should have been irritated, she was certain she'd have enjoyed doing the exact same thing.

"What the fuck just happened?" BJ asked.

He was far more inconvenienced by the punishment. Sure, she wasn't thrilled by the idea of spending hours busting her knuckles on these walls, but she had to appreciate the creativity. Although having it doled out by such an attractive woman might have eased some of the pain. If she hadn't known how bad she had it for Jillian before, she pretty much did now. "Could be worse," she said as she shrugged.

"Worse? We have to scrub permanent marker off concrete with nothing but a sponge and Comet," he said, holding up the supplies for reference.

"Well, if you had charged your phone last night or set a real alarm clock, we wouldn't be here. Would we?" Laura smiled and snatched the sponge from him. Brooke let out a burst of laughter from the corner where she'd already begun scouring.

"Yeah. We, err, I shouldn't have stayed up so late," he said, glancing over at Brooke quick enough that Laura almost missed it.

They went to work on removing the marks. It had taken them close to every minute of the allotted time, all the way up to lunch.

Minus the light and lingering fish scent, the room was spotless. Or in this case, scaleless. They had about five minutes to admire their handiwork before the second shift was due in to begin preparation of PM nutrition. While their shift had been delayed, second shift was right on time. Rounds of hoots and whistles echoed through the spotless room. Laura wanted to be proud, but she was too exhausted. Plus, it's not like they had any option other than perfection when it came to Jillian's directive.

Laura cringed as the crew began their work. Within minutes, all their hard work would be gone, and it pained her a tad to stay and watch.

"Wait," Jillian called out when she came through the door. Everyone froze at her command. She made her way around the room quickly. It was easy to see that there wasn't a single black mark remaining. Jillian smiled and nodded at them. Now Laura was proud. Despite her fatigue, she stood taller and pulled back her sore shoulders. She hoped to earn many more of those smiles from Jillian over the next four weeks.

CHAPTER TEN

The sun was barely up this morning as Laura made her way to the fish house. The difference on this day was that normally she'd be covered in squid guts by now. Today she got to sleep in, though unlike BJ the day before, she had the day off. Her knees were still pink and tender from spending three hours as Cinderella, thanks to him. Her neoprene wet suit was soft, but also tight enough to remind her every time she bent her legs.

Laura had no idea what Jillian had up her sleeve for today. But given the sadistic enjoyment she got out of circling fish scales, Laura was apprehensive to say the least. Jillian was waiting outside the building with two silver buckets under her arms. "Are you ready?"

"I'm not sure how to answer that." It was the truth. She should have said something like "hell yeah" but felt more like saying "nope, not at all." The one thing she could assume was that it was in the water as Jillian's express instructions included the words "full wet suit."

"Honestly would be the best way," Jillian said.

"Okay, then. Not really. It's hard to say you're ready for something when you don't know what that something is. Am I ready to try whatever cockamamie idea you have up your sleeve? Definitely not. But for some reason I trust you anyway."

"Good. I'd never put you in a situation I didn't think you could handle. Although I don't know what that threshold is. At least not until we have evaluated you, right?"

Laura's pulse beat harder in her throat. "Right."

"Good. As you know, all animals respond pessimistically, and that includes humans. We've evolved to expect the worst following a bad experience."

"Yes, it improves our survival rate." Laura hadn't expected the behavioral psych lesson, but she should have.

When they reached the edge of the lagoon, Jillian set the pails on a large rock outcropping on the sandy beach. The air was calm and quiet. In the distance, trainers worked along the edges of the water with their pods, splashing and greeting the eager dolphins. On the beach, however, it was just the two of them. Jillian faced her and took Laura's hands in hers. Her large hands were strong and steady as Jillian's long fingers intertwined with her own.

"You are safe," Jillian said as she stared into Laura's eyes. It was almost as if she was trying to speak to her very soul.

Looking into Jillian's unwavering gaze, Laura spoke the words, "I am safe." She could almost feel Jillian inside her. She had never felt more invulnerable as she did in this very moment

"Now are you ready?"

Without hesitation, Laura answered, "Yes."

Jillian scooped up both buckets with one arm and held Laura's hand with the other. "The water is a constant seventy-three degrees. The shallows stretch about a hundred and fifty feet across and seventy feet out. There are three drop-offs. One at three and a half feet, then at fifteen, and finally at seventy-five. Okay?"

"Okay," Laura said. Jillian had distracted her with facts until they reached the first drop-off point. She hadn't felt the initial chill of the cool water until it had seeped through her wet suit. She was glad of the absence of the paralyzing sting of the cold against her warm skin, kept warmer by the firm and gentle hold that Jillian had on her hand. The waves lapped just beneath her breasts, and her nipples were thankful. She paced her breathing, making sure not to fall victim to her anxiety by holding her breath.

"Do you want to keep my hand or can you hold one of these?" Laura wondered for a second if she couldn't just do both before releasing Jillian's hand and taking the bucket from her. "Wait, this one's yours," Jillian said, trading pails with her.

"I respond to many things, but raw fish and clam Jell-O are not any of those things."

"That's too bad, because it's all you can eat clam Jell-O day."

Laura couldn't even fathom such a thing, even as a joke. "More for you then."

She was surprised and encouraged by how comfortable she was. Jillian had a way with humans as well as animals. Laura jumped when Jillian slapped at the surface of the water and called out someone's name across the pool.

"What the hell?"

Jillian laughed. "Sorry, I'll warn you next time. Here, let me take that." Jillian took Laura's pail and set it behind them on the wall. She turned back just as a large gray mass appeared before them.

Laura's voice caught in her throat. Jillian reached into her bucket and welcomed Pepper with a small capelin. Laura kept her fists clasped to her sides to keep from reaching out and touching her. There was no book or photograph in the world that could describe what six hundred pounds of dolphin looked like right there in front of her. She could feel the sting of tears in her eyes. There she was after all these years, living her dream.

Jillian put her hand below the surface and directed Pepper around in front of them. Gracefully, she turned and brushed up against their legs, and Laura could feel her solid and powerful body against hers.

"Go ahead. Touch her," Jillian said, reaching out and stroking Pepper's head right behind her blowhole.

Laura hesitated, trying to hold back her excitement so she didn't scare this gorgeous creature. Her hand trembled as she touched her. Pepper eyed her curiously as Laura spoke to her with awe. Jillian maneuvered her around again and let Laura run her hands along the length of her cool, smooth body. She looked at Jillian who was staring at her, and she pulled her arms back tight against her body. Jillian laughed, and Laura felt her face warm. Although covered head to toe in neoprene, she felt naked and exposed in her pure elation as Jillian stood watching her every move and reaction. She wasn't sure any of her most intimate partners had ever seen her soul as bare.

"I wonder how different things would be had I gotten this chance ten years ago?"

"What do you mean?" Jillian asked as her hand glided through the water to reposition Pepper once more.

"I wonder would I still be ten years behind on my life?" Jillian took her hand and ran them together along Pepper's side tracing along the unique markings and colorations.

Jillian stepped behind Laura and gripped her wrist. "Point your finger," Jillian said before guiding Laura's hand with two swift motions, down at the water and then out at the horizon. Laura was surprised by the control she allowed Jillian to have over her. With a strong flick of her tail, Pepper bolted toward the distance and disappeared beneath the surface.

"Where'd she go?"

"Just watch," Jillian said into Laura's ear just before Pepper leapt out of the water at the center of the lagoon.

An intense heat ran the length of Laura's body and back again. Her core was set alight, and she could feel her skin burn with exhilaration. "Holy shit, that was amazing," Laura said, spinning around in Jillian's arms. She held her breath, and Jillian's dark gaze flicked to her lips and back. She licked them instinctively as if under some sort of siren spell. She regretted it almost immediately when a devilish smile spread across Jillian's face. Thankfully, Pepper's return broke through the enchantment, and Laura stepped away from Jillian.

"And here I was about to say that you are right where you belong."

Laura's belly set flight with a flutter of a million butterflies, and she thought for the first time that maybe that was true.

❖

For those few fleeting moments, it took every bit of reserve that Jillian had to keep herself from wrapping Laura in her arms and kissing her full, pink lips until they were both breathless with need. Jillian was captivated by the pure joy that filled Laura. Over the years, she had witnessed hundreds of people encounter these beautiful animals for the first time, but it was rare to see those raw emotions flow out of them so freely.

She was so caught up in the moment and the sparkle in Laura's glistening eyes that she almost forgot why they were there. While Laura seemed at ease in the water now, the truth was that beneath the excitement there was a dark and sinister monster lurking within her. Jillian didn't know if she could help Laura overcome her fear, but she wanted to try.

"Can you tread water?"

Laura opened her mouth to respond, but no words came out. After a few seconds, she answered, "I used to."

It wasn't a skill one usually lost. However, considering the circumstances, Laura probably hadn't even attempted it in years. The glow on Laura's face began to fade. "Okay. Then we'll spend a little more time here in the shallows."

She needed to keep Laura out of her own head, at least for the time being. Running Pepper through a few of her husbandry behaviors would work for all of them. She held out a bucket to Laura who pulled out a large mackerel and tossed it into Pepper's wide-open mouth. When Laura's smile returned, a rush of warmth washed through her. Jillian wanted to make that feeling last as long as possible, for both of them.

"Put out your hands like this," Jillian said, laying one hand over the other and cupping them ever so slightly. Laura mimicked her as instructed. Laura set her hands into the water, and Pepper rested her snout into them.

"Oh my God," she cooed glancing back-and-forth between Pepper and Jillian.

"Give her a kiss."

"What? Really?" Laura asked. Her eyes were wide with wonder.

"Yes. Right there on the rostrum. It's not nice to keep a girl waiting," Jillian said. How lucky was the girl who got to kiss Laura's lips? Laura pressed her lips to Pepper's. *Well, that's a first.* Jillian was jealous of a dolphin. She blew her bridge whistle, and Pepper popped open her mouth for a reward.

Laura tossed in a capelin and thanked her for her kiss. "One of the best I've ever had," Laura said before wiping her fingers across her wet lips.

Jillian's foothold was weak, and it had nothing to do with the natural layer of algae covering the bottom. A rush of heat spread up inside her thighs and settled warmly between her legs. She could taste the salty tinge that would linger on Laura's lips long after she tried to wipe it away. She coughed and pulled at the tight collar of her wet suit that was cutting off the oxygen to her brain. "Okay, uhm, right."

To help her refocus on the task at hand, Jillian ran through a variety of basic commands. After flipping Pepper over in a present fluke's position, she showed Laura how they perform blood draws and urine collections. Jillian hoped that turning their attention toward a more scientific course, she could regain some control over her raging hormones. Thanks to Pepper, that was easier than she'd expected when she decided now was the perfect time to release her bladder, tingeing the water around them with a yellow haze. "Thanks for that," Jillian said, waving her hand through the water to help with the dispersal.

"Oh, the glamour of working with animals," Laura said with a chuckle.

"Could've been worse." Jillian sent Pepper off for a quick playful lap as she led Laura closer to the drop-off.

"Now the real test begins, huh?" Laura said quietly.

"Soon. But not quite yet." Jillian saw the doubt begin to creep in again, and she cupped her hands against Laura's cheeks. She shouldn't have, but it was too late to pull away. "Look at me. You're safe. I'm not going to make you do anything you aren't ready for. Okay?"

"I'm not even sure I'm ready to be *here*, but I am." Laura put her hands on Jillian's and took a deep breath. "I'm scared," Laura said almost too quietly to be heard.

"I know you are, but look at where you are. See how far you've come. The most important trait to have in this field is initiative and you've got it in spades. You are fearless."

Laura squeezed her eyes closed. "I wish."

Jillian resisted the urge to brush her fingers across to Laura's face. "Is there anything in this life worth doing if it doesn't scare the shit out of you?"

Laura dropped her hands from Jillian's, but she didn't move her own. "Easy for you to say. I bet there isn't a thing in this world that you're afraid of."

You, for starters. "Not true. But this isn't about me."

Laura sighed. "I can tread water. Not forever, but for a bit."

Jillian took her hands away from Laura's face and smiled. "Good, that's my girl." Why did she just say that? She cringed inside but pushed past it quickly. "We're going to swim out to the center, there," she said as she pointed toward the middle of the lagoon. "We'll tread just long enough for Pepper to set up. About thirty seconds or so."

"That's it?" Laura asked with a faint rattle in her voice.

"Yep." Jillian signaled for Pepper to return from her free swim and tossed her a block of Jell-O.

Laura gave Pepper a good rub near her dorsal. Jillian was encouraged by how Laura's demeanor changed just having Pepper near. She positioned herself on Pepper, showing Laura how she needed to place her own hands when it was time.

"Shut up. I'm doing that? Shut the hell up."

Jillian laughed at Laura's absolute inability to hide any emotion, or willingness to for that matter. Jillian called out to one of her nearby trainers, "Ben, set up for me? Dorsal pull."

"Wait. What? You're not going out there with me?" Laura's face blanched.

"It's okay. I'm going to be right over there," Jillian said, pointing toward the shore where they'd entered the lagoon. "Ben's going to set you up and then Pepper will bring you straight to me. You'll be able to see me the whole time I promise." Laura's expression softened and the color began to return to her face.

"Oh...uhm. Okay." Laura's voice still trembled.

"Get on with Ben, get off with me." Jillian closed her eyes and shook her head in disbelief at what she had just said. "That's not...I didn't mean..."

"Get off with you. Got it." Laura laughed wickedly, and Jillian's knees nearly buckled. Her color was back to normal now.

"Go. I'll be waiting for you over there." Laura paused at the edge of the drop, and turned to look back at Jillian for reassurance.

"You've got this." Jillian waded over to Laura's side. "Just ease yourself in," she said as she demonstrated a slow squat into the water. When she was shoulders deep, Jillian pushed herself out toward Ben. She spun around to face Laura and waited for her to do the same.

Laura's eyes locked on to hers, and Jillian refused to break that connection. If Laura needed to know that she was there for her, she would stare forever. Laura began to sink, and Jillian nodded. When she pushed herself out toward Jillian, she gasped at the shock of the cool water enveloping her. Jillian could hear Laura's short, puffing breaths as she paddled toward her. Their eyes still locked on each other, Jillian moved backward through the water as Laura got closer.

Jillian didn't dare take her eyes off Laura's until they made it the entire way. She welled with pride for Laura, and for her determination to fight her illness at every turn. When she could give up and retreat, she pushed forward. Jillian was in awe of her.

"Guess what?" Jillian asked, having reached the setup point.

"What?" Laura's breaths quick and shallow.

"You did it." Jillian pushed away from Laura who looked around in surprise. As Ben and Laura waited for Pepper, Jillian swam back to the shallows to wait for them. Laura grabbed Pepper's dorsal and pectoral fins and within seconds, she was riding Pepper's wake as they raced toward her. Laura's smile spread wide across her beautiful face, and she squealed in delight. Jillian was certain she'd never seen anyone or anything more perfect.

CHAPTER ELEVEN

A mazing? That's all the detail I get?" BJ said as he tossed out several items from the storage room.

Laura picked up a giant Kong big enough for an elephant and tucked it under her arm like a basketball. "Well, it *was* amazing."

First, he handed her one of the two orange mooring buoys. Then, he tossed the rope that held together what looked like dolphin-sized nunchucks over her shoulder. "I have no doubt. But you're being weird about it."

She groaned under the weight of all the stuff he was piling on top of her. "I'm not being weird. And will you stop giving me all this shit?" She shifted her shoulders to adjust her load.

"I'm only giving you shit because you're being vague and cagey."

"Not that kind of shit." Laura raised her arms as best she could with everything she had in them. "This shit."

"I know," he said, picking up the other orange buoy and the large white docking cushion.

It wasn't like she didn't want to tell him about every single thing that had happened. She'd replayed it over and over in her head about a thousand times by now. But how could she explain to him what had happened if she left out all the stuff about Jillian? About how she'd held her so protectively and given her the strength she needed to push through. How she had held her face in her strong hands and stared deep into her soul. How their bodies had pressed into each other so perfectly in those brief moments when she swore that Jillian was going to kiss her.

"Yo, Laura. Where are you going?" BJ called out to her as she missed the turn onto the path that led to the modules.

"Sorry," she said as she hustled under the weight of her load to catch up.

"That's not good enough. We have two whole hours of babysitting ahead of us. You're going to spill, so just start now."

"It was a—"

"I swear to God if you say amazing one more time."

But it was. Sure, she could find other adjectives to describe it, but they'd all mean the same thing. Maybe she could tell him that it was life changing, inspiring, unbelievable, a dream come true, but Laura knew what he really wanted to know. Her attraction to Jillian was no secret. At least not to BJ, or Brooke for that matter. He had pretty much called her out on that day one.

The problem wasn't that he knew. It was that her feelings for Jillian were far from appropriate. That much was evident the day in the parking lot with Officer Williams after making herself look like a complete ass because of an ass. Oh, but what an ass it was. However, now Jillian had become so much more than just a delectable body part.

"It was the best day of my life," Laura said when they reached the series of octagonal honeycomb enclosures where the animals could be observed in a more controlled environment.

"Now we're talking," BJ said as he tossed his buoy and cushion into the water. "Play time, my lovelies."

Laura threw in the tethered rolls and set the others up on the step of the observation chair. She leaned forward against a wall while Kaipo, Kaius, and Pepper each picked out their favorite toy. Laura almost couldn't believe that she'd been in the water with Pepper. So much had happened in the short time that she'd been at the institute. She still had trouble accepting that it wasn't a cruel illusion.

"Have you told Brooke how you feel about her yet?" Laura asked.

"What? No. Why would I do that?" BJ's eyes almost popped out of his head.

"Since you're forcing me to talk about my feelings for Jillian I figured turnabout was fair play."

"First of all, I never even mentioned a thing about your *feelings* for Jillian. I just wanted to know how your day went because you were avoiding it. But it makes much more sense now."

"You can't say anything. To anyone," Laura said, pointing her finger at him. She thought that it was almost guaranteed that he'd tell Brooke before the day was out.

He cocked his head, pursed his lips, and leered at her. "Fucking seriously?"

"I'm still trying to wrap my head around everything. It's all moving so fast. For the first time in years, I swam. Not like shallow, kiddie pool swimming. But like, can't touch the bottom, treading water, kind of swimming." Laura wouldn't have believed it if she hadn't been there herself. "Granted I didn't go under and had Jillian there with me, but I did it."

BJ grabbed her by the shoulders and gave her an excited shake. "That's amazing," he said and then laughed once he realized what he had said. "You know what I mean."

"I told you. But…"

"But what? No buts."

"What if Jillian hadn't been there? I don't think I could have done it without her." Jillian had her so distracted the whole time that a few times Laura nearly forgot where she was. All she had to do was touch her or look into her eyes, and it was like she was under a spell. As if Jillian was somehow giving her the strength she didn't have within herself.

"Of course, you couldn't have. That's kind of the point isn't it?" he said.

She supposed he was right. Laura knew she wouldn't have been there without her. But that's not what she meant. She tried to imagine having anyone else holding her, supporting her, or believing in her more than she believed in herself. What if *that* was the illusion?

"What happens when the day comes that she isn't holding my hands in hers? When I'm standing on the ledge alone?"

"You seem to be under some ridiculous notion that she somehow kicked your arms and legs for you or some shit. You did that, Laura, not Jillian."

"Yeah, but."

"No. Stop with the fucking buts already. Sure, she was there holding your hand. Yes, she kept you distracted by her bangin' body and smoldering eyes, or whatever. But you can't possibly think that she's what kept you afloat out there, can you?"

Laura caught the flying nunchucks as Kaius whipped them at her head like a water ninja. "Not today, buddy," she said, tossing them back into the pool where he was waiting.

"See, even he was trying to knock some sense into you." BJ bent over the wall to push a rogue cushion back into the water.

"I know. I know. She just has me so twisted around. And then when I thought she was going to kiss me, I—"

"What?" he said, springing up off the wall from the other side. "Shut up."

Butterflies swarmed in her belly just thinking about it. The way Jillian had licked her own lips and bit down on the plump bottom one so softly. Her body had reacted with a hunger that rippled through her. A feeling not much different from the one she endured now. "Oh yeah. Thank God one of us had our wits, because I'm not sure I'd have been able to stop what she started."

"What *she* started?"

"Yes. She started this nonsense two months ago with her charming smile and tight ass while making delightfully random conversation at the coffee machine."

"That's not weird and specific or anything," he said, raising his eyebrows.

It might have been so. But since that moment Laura had been both unable and unwilling to get Jillian out of her mind. With every encounter they had, she managed to ingrain herself more firmly within Laura's very being. The truth of it both thrilled and terrified her for reasons that she wasn't sure she understood.

"So, Brooke. What's going on there?"

"Nothing." BJ smiled and his face flushed, contradicting the tone in his voice.

"Oh, hell no, man. After the coals you just dragged me over? No such luck, buddy."

"Dude. Our situations are hardly the same." He rested his elbows on the wall and leaned forward onto them.

Laura did the same. "They're identical. We both have crushes on women who already know even though we like to pretend they have no idea."

"That's a gross simplification of the facts, and you know it."

Sometimes Laura forgot that BJ had to hide a part of who he was out of fear and misunderstanding. He was such a genuine and attractive man who was wise beyond his years. She just adored him so damn much. "Do you trust her?"

"It's not always about trust. But yes, I do," he said.

"And you like her, right? As in romantically," she asked.

"I know what you're going to say. It's better to know now than to wait."

"Not at all what I was going to say, but I like it so pretend I said it."

"Zeno thanks you for that, Pepper," BJ said after she had bumped the buoy over into the adjoining module.

Instead of fishing it back from Zeno's pool, Laura chucked in the dolphin-sized Kong. "Look, she likes you. That's obvious. Just be honest with her, like you were with me."

"And if she doesn't respond like you did?"

"Then she's not as cool as I am and not worth another second of your time." Laura smiled and bumped his shoulder with hers. "Right?"

"You do know that cool people don't actually call themselves cool, right?"

❖

Jillian leaned over the stack of books and papers that were piled all around her dining table. She stretched for her open laptop trying not to topple any of them over in the process. She sat and opened her computer in front of her, there was a knock at the front door. Jillian paused for a moment knowing that she'd left the door unlocked earlier, and if it were anyone she knew, they'd just let themselves in.

When she heard the door open, she was surprised to feel a twinge of disappointment that it wasn't an impromptu visit from Laura. Disappointment made way for a tingle of curiosity at the thought of having Laura alone in her home. That feeling was brushed away when Diana came into the kitchen. Jillian closed her laptop and leaned against the back of the chair.

"What's all this?" Diana picked up a couple of the books and turned them over in her hands.

"Just some research for a project I'm working on," Jillian said, reaching out to take the them back from Diana.

"That project wouldn't happen to have a name, would it? Maybe, I don't know, Laura Carter?" Diana set the books back down instead of handing them to Jillian.

Laura was the inspiration for expanding her research idea, but it wasn't about her. And besides, where would Diana even get the idea that this stuff had anything to do with Laura? "What are you talking about?"

"I saw the two of you working with Pepper the other day. A rather intimate little one-on-one session it seemed."

Jillian had been there. She'd also replayed the entire day in her head several times since then, but she would hardly have called it intimate. Except for those few fleeting moments she held Laura in her arms resisting the urge to kiss her. "I'm not sure what you saw, but it wasn't that."

"You seem to forget that we used to be a thing. I'm more than qualified to make that call." Diana set her hands on Jillian's shoulders. She purred into her ear, "Remember?"

Uncomfortable with the contact, Jillian stood and took her coffee mug to the microwave. She noticed that it was just about empty, so she poured a fresh cup instead. "Well, it's the wrong call. I guarantee that whatever you thought you saw was well… not what you thought you saw."

"Okay. Then what was it?" Diana sat at the table intent on getting to the bottom of something. "Why would the director of education be taking such an interest in one particularly attractive trainee?"

Jillian had two options. She could either let Diana continue with this uncomfortable and invasive investigation or she could just tell the truth. The problem was that both had the potential to blow up in her face.

Diana wouldn't let go until she had the answers she sought, even if she had to twist and tie Jillian into some sort of confession that corroborated the ideas she had in her head. "Look, Jillian. I get it. She's young, smart, beautiful, and has one hell of a body."

"Come on. Don't talk like that about her." It was true, and Jillian was very much aware of each dip and curve on Laura's body. She just didn't want Diana to covet it so carelessly.

"Jillian, we've known each other for a long time. I can tell when you've got more on your mind than the usual. What's going on?"

In spite of their romantic history, she considered Diana her friend and a close one. Jillian told her about Laura's illness and how she'd arranged time for them to work together to see if Jillian could help her. "I've taken it a step further here," Jillian said, handing her a book on animal assisted therapy and sitting back at the table.

Diana looked at it skeptically and fanned through the pages. "Wait a second. I need to understand something first."

"And what is that?"

"Why are you willing to risk the last twenty years of your life and career for this girl? You do realize that nothing about this looks good from the outside looking in?" Diana leaned back in her chair and crossed her arms.

Jillian was aware of how it looked. She had no doubt that she'd taken a special interest in Laura, and while she wasn't violating any policies that she knew of, she wasn't oblivious to the perception. Without her, Laura wouldn't have a chance at the institute or in this field. Laura knew that too, and yet she kept trying despite it. If Jillian could help her even a tiny bit, why wouldn't she? "I'm not risking anything. I'm just trying to help her."

"I get it. And it's wonderfully noble of you. That's always been an admirable trait of yours. But what if it were anyone else? BJ? Steven? Would you be so willing to help them?"

"Steven was an ass," Jillian said without hesitation.

Diana laughed and nodded her head. "You know what I mean."

Of course, she did. Diana was fishing. So much for avoiding the awkward and annoying interrogation part of this conversation. "Yes, I do. Would I help anyone else? Yes, I probably would. Laura has been through a lot. She's more than qualified to be here and refuses to let this thing beach her. If anyone else had that same determination against such impossible odds then yeah, maybe I would help them too."

"At least tell me that you are not sleeping with her."

Why was that always the way? It was possible for two lesbians to be in the same room and not want to have sex with each other. That wasn't necessarily the case here, but sometimes it was. Either way she wasn't about to confirm or deny that with Diana. "You're being ridiculous. And I'm not answering that."

"Holy shit, Jillian. You're fucking her?"

"Good grief, Diana, stop yelling. It's none of your business. Seriously. Do I ever ask you which one of my staff you're sleeping with? And besides don't get self-righteous with me because you didn't get your paws on her first."

Jillian was beyond over with this conversation, and Diana had more than overstayed her welcome. Laura would be horrified to know that she had been the subject of such a discussion, regardless of whether anything had happened between them. Besides, Jillian was positive that whatever they would be doing would be much more than mere fucking. Laura was far too passionate not to put some or all of that into her private life. The thought sent a tingle dancing over her skin.

"Well, I'll have you know that neither my paws nor any other part of my body is interested in her. I was just looking out for you."

"Everything's fine. You don't need to look out for me. I've been training animals for twenty years. Conditioning, repetition, reinforcement, exposure. That's all it is."

"Throw a few smelt in her mouth and you've got yourself a talking dolphin."

"Diana." Jillian was appalled by the insinuation.

"What? All I'm saying is that you may need to rethink this idea of yours. Let her sink or swim on her own. Literally. I know you want to help, but there are some things that are outside our expertise. This is definitely one of them." Diana showed herself out.

Jillian had thought about that more than a few times. She contemplated letting her go the same night she'd expelled Steven, but she didn't. She made the deal with Laura for four weeks. Jillian would give her whatever she could in that time. If they succeeded, Laura had the rest of her life to live her dream. If not, then Jillian imagined it would be a matter of time until she found another way. Jillian was determined to do everything she could in the next few weeks to give her the dream. After their interaction with Pepper, she felt that they were well on their way.

CHAPTER TWELVE

Once everyone was herded into the conference room, all eyes were focused on the individuals at the front. Laura and her seven fellow trainees stood pressed against the back wall behind Jillian and Fletcher. Diana was at the front of the room alongside two officers from the Florida Wildlife Commission. They'd all been pulled from their current assignments and duties by Jillian who said little else except, "Follow me." Which every one of them had done without hesitation.

One of the most important programs conducted at TMRI was the manatee rescue and rehab initiative. As one of the few federally regulated marine life critical care units in the state, their team of emergency responders were dispatched to every rescue and stranding call within a hundred miles of the facility. And today they received one of those calls. According to Diana and the FWC, seven West Indian manatees had found themselves trapped in a shallow pond after swimming over an embankment when the river swelled earlier in the week.

The energy in the room was electrifying. Moving seven, thousand-pound animals was going to take the combined strength and knowledge of both the institute and the wildlife commission, as well as teams from SeaWorld Orlando, the University of Florida, and the US Geological Survey. The coordination effort that was getting underway was energizing, and Laura was buzzing from the activity. She was excited to be witnessing such an important and integral step in the mission to ensure the survival of these threatened animals. It made her even more proud to be a part of the TMRI family.

"Is it just me or are you a bit bummed that we aren't going with them?" BJ said just loud enough for those next to him to hear.

"Like they need a bunch of newbs like us getting in the way," Brooke said.

Laura agreed with both of them, but she had to admit she was more disappointed about not getting to witness the rescue.

When Diana dismissed the team, Laura and the others pressed themselves tighter against the wall and out of the way. The room emptied as fast as it had filled in a controlled chaos.

Jillian followed the mass and then stopped in the doorway. She turned around and looked at them all with impatience. "What the hell are you people waiting for? Load up."

All eight of them hopped to attention and scurried out the door behind Jillian. The disappointment that they had been feeling was replaced with disbelief as they raced after the others. A convoy of vehicles was staged along the alley between the fish house and the medical building. Team members and staff jumped in and out of trucks with nets, slings, buoys, and crates of every size. If it wasn't bolted down it was being loaded into a vehicle, and within minutes, they were ready to go.

Fletcher and Jillian hollered to Laura and the others from a white cargo van at the end of the line. Metal latches clanged and doors slammed along the row of vehicles. The last of their group filed into the van as the first truck began to pull away.

"Get in the van," Jillian bellowed at the stragglers. She was already pulling away from the curb before the door was closed. Laura had no doubt Jillian would have left whether the last of them had made it into the vehicle or not.

From the far back seat, she could see Jillian's face in the rearview mirror. Her eyes were shaded with sunglasses, but Laura could see the intensity and focus in her angular jaw and the taut muscles of her neck. Her lips were closed tightly but still full and pink. When Jillian's tongue ran slowly across her bottom lip, Laura did the same out of instinct. When Jillian raised her eyebrow and grinned ever so slightly, Laura knew she'd been caught. It was confirmed when Jillian pulled her glasses down just enough to make sure Laura knew she'd been busted. Jillian laughed out loud, causing Fletcher to look at her curiously, but she said nothing.

A red-hot flash worked its way up Laura's neck into her cheeks, and she slid in her seat just short of melting into a heap on the floorboard.

"What are you doing?" BJ asked, looking down at her.

"Wishing these windows opened so I could toss myself out onto the road." Before BJ could give her shit about getting caught ogling Jillian, Fletcher turned around to face everyone in the back.

"When we get to Crystal River things are going to look and feel pretty hectic. With the different agencies, there's going to be about forty or fifty people working to trap, assess, and hopefully relocate this aggregation."

"What?" Laura asked, deafened by the rushing sound of blood in her ears. "Where?" The rattle in her voice was noticeable even to herself. She grabbed BJ by the arm, and he winced. "Where? Where did he say we were going?" She squeezed his arm tighter until he yelped.

"Crystal River. Why?" As soon as he said it, his face went white. "Oh God." He grabbed her hand and squeezed it. "Fletcher, did you say Crystal River? As in Crystal River Springs?"

"That's the one," Fletcher responded before continuing with his briefing.

"Okay. It's fine." BJ comforted her. "It'll be fine."

Beads of sweat were building on Laura's upper lip and forehead. She wiped her clammy hands on her pants before swiping them across her brow. "BJ that's…that's…" She choked on the words.

"I know. Don't worry. When we get there, we'll let Jillian know and you can just stay in the van."

She took several deep breaths, exhaling slowly through pursed lips. She told herself to keep breathing though she wanted to hold her breath. "I can't do that. Nobody knows, BJ. Just you and Jillian." She let out a shaky exhale. "I'm not ready."

"I know. But you don't have to get in the water. There are going to be so many people there, and we don't even know what we'll be doing. I'm sure we're just extra hands."

She had to know for sure. He was trying to help, but he would say anything to keep her from going into a full panic. "Ex... excuse me...Fletcher?" She didn't care that the whole van full of people turned to look at her. She took a ragged breath, and her eyes were drawn to Jillian's who was looking back at her through the mirror. At first her unshaded stare was one of confusion, but then realization struck and her eyes expressed the fear that BJ had vocalized. Oh, shit.

Jillian turned to Fletcher and mumbled something no one could have heard, certainly not Laura all the way in the back. It was Jillian who responded to the question, "We'll let you know more of what our role might be when we get there," she said before making Fletcher turn back around in his seat.

"Do you have anything?" BJ asked.

"Huh?" she said, looking away from Jillian's gaze.

"Pills? Xanax. Klonopin? Anything?" he asked.

"Yes. In my bag, but I don't like to take them during the day while I'm working."

"Take one, or half of one. We have at least an hour until we get there. You cannot put yourself through this for that long." He picked up her bag off the floor.

He was right. She would either go mad with anxiety or pass out from trying to hold her breath for the whole ride. As she set the tablet under her tongue to dissolve, Laura wished that she was back in the lagoon with Jillian's strong arms wrapped around her. She closed her eyes and imagined herself there.

❖

Jillian tried to keep her eyes on the road, but she kept looking back at Laura in the mirror. Her face was ashen and the wild panic in her eyes called out to her. She wanted to pull the van over and hurdle every seat to get to her. Jillian couldn't begin to imagine what Laura was feeling, but her heart beat harder and her breaths came quicker as Laura tried to get a handle on her own. Jillian paced her own breathing with Laura's and tried in vain to control it and help her through the fear.

She caught BJ's eyes and he nodded at her. Laura's were still closed, but her shoulders had begun to dip into a more relaxed posture. Jillian was glad that he was there with her since she couldn't be. She wanted to kick herself for not catching this before they got on the road. Jillian had to wonder how they even got this far before Laura connected the dots. Jillian tried to recall if Diana had even given a location during their briefing. Either way, it no longer mattered. Laura was about to confront her demons head-on without any warning, and Jillian didn't know what she could do to stop it.

During the ride she looked back often at Laura but never saw her eyes. Her head hung forward with her eyes closed for the remainder of the drive. An occasional glance at BJ assured her that she was all right. After what seemed like a hundred years, they arrived at the staging area. A temporary command center was established in the parking lot where they could coordinate their teams once they assessed the situation on the ground.

Jillian ordered her group out of the vehicle and sent Fletcher to be her ears among the action. At first glance, she estimated no less than ten people per agency had responded. Their distinctive colored shirts set them apart from each other, as well as the handful of divers standing by with full scuba gear just in case. There wasn't any situation that they weren't prepared for.

"You can go observe, but do not get in the way. Once the briefing is finished, Fletcher will return with our assignments if we have any. If you're pulled into service or given a directive, don't ask questions, just do it."

As expected, everyone except BJ and Laura rushed toward the action They lingered behind the van hoping not to be seen. "You can head over with them if you want. I'll stay with her," Jillian said to BJ.

He looked at Laura and rubbed her arm. "Are you okay if I go?"

"Go ahead. I'm fine," Laura said.

As soon as BJ was out of sight, Jillian slipped two fingers under Laura's chin and raised her hanging head. "Hey, you." Tears formed in Laura's eyes, and that ripped at her heart. "I am so sorry."

"It's just that I haven't been here since, you know."

"I was so caught up in the momentum that I never even thought about where we were going."

"Why would you?" Laura asked, pulling Jillian's hand from her face.

The idea that Laura didn't want Jillian to touch her hit her harder than she could have expected. "I should've asked. You wouldn't have to be feeling like this."

"That isn't your responsibility, Jillian. Your job isn't to babysit and protect me. What if you weren't here?" Laura's voice was shaky but not from nervousness, and it crackled as she raised her voice in frustration.

"It is my responsibility to protect you. As a trainee in my program it most certainly is my job." Jillian kept her voice low and calm.

"But why? Why are you giving me so many chances? Me?" Laura tapped hard on her own chest. "You've gone so far out of your way to help me. Why?"

Diana had asked the exact same question the day before. So many potential answers flooded her mind. *Because you need me. Because I want to feed the fire burning inside you. Because I think I'm falling in love with you.* Jillian shrugged and just said, "Because I can."

"But we don't even know that. We're just throwing shit at the wall and hoping it sticks."

A painful pang twisted her heart. "Is that how you think I would approach something so important?" she asked.

"I don't know. What do you even know about PTSD? About fear or anxiety?" Laura's voice grew louder.

"What makes you think that you're the only one who's afraid of things? Everyone's scared of something, Laura."

"Tell me. What could the incomparable Jillian Marshall be afraid of? What paralyzes her with fear and anxiety?"

"Plenty of things," Jillian said, hoping that Laura wouldn't press her. She had only ever been afraid of one thing, but since the day Laura entered her life her fears had multiplied. She was frightened of her attraction to Laura and of her desire to just be near her whenever she could. She feared losing her heart and then losing Laura to her dreams. Not to mention losing her career when everyone at the institute found out that she was falling for a trainee. How could she possibly tell Laura that she was her biggest fear? She couldn't, and she wouldn't.

"Like what?" Laura asked after several moments of silence.

"Heights," Jillian said.

Before Laura could ask any more questions or demanded details, Fletcher returned. The rest of the group scurried along behind him. She had tried to calm her down in these few minutes they had been alone, but had just managed to get her more agitated. It wasn't going to help her with whatever she was about to be confronted with.

"We've got seven of them. Five cows and two juveniles. They're in a receding retention pond near a subdivision on the north fork of the river. Seems to be as low as three feet in most places. It looks like they washed up over the embankment during the surge last week."

Several box trucks and a medi-van drove out of the park to set up down river, where it would be easier to access and examine the animals. "What do they need from us?" Jillian asked.

Everyone stepped closer hoping to hear that they'd get some hands-on experience instead of just standing around.

"They need a few hands in the water to help herd them into a confined space. And of course, there's no shortage for anyone willing to do the heavy lifting. There's at least one nursing cow and she's pushing two thousand."

"And vet staff?"

"Two vets are on hand from SeaWorld with a few technicians, and FWC will be tagging the calves before release," Fletcher said.

Jillian was pleased to hear that the agencies were in full cooperation and rescue was imminent. It would no doubt be a long and arduous day, but also a rewarding and memorable one. "Who wants to get muddy?"

Everyone including Laura raised their hands. "Then let's go." Jillian shooed everyone back into the van waving her hands at her sides like she was herding ducks.

She was relieved that they were moving downstream away from the place of Laura's worst nightmare. The terror she saw in her face was heartbreaking, and Jillian somehow succeeded in turning her fear into anger instead of dispelling it. She hoped that the detailed information from Fletcher as well as the site change would allow Laura to regain her focus and forge through.

CHAPTER THIRTEEN

After nine hours wading through muddy, waist deep water and lifting over four tons of manatee, Laura was ragged, but she wasn't alone in her pain. The van was filled with nine other filthy, weary, and wild individuals. The energy in the vehicle was energized and joyful, with everyone retelling the day from their own personal and unique perspectives. Laura was positive that while they were all a part of the same rescue, no one had the same story to tell.

BJ was sitting next to her picking flakes of dried mud off the back of his arm. Laura on the other hand was content to let the hardened muck solidify and serve as her temporary memento until the shower washed it away. However, she still didn't appreciate BJ adding to it by brushing his own crustiness off onto her.

"You're making a mess. I hope you get stuck cleaning that out of the van," she said, nudging him to stop.

"I can't believe you're just sitting there covered in swamp sludge and manatee shit like it's totally normal."

"Dude, this is my badge of honor, and I'm going to wear it proudly. At least until I strip down naked and burn these things in a trash fire." While she was proud of her disgusting shell, she couldn't deny that she smelled like a skunk ape and there wasn't a shred of hope of washing it out of her clothes.

"You were so great out there today. I admit I was really nervous for you. I had a whole plan worked out in my mind in case you had an attack or something."

"Aww. Thanks. I did all right, I think." Laura had done all right. She waded into the sludge and helped lift thousands of pounds of unimaginable weight onto her shoulders. She had a hand in one of the most rewarding endeavors she could ever be involved in.

"All right? You are a rock star, Laura. You didn't even hesitate when they told you to get in. Even I was overwhelmed by the whole chaos of it," he said.

Laura knew that wasn't entirely true. She had plenty of doubts and wanted on more than one occasion to throw up her breakfast. "Wading through water isn't the problem anymore. It's as soon as I go under. My face touches the water and it takes me right back there."

"That's good though. You used to not be able to go anywhere near the water. Now look at you! Rescuing manatees and swimming with dolphins and shit." He gave her a light punch in the arm.

Laura laughed at the simplicity of it, although it was anything but, and it had taken her a decade to get that far. "Yeah. But at this rate I'll be forty before I can put my face under water."

"I think your math is off. But I get it."

Laura wondered if she would ever get there whether it was by the time she turned forty or not. She had to hope that if she had gotten this far in the last few weeks that she wouldn't still be trying after twelve years.

"Maybe I'll just keep my day job and hang around shallow ponds on the weekends saving manatees."

"Shut up. You've made more progress in two weeks with Jillian's help than you've done in a decade on your own. It's clear that something is working."

Laura hadn't seen Jillian except for a few moments the entire day. It almost felt as though she had put as much space between them as possible. And considering that they were working within a relatively limited area, she did it well. Laura had attempted to get Jillian's attention when she could, but her eyes were anywhere other than Laura. She had hurt Jillian's feelings that morning. It had been obvious when she removed her hand from her face. It wasn't that she didn't want Jillian's touch on her skin, it was very much the opposite, and that's why she had gotten angry.

She'd already been feeling overly dependent when Jillian had touched her; she could feel a need rise inside her. But Laura couldn't need her. Needing her would mean that everything she'd worked for relied on someone else and was so easily lost. Yet today she had gone in the water, schlepped through the muck, and rescued seven helpless animals all because of her.

Laura looked up into the mirror, and to her surprise and delight saw Jillian staring back at her. The gaze that she'd searched for all day was there, waiting for her. This time she didn't shy away when Jillian smiled back at her.

The energy in the van was beginning to settle as the excitement of the day wore off. The sun had dipped below the horizon, turning the sky outside into an abstract painting of orange and purple. The glow illuminated Jillian's face in a warm, ethereal light. The loud conversations faded into mumbles and murmurs as passengers began to succumb to exhaustion. But not Laura.

She fought against the urge to lean back and let the hum and sway of the road lull her to sleep. She wanted to spend this time memorizing the lines and edges on Jillian's face as if she'd never again have the chance. The lights and shadows flashed and danced over her unique features and her tightly clenched jaw. She'd become rather fond of the small scar beneath her eye on the ridge of her cheekbone that she'd never noticed until now.

When the bright interior light of the van blazed through her eyelids, she realized she'd lost her battle to stay awake. As she climbed out behind the others, her muscles screamed with stiffness and the hard, dry mud cracked and crumbled from her skin. It wasn't even seven o'clock, but Laura couldn't wait to get into her bed. After she showered off whatever Florida microbes had begun to set up residence on her body, she would do just that.

Everyone else had the same idea and were practically stripping as they sprinted toward the dorms. Not even Brooke or BJ waited for her to get all the way out of the vehicle before they took off without her. She didn't even bother with rushing, as there weren't enough shower stalls for everyone at once anyway. She might have to wait, but the perk was that she could take her sweet time.

A hand reached out for her as she stepped out of the van. Laura recognized several scattered freckles and smiled before she even looked up. She was quite capable of getting her aged self out of a car, but took the opportunity to hold Jillian's hand anyway.

"Thanks," Laura said, stepping down but still holding on to Jillian.

"My pleasure."

Whoa. Those words were guaranteed to echo in her mind all night. When Jillian made the move to release her, Laura held fast. She wanted to apologize for her behavior earlier and that included pushing Jillian's hand away. "About this morning—"

Jillian interrupted. "It's fine." She tugged at her hand, but Laura squeezed tighter and stepped toward her.

"No. It wasn't." She now held Jillian's hand in both of hers. "I was scared and frustrated, and I lashed out at you. I didn't mean it."

"You weren't wrong though. I don't know what I'm doing, Laura. Not really. But I know that I wanted to do something."

"Well, it's working. Shit is sticking, or I wouldn't have been able to do what I did today. Not without you."

"But you did do it without me. I made sure I didn't get within a hundred feet of you today. That was all you, my sweet girl."

Laura stomach somersaulted and a knot formed in her throat. *Her* sweet girl? *She just called me her sweet girl.* Laura's mind was blank.

"I'm proud of you, Laura."

The butterflies in her belly were in full flight, and she couldn't think of two words to string together. "I…stink," Laura blurted out, and Jillian laughed. "Christ almighty. I'm a train wreck. That was supposed to be 'I need a shower,' but…yeah." If anyone could ruin a moment it was Laura.

"I agree. Not that you stink, but about the shower."

"Right. Well, I should go now."

"Me too," Jillian said, closing the doors to the van. "Hey, wait."

Laura had taken just a single step when Jillian called her back. "Yeah?"

"Will you help me with something tomorrow?"

"Of course, with what?" It didn't matter what it was, Laura was going to do it.

"Just a thing" Jillian said.

"Okay." She had no idea what it was and was excited about it anyway.

❖

The common room of the residence hall was quiet when Jillian arrived to pick up Laura. She at least expected two or three people to be milling about or plopped on the couch watching television or something. But there was no one. It seemed that the older she got the less she understood the younger generations and their addiction to sleep. Jillian tried to remember the last time she'd slept in, as even on her days off she was out of bed with her first cup of coffee by six a.m. Here it was nine and not a soul had roused.

As she headed toward Laura's room, she hoped that she wasn't one of them.

To Jillian's relief she hadn't even knocked when Laura stepped out into the hall already dressed and ready to go. Jillian's heart skipped a beat at seeing her in something other than institute blue. While Laura could probably make a straightjacket look attractive, the hot pink T-shirt and form-fitting jeans were far more beckoning. "You look nice."

Laura smiled, and her face brightened a few shades closer to the shirt, and she thanked her. Jillian almost felt like she should've handed her flowers or a corsage as they stood there awkwardly at Laura's door. Of course, she hadn't intended on this being a date, or even date like. Except she wasn't sure what else to call it. Although why did she have to call it anything? It was just two people going out for the day. But not going out like on a date. Her mind was a whirl. Jillian had plenty of reasons to be nervous, none of which had been because she didn't know what to call this other than a date. That was until now, of course. *Oh, for goodness sake's, what's wrong with me?* "Shall we go?" Jillian asked.

"Yes. Unless your plan had been to stand here in the hallway all day."

Jillian laughed. "Well, not anymore." What she had in mind was the opposite of standing around all day. So long as she could make it from there to her truck without backing out, it would prove to be much more exciting as well.

Laura paused when they got to the parking lot, and Jillian looked at her. "What's wrong?"

"Nothing. I just don't have any idea what you drive."

Jillian hadn't even thought about it, but she was feeling playful. "What do you think I drive?"

"Seriously?" Laura raised her eyebrow.

"Yes. Which of these do you think is mine?"

"All right. I'll play," Laura said, tapping her fingers on her lips as she perused the cars in the lot. Jillian crossed her arms and chuckled at her serious contemplation. "Hmm. It must be something practical, but not dated, like an old Buick."

"Right, and because I'm not a silver haired, eighty-year-old," Jillian said.

"But you are older so it's not going to be a bright orange Mini Cooper either."

"Hey, I could drive one of those."

"No. Because that's BJ's car. Yours is practical, dependable, useful but strong, attractive, tough, and shiny," Laura said.

"Shiny?"

"Yes. The woman who would circle a million invisible fish scales wouldn't possibly have any spots on her black Silverado 1500 backed into that corner spot under the lamppost."

Jillian's mouth fell open. "There's no way you just guessed that. Impossible."

"I didn't guess. I made several very keen observations based on the most dominant traits of your personality and deduced the most obvious answer from the choices available." Laura smiled and headed out toward Jillian's truck.

"No. Way."

"What? I have a graduate degree in animal behavior, I know a few things." Laura stopped at the front of Jillian's truck with a cocky smirk on her adorable face.

"So, you're telling me that you somehow psychoanalyzed me with your shrinkie brain tricks to figure out which of these forty cars was mine." Jillian set her hands on her hips.

"Sorta." Laura was clearly amused with herself, but Jillian found it impossible to believe that she'd done anything but guess that the truck was hers. Jillian poked Laura's side, and she almost leapt out of her skin.

"Oh my gosh, you're ticklish," Jillian said as she stepped closer to Laura.

"Don't. No." Laura backed away, but she was trapped by Jillian's truck. One arm was wrapped around her waist and held her side, while she held out her other hand to stop Jillian.

"Tell me how you knew and I'll spare you." She took another step closer.

"Jillian, don't. Oh my God." Laura laughed nervously as she pressed both hands against Jillian's chest.

"Tell me." Jillian's hands hovered at Laura's sides.

"Okay. Okay. I'll tell you," Laura said, but Jillian didn't withdraw or back away.

She was enjoying everything about having Laura in her arms pleading with her. She set her hands on her waist but didn't tickle her. Instead she pulled her tight up against her body and looked into Laura's surprised eyes. Jillian tilted her head and Laura's hand slid up to her shoulders. Their lips were but a breath apart. "Tell me," she whispered against her mouth.

Laura's lips parted ever so slightly in response. Her darkened eyes called to her, and she was afraid that she'd started something she couldn't finish. Jillian's legs shook, and a flood of heat rushed between them. She wanted to take Laura right there against her truck. The feeling of Laura's soft breasts pressed against her fueled the need building inside her.

"I cheated," Laura said, breaking the spell between them.

"How?" Jillian's fingers dug into Laura's side, eliciting a high-pitched screech.

"Your...your shirt," she responded laughing breathlessly.

Jillian let Laura go and looked at herself. She stretched her shirt out before her. "Well, I'll be dammed." On the front of her black vintage T-shirt was a faded image of a Chevy logo and the word Silverado running down the left side of her chest.

"Only lesbians and rednecks wear shirts advertising what they drive."

Jillian lunged for Laura who narrowly escaped her grasp. "Get in the truck before I change my mind about today."

Laura opened the door and jumped into the vehicle. "Where are we going?"

As she got into the truck, Jillian almost changed her mind. Not because she didn't want to fulfill her plan, but because she just wanted to be with Laura, and it didn't matter if they just spent the whole day driving aimlessly across the state. "Remember when you asked me if there was anything I was afraid of?"

"I do, and I'm sorry about that. I didn't mean anything by it."

"No worries. It's a fair comment to make when someone without any fear is telling you how to overcome it. But I'm not without fear."

"Heights, right?" Laura asked.

"Yes. But unlike you I've never confronted it," Jillian said.

"Never?"

"No. Not head-on the way that you do, that's for sure."

"Oh, dear God, don't tell me that you've gotten some wild hair up your ass to go sky diving or some shit?" Laura looked over at Jillian with wide eyes.

"Oh, hell no." The thought of getting in a plane made her queasy, jumping out of one was out of the question. "But it's still sort of a wild hair idea. Just wait. There's some back story." Jillian started the truck and they were on their way.

"Uh-huh."

"When I was ten or eleven, I had the worst crush on my oldest brother's girlfriend. One day he busted me drawing her name on my notebook with little hearts and flowers all around it."

"Oh, man." Laura cringed.

"Yeah, well, turns out he wasn't so concerned about my crush on her as much as he was about the fact that I liked another girl. I'm not sure I thought much about liking other girls and that it wasn't 'normal' until he told me that it wasn't. I just knew that I had two older brothers, and I wanted to be just like them."

"Aww, a little tomboy Jillian."

"Very much. So much so that I'd do anything to prove just how much like them I was. Well, when he told me that I wasn't 'man' enough to get a girl like Rachel, I thought he meant I didn't have the guts or whatnot. I told him I could do anything he could but better, and I'd prove it."

"And what could go wrong with that?" Laura chuckled.

"Right? So, on our way home from the bus stop that day we passed by a vacant construction site where they were building a new house. A huge one, with the fancy Spanish tile roof. So, he dared me to climb up onto the roof to prove myself."

"You didn't."

"Of course I did. And it was fine going up. I climbed out a loft window on the second story and then scaled up the side of the eve to the peak that sort of hung out over the front." Laura gasped next to her. "Yep, and that's where I lost my nerve. As soon as I looked down I froze. My brother looked like a tiny ant on the ground looking up at me."

"Oh, Jillian." The concern in Laura's sweet voice was comforting.

"I tried to get down, but my feet kept slipping on the tiles and it was so much more steep looking down than up. It could've been the roof of the Empire State Building, that's how it felt. My fingers were tucked under the lip of the rough tile and it was cutting into them because I was holding on so tight, and the tiles were so hot they were burning my legs through my shorts. All I could do was scream for my brother to save me." She remembered how scared she had been but also how helpless her brother looked when he couldn't save her.

"That must have been awful for both of you." Laura ran her hand down the length of Jillian's forearm. She laced their fingers together and pulled her hand over onto her knee.

"I just kept screaming for somebody to help me. After a few minutes, he came racing back along with my dad. Mark just stood there with his arms crossed as my dad climbed up onto the roof to get me. I couldn't even tell you how long I was up there, and I still have the burn scars on my legs. So now I'll do just about anything to avoid getting more than three feet off the ground."

"Well, it's a good thing that you don't work on roller coasters or at one of those zip line parks because that would be as silly as me training to swim with dolphins for a living." Laura laughed.

How could she know that? Before Jillian even had the chance to respond in surprise to Laura's statement they'd arrived at their destination.

Laura looked over at Jillian and said, "I swear, I had no idea."

CHAPTER FOURTEEN

Neither of them said a word as they made their way up the long dirt road to the main lodge of Florida Forever. Laura had to wonder what the hell Jillian was thinking. She had just spent the short drive reliving the moment her fear of heights was born, and now they were in the parking lot of a zip line adventure park. Up until now, Laura thought Jillian was the sane one between them. Although by the looks of her white-knuckle grip on the steering wheel, she might have been having second thoughts.

"I'm going to assume we're here for the swamp buggy tour or the horseback riding?"

Jillian turned her head toward Laura but didn't unlock her fingers from the wheel. "Why would I need your help with riding a horse?"

"I don't know, but it seems like you might need my help driving you to the hospital because I think you've lost your damn mind. Zip lining?"

Jillian let go and turned in her seat to face Laura. "When you asked me what I was afraid of I realized that here I was trying to help you overcome this monster you've been fighting for a decade, and I had no point of reference."

"So, you thought this would what? Help?"

"Basically. Although now I'm wondering why I thought that." Jillian scrunched her face.

"Look, it's a sweet gesture. But you don't need to do this."

Jillian took Laura's hand in hers. "No, I don't need to. But I want to. You're the bravest, most fearless woman I've ever met."

Laura scoffed. "I'm absolutely not fearless. Stubborn, emotionally unstable, and delusional, yes. But not fearless."

"Except you are, and in spite of it you keep going. Every day you wake up with the courage to try even when all the odds are against you."

The words took Laura off guard. She only ever counted her successes as worthy of her end goal. She never considered that the simple act of trying at all was in itself an achievement. Her failures so often outnumbered her accomplishments that she always felt two steps behind on progress. Yet here Jillian was, knowing all of Laura's attempts and setbacks, and still giving her credit for all of them.

"Jillian, that doesn't mean you have to throw yourself off scaffolding. Why not start small, like climbing a ladder or something?"

"Is that what you would do? Start small?"

Laura never did anything small. Which explained why all her mistakes were so big. "You're taking advice from the train wreck with PTSD? What are you trying to prove? You haven't been concerned about heights since you were twelve years old. Why now?"

"You've put more faith in me than anyone ever has, but I've done nothing to earn that."

"And you thought this was the best way to do that?"

"You know I was trying to make this a grand gesture of trust, and you are screwing that up for me." Jillian waved her arms around and they both laughed.

"Well, why didn't you just say that?" Laura asked as she got out of the truck. "But don't expect me to stand under you and catch you if you get stuck up there."

Once they made it from the parking lot to the registration desk, Laura was excited about the idea. She was almost positive that Jillian wasn't, as she hadn't said more than three words since the truck. When she stepped off the scale, Laura stopped her with a hand on each arm. "Are you sure you want to do this? Because we can go find something else to do."

"Yep. I'm sure." Jillian signed her name on the release form. "Your turn," she said, stepping out of the way so that Laura could get on the scale.

They waited for a few minutes for the rest of the group that made up their party. A strong, pungent odor of horse manure wafted by on a light breeze, and Jillian groaned beside her. The way she was leaning over the porch railing made Laura wonder if she was about to be sick.

"Are you okay?" she asked, rubbing her back gently.

"Just a little queasy. I'll be all right."

Laura knew the feeling all too well. "Let me go see if they have any water, or maybe some ginger ale." She didn't dare ask Jillian one more time if she was still up for this crazy idea. But if she could help her through it, she'd do whatever she had to. She left and returned with a water just as their ride arrived. A scrawny young man hopped down from an enormous vehicle on four monster truck wheels, and the day got that much better. The smell of burning diesel exhaust overpowered the manure scent as they boarded what Laura guessed was a school bus stripped of every bit of its protective yellow skin. She laughed as Jillian hesitantly took a seat next to her on the weather-beaten bench seat. There was no doubt in Laura's mind that Jillian was regretting everything about this decision. For Laura it was quintessential Florida, just like the place promised, and she loved it.

She was glad to see much of the concern on Jillian's face replaced with amusement as they bumped and swayed through cypress hammocks and sand dunes active with wildlife. Their driver kept them entertained with bad jokes along the way, which

Jillian was, of course, a huge fan of. The buggy stopped at the start of a neatly mulched trail that disappeared into the wiry brush. They followed the signs along the paths as the scent of pine sap and palmettos welcomed them.

Laura took a few long cleansing breaths to clear her lungs of the fumes left over from their ride. She heard Jillian do the same although probably more for the calming benefits. She hooked her pinky with Jillian's to provide her a small link in reality as her mind no doubt raced with anxiety. The sting of rejection zipped through her when Jillian pulled her finger away. However, it was a short-lived pang when Jillian intertwined her fingers with Laura's.

She could feel the tension in Jillian's tight grip and rubbed her thumb along the side of her index finger in slow, soothing strokes. She reluctantly let go of her hand when they reached the open-air pavilion where several long haired youngsters mingled about.

"Are there any actual adults who work here?" Jillian asked.

Although she'd said it in a joking tone, Laura knew she was at least half serious. They lined everyone up at the benches that ran the length and width of the building. Every station had a few hooks that held a serious collection of ropes, straps, and buckles. There was no use trying to keep her mind out of the gutter as Jillian ran her fingers along the thick canvas belts. The throbbing pulse began between her legs, and now she was the one second-guessing this wild idea.

Their zip guides introduced themselves and the outfitting began. Jillian skillfully stepped into the heavy-duty harness and pulled it up around her hips. For someone who had never done this before, Laura could only imagine how she'd become so adept at gearing up. As she slid her own harness on and pulled the belts tight around her thighs, her rigid knot pressed against the seam of her jeans and she shuddered.

If Jillian was feeling anything like this her fear of heights might be the furthest thing from her mind. When Jillian tugged at her straps and her hips thrust forward, Laura had to sit .

"Are you all right?" Jillian asked when Laura squeaked out a noise as she fell onto the bench. She was most definitely not okay. Sitting had just added to the tension between her legs as the thigh straps rose higher and pressed the ridge of the fabric right against her clit. Laura wasn't sure that she wouldn't come just sitting there.

"Mmmm. Fine," she said. If she didn't move, she was okay. As her luck would have it, when the guide came around to check their gear her plan failed. She stood up, and he loosened the loops around her legs giving her instant relief. God only knows why she hadn't done the same. But then he grabbed her by the belt around her waist and gave it a few aggressive yanks which caused her to howl out at him to stop.

"Just making sure you are in."

"Trust me. It's good," she said, and he moved on to Jillian and the others.

When he was gone, Jillian leaned over to Laura and hummed in her ear, "Is everything okay? You seem—"

"It's…it was pinching my…you know."

"What?" Jillian asked.

"My…" Laura pointed at her crotch. "My lady business. The straps were too tight, and my jeans were riding up."

"Oh." Jillian's cheeks blushed crimson with the same heat Laura felt in her own face.

"I probably should have worn different pants," she said in a pitch higher than normal.

Laura could see that Jillian was near to bursting trying to hold back her laughter. She wanted to crawl under the bench and die. Why did she even tell her?

"You might need different panties now, too." Jillian burst out in laughter, drawing the attention of everyone around them.

Laura didn't know if she was more aroused or horrified that Jillian was enjoying her situation so shamelessly. Although the fact that her attentions were anywhere except on her fear was all that mattered.

❖

Jillian stood at the base of the towering monolith. It was over seventy feet high with hundreds of steps winding upward through the trees and into the blue sky above. If she stared too long at the platform perched at its top the whole thing seemed to topple over onto her. Jillian turned her eyes to the ground until her head stopped spinning.

She took a few long, slow breaths through her nose as the others began their ascent. A bead of sweat trickled down the middle of her back. Laura was standing on the bottom step waiting for her, but she couldn't move. Her lightweight running shoes felt leaden and held her steadfastly to the spot. Laura stepped down from the staircase and came to her. She brushed her soft hand along Jillian's arm but said nothing. She looked deep into her eyes as if speaking words of understanding only their souls could hear.

Laura didn't ask to retreat nor did she urge her to advance. She just waited. She stood there giving Jillian all the time she needed to trust and let go. The rest of the group they were with weren't as patient as they paused a few flights up looking down at them. Her gaze flicked between Laura and the group as the seconds ticked by. Jillian took her hand and nodded as words seemed to be stuck beneath the tennis ball wedged in her throat.

Laura squeezed her hand and led her up the stairs. Jillian took each step with caution, gripping the handrail with her free hand. There wasn't a force on the planet strong enough to make her let go of Laura's. With each rise, she thought about Laura and how she lived with this constant state of anxiety every time she was near the water. Jillian couldn't even remember the last time she'd felt this all-encompassing fear. If she had to guess, she'd imagine it was the last time she'd been on a plane, but that had been years ago.

A breeze blew through the steel scaffold and made an eerie whistle bringing her upward climb to a halt. The sudden stop jerked Laura back unprepared, and she yelped but didn't let go. Instead she gripped Jillian's hand tighter.

"You're good," she said, offering Jillian a kind smile.

She was good, except for not having her feet on the ground where she preferred them. She pulled Laura's hand to her lips and kissed it. The sweet, clean scent of her skin tingled her senses, and for that moment she'd forgotten where she was. Laura never moved to pull back her hand, and Jillian's devilish mind wondered if she'd have let her kiss as far up as she desired. Given their current situation it would have to remain a mystery, but by the way Laura's eyes had darkened Jillian already knew the answer.

Like an obedient albeit nervous puppy, Jillian followed Laura step-by-step all the way to the platform on top of the tower. They stopped on the last step and waited for their guide to clip and lock each carabiner securely to the safety cables. There was little point in trying not to look down. They hovered above a clearing with acres of forest canopy stretching out in the distance. And focusing on her feet was useless as the deck was made of a steel mesh that did nothing to disguise the distance between her and the ground.

While he had connected her harness to the cables, Jillian had been forced to release Laura, who was now standing away from the railing well out of her reach. In spite of the light breeze, Jillian was sweating through her shirt. She pinched her collar and pulled it up to wipe off her upper lip. What she'd give to be at sea level, or below, and in a pool of cool water. "This shit is for the birds," she said still standing on the last step, and Laura laughed.

"Ladies and gentlemen, she'll be here *owl* week."

"Funny, but no. I most definitely will not." To her dismay, she was forced to abandon the safety of her step and joined Laura and the rest of their group out in the wind with nothing but two wires and a couple of clips to keep her from certain death. She jerked on the lines, and the carabiners clanked around. Sure, they were heavy duty, but she balked a little at betting her life on some lesbian's key chain accessories.

When she took that last step up, Laura was there with an outstretched arm. Jillian took her hand without question. She squeezed in tight with the others as instructed and listened intently to every word the guide said. Earlier, they'd spent thirty minutes going over the same information and practicing several runs on a mini-line that wasn't more than a foot off the ground. It had all seemed rather elementary, yet here she was, seven stories in the air, and struggling to remember what she'd been told. Someone beside her shifted their weight and bumped into her causing her to step back. It was only after she had done so that she realized doing it could have been a terrible mistake.

Laura's arm wrapped around her from behind and clasped securely around her waist. "I've got you," Laura said as she pressed into Jillian's back.

She closed her eyes and listened to the guide as she relaxed in the safety of Laura's embrace.

When the time came they decided they would go in the order they had come onto the platform. This meant that she would be last. Jillian was relieved by this, as it gave her the advantage of watching the techniques of the others, but it also gave her some extra time to hightail it back down the stairs when her turn came.

With each person who stepped off the edge and went zinging off into the forest, Jillian got closer to the point of no return. Literally. Once they left this tower the only way back to the ground was to finish the course. There was one set of stairs, and they were the ones behind her.

When it was Laura's turn, Jillian's heart ached. She'd been okay being the last one in line until now. The realization hit her that she would be alone once Laura had gone. She would have to let go on her own without anyone except the guide as her support.

"One sec," Laura said when he called her forward. She looked at Jillian and said, "I know I shouldn't ask again, but are you sure you want to do this?"

"No. Yes."

"Do you want me to go after you so I'm here with you?"

Jillian wanted to say yes. But more than that, she wanted it to be Laura's face she saw when she made it safely to the other side. "No. You go first, but you have to promise to catch me. Okay?"

"Always."

Jillian's skin tingled. She wanted to take Laura in her arms and kiss her until one of them begged for air. As Laura stepped to the ledge, Jillian held her breath, and then she was gone. She had never met anyone as unbelievable as Laura and every part of her knew it. With every ounce of strength and bravery she could gather, Jillian approached the ledge.

He worked quickly, snapping and clipping her safety wires to the thick metal cable. He lifted the trolley system that hung at her side up onto the wire. Jillian could feel the bounce and vibration of Laura's run as it reverberated through the line. He squeezed her grip tight as she clutched the tether in her gloved hands. He hollered commands for a clear zip and gave her the all clear, but she didn't move. Her heart pounded in her chest, and she could feel her pulse throbbing throughout every vein and vessel.

"Whenever you're ready," he said.

"Mm-hmm."

"Do you want me to push you?"

"What?" She thought he had to be joking with her.

"Sometimes it's easier if we give you a little nudge if you need help with that first step," he said.

"You're kidding. People actually want you to shove them off a seventy-foot skyscraper against their will?" Jillian wrung her hands tight around the lines in her hands.

"Yes. More than you'd think. Especially men."

"No. I…I can do it," Jillian said, looking at the ground so far below them.

"Whenever you're ready."

"You already said that." Jillian took a deep breath and blew it out.

"And I still mean it." He clicked the clip on his belt over and over.

"So, if I opted for the push, how would we do that exactly? Like a countdown, three, two, one, go? Or what?"

"You sit back in the harness. Like it's a chair." She leaned back as he demonstrated. "Right, like that. Let it support your weight. Trust it." He gave his contraption a healthy bounce.

And then before Jillian could ask another question, he shoved both hands against her back and pushed her off the damn thing. For the first twenty feet she wanted him dead. Maybe it was a hundred, she didn't know. All she knew was that she could see Laura in the distance waving her arms like a lunatic. A remarkable lunatic she would do anything in the world for.

CHAPTER FIFTEEN

For just about the entire ride back to the institute, Laura laughed. Not only because she was in such a great mood, but because every few minutes Jillian would burst out with some random exclamation of excitement or disbelief. And just like clockwork, Jillian hollered out, and Laura cracked up once again.

"Why do you keep laughing at me?"

"Because you're so damn cute, and I can't help it," Laura said.

Jillian blushed. "Oh yeah? Cute huh?"

"Adorable."

"Did you think it was cute when I sped right past you on that double run and left you in my dust?" Jillian demonstrated by thrusting out her hand and making a swishing sound.

This was a new side of Jillian that Laura was enjoying immensely. She was free and joyful, like she'd discovered a part of herself she never knew. "I like this. This new, wild side of yours."

"You didn't like me before?"

"Pfft." If anything, she liked her more, but that in no way diminished how much she liked her before. "I liked you. Well, like you. I like you." *Christ, Laura, say like one more time, you idiot.*

"Good to know," Jillian said without mention of her embarrassing language skills. "I can't believe I actually did it. I spent my whole life content with being afraid, and then I meet you and…I don't know. You inspire me, Laura."

"I'm so proud of you."

As they pulled into the parking lot, Laura's mood turned sullen. Although they'd spent the entire day together, she wasn't ready to say good-bye. Even as the exhilaration had worn off and her muscles began to stiffen up, she wasn't at all tired. If Jillian had decided to speed past the entrance and off into the darkness Laura would have driven all night. It didn't even matter where.

Jillian took the time to back her truck into the same spot as it had been that morning. When she put it in park and cut the engine neither of them made a move. The air in the cab was still and quickly began to grow warm. In the silence Laura feared that Jillian would be able to hear the steady pounding of her heart through her chest.

The yellow streetlight cast a romantic haze through the deep-tinted windows that were beginning to fog. Laura fiddled with the velvet fabric of the center console trying to think of anything to say. Jillian lifted the divider and eliminated the offending obstacle between them. Laura's stomach fluttered as Jillian shifted in her seat and reached for her hand. She rubbed her fingers over Laura's before linking them together.

Jillian brought Laura's hand up to her lips and closed her eyes before kissing it softly. While she'd done this earlier, this time it was on the sensitive flesh of her palm. But she didn't stop there. Jillian placed soft pecks on her wrist and worked her way up the length of her forearm. Her breath caught when she looked up at her with dark eyes full of desire. She had never had anyone look at her with such hunger.

Laura's arm was stretched as far as it could go, but Jillian wasn't discouraged. She let go of her arm long enough to slip hers around the small of Laura's back and pull their bodies together. Jillian cupped Laura's face in her hands. She brushed the wild strands of hair from her face and ran her fingers across her cheek, tracing each mark and line.

"Do you know how amazing you are?" Jillian asked, staring into Laura's eyes.

Laura had never thought of herself as such, yet here in Jillian's arms that's exactly how she felt. "It's not hard to when you look at me that way."

Jillian's gaze dropped to Laura's mouth and her heart skipped. They'd been here before teetering on this cusp of a kiss with the potential to change everything in an instant. There were no crowds, no onlookers, or places to be. They had all the time in the world, yet Laura was breathless and paralyzed with anticipation.

When Jillian leaned in, Laura held her breath. *It's happening.* She closed her eyes and Jillian's lips brushed against her mouth. "May I kiss you?"

Without answering, Laura pressed her lips to Jillian's. They were softer than she could have imagined, warm and perfectly wet. Laura wrapped her arms around Jillian's neck and pulled her closer. She moaned with delight when Jillian's tongue parted her lips and slipped inside. Their tongues danced together in sweet pleasure.

A rush of wet heat flooded between Laura's legs, and her clit throbbed with need. Jillian grabbed her by the waist and shifted their bodies until Laura straddled her lap. When her hard clit rubbed against the rigid seam, she purred; for the second time today, her desire was determined to make a scene. When Jillian nibbled into Laura's neck, she was afraid that moment would be now. Her nipples stiffened as they brushed against Jillian's chest.

A shiver ran through her body when Jillian's hands worked their way under her shirt to tease her through the lace of her bra, and she cupped her breasts firmly in her warm hands. Laura kissed Jillian again, more fiercely than before. She wanted her, right there and now. She reached between their bodies and pressed her fingers between Jillian's legs. She was just as hot and wet as

Laura, and she could feel it through her jeans. Jillian's head fell back, and she groaned with want. The sound urged Laura to press harder into her.

But then Jillian grabbed her hand, stopping Laura's fingers from moving against her. "Wait. Please," she said, pulling their hands up from between them.

"What's wrong? Did I hurt you?"

"No. No, I just need a second." Jillian kissed Laura's hand and set it on her leg.

"Okay," was all she could say as she slipped off Jillian's lap and back onto the seat next to her.

Jillian squeezed Laura's leg. "Please don't be upset. I want this. I want you. I just…we need to slow down."

Laura felt embarrassed and ashamed at how unglued she'd become. "I'm sorry." She hung her head.

"Oh, my sweet girl. Please don't be sorry," she said as she squeezed Laura's knee. "I've never wanted anything more. But not here, not like this." She kissed her slow and sweet with the hope of another time.

"I should probably go. I think the day is catching up to me." Laura said it, but it wasn't true.

"Me too. Thank you for today, for everything."

Laura said, "Mm-hmm," and gave Jillian one last kiss before she got out of the truck. She needed a long, cold shower. Alone.

As Laura walked away, Jillian sat in her truck staring blindly at the fogged windows. The aching between her legs was beginning to subside, but not the feeling of Laura's hands pressing against her clit. She slapped her hands along her thighs trying to return the blood flow so she could walk. If she got out now, she was afraid her legs wouldn't hold her up, let alone get her all the way to the house.

Jillian was overwhelmed by the rollercoaster of emotions she'd been on all day. Although every day with Laura was a struggle against right and wrong, desire and duty. Never had she been so out of control with need as she had just been with Laura. She wanted to feel her soft skin against her and slide her fingers through the liquid heat that she knew flooded her center. The problem was that she didn't want it to be because they were just riding an adrenaline high. Of course, now that her rational mind let Laura walk away, her throbbing clit was rightly annoyed.

The longer she waited and regretted her decision to send Laura away, more than her libido became frustrated. Jillian hopped out of her truck and stomped off toward her house. She tried to convince herself that it was the only option, as much as she wanted Laura this was for the best. When she reached the fork in the path that would have taken her to Laura, she forced the idea from her mind and kept on for home.

As soon as she was inside, she began to strip off her clothes. Her entire body was begging for release including her skin. By the time she reached the bathroom she was stark naked. Jillian looked at her wild reflection before starting the shower. The bathroom mirror fogged almost as fast as the windows in her truck had. The hot steam billowed out when she pulled back the curtain and stepped in.

The water scorched her sensitive skin, and she hissed. The added heat on her already inflamed nerve endings was almost too much to handle as she soaped up her cloth and lathered herself. Rivulets of water ran over her shoulders and breasts flowing off the stiff peaks of her nipples. Following a stream of water, Jillian slid her fingers along the curves of her chest to her belly and beyond.

She could still taste Laura's sweet tongue on hers and feel the hard nipple under her thumb. Her mouth watered at the thought of sucking that tight tip into her mouth. Her pussy throbbed, and Jillian could feel that she was wet from more than just the cascading water. She hesitated for a moment before sliding the tip of her finger between her folds and pressed against her swollen clit. She moaned with delight as she slipped her fingers deeper into her wetness and cupped her swollen lips. She flicked and circled her clit roughly with her thumb as her middle finger pushed farther inside.

Jillian imagined it was Laura's hand that stroked her so perfectly. A loud knock startled her, and she froze. She didn't move a muscle as she listened for another and hoped that whoever was at the door would go away, especially if that someone was Diana. When they knocked again, Jillian hollered out for them to wait. She mumbled under her breath as she rinsed herself and slapped off the tap.

Diana was the last person she wanted to see while she was horny and irritable. Jillian wasn't in the mood to answer a million questions about how close she was with Laura or where they had been today. She slipped on a pair of shorts and a loose T-shirt, forgoing a bra or panties. Jillian hoped she could chase the visitor away quickly and finish what she'd started in the shower.

She leaned to pick up her discarded clothing as she opened the door. When she stood up, she came face-to-face with Laura. She stood on the stoop illuminated by the escaping light from the house. Her hair was wet and wild as if she too had just stepped out of the shower. Her arms were crossed in front of her, and she turned one leg back-and-forth on the ball of her foot. Jillian wanted to ask what she was doing there. She wanted to ask what had taken her so long. But instead she tossed the clothes onto the floor, wrapped an arm around Laura's waist, and pulled her inside.

Jillian slammed the door shut and turned the deadbolt. She pushed Laura up against the door and claimed her mouth hard. When Laura opened to her, Jillian slid her tongue inside. She used her knee to spread Laura's legs and then pressed her thigh between them. Laura moaned into her mouth and grabbed Jillian's hips to pull her in harder against her.

Jillian ran her hand up Laura's back and wrapped a fist into her wet hair. Laura gasped when Jillian pulled her head back to expose her neck. She remembered how Laura responded to the playful bite she'd given her earlier, and just as she'd done then, Laura pressed herself into Jillian. She could feel her hot, wet heat against her bare thigh, and she wanted more. She wanted to feel her in her hand, in her mouth, and on her tongue.

Laura grabbed the hem of Jillian's T-shirt and slipped it over her head exposing her bare breasts. She slowly drew her finger across Jillian's collarbone and then along the curve of her chest following the same track that the hot water had. When she reached the taut, pink peak, Laura lowered her head to take it into her mouth. Laura flicked her wet tongue across Jillian's nipple and teased it into the tightest knot. Her clit throbbed, and she soaked through her flimsy athletic shorts.

There were too many clothes between them, and Jillian needed more of Laura's body in her hands. She walked them away from the door to the couch and slipped her wet shorts off, standing naked before Laura who took several moments to get her fill before removing her own clothes. Jillian could've spent hours gazing at her body as she presented it to her, but she'd rather spend that time touching and licking her way over each arch and line.

Jillian took Laura's hand and knelt on to the floor pulling her gently down with her. On their knees before each other, their breasts and thighs pressed together, Jillian traced along Laura's shoulder and arm to the tender flesh of her side and her hip. She leaned back and ran her finger across Laura's belly and down to a small delicate patch of hair between her beautiful legs. She looked up to see that Laura's eyes were closed and her lips slightly parted. As her fingers moved lower, Laura's eyes opened, and Jillian paused. "Please touch me," Laura begged, and Jillian obeyed.

❖

Laura's whole body was throbbing with anticipation. Jillian's fingers hovered just above her center driving her mad with desire. She begged her to continue. When Jillian parted her lips and slid between her folds, Laura's knees trembled. She grabbed on to Jillian's shoulders for support. When Jillian made several smooth strokes over her clit, she could no longer hold herself up. She pulled Jillian down to lie with her on the plush rug in front of the sofa.

Their bodies pressed together on the floor as Jillian's hand continued to stroke her. Laura's mind was whirling with pleasure and burning desire. She needed to touch Jillian the way she was being touched. She slipped her hand down her belly and over her soft mound. Laura could feel that Jillian's fire matched her own. She slid her fingers into the wetness coating her hand with a flood of liquid heat. She teased the tip of her middle finger closer and closer until she slipped inside and drew a gasp from Jillian. Laura moaned when Jillian wrapped her leg over Laura's hip and opened herself up to her.

As much as Laura was enjoying the smooth, controlled strokes from Jillian, she was ravenous and needed to take control. She rolled over, pushing a surprised Jillian onto her back. She set herself firmly between Jillian's legs as she pulled them both up around her hips. There was just enough space for one hand between them, and Laura took it. She plunged deep into Jillian drawing out a cry. Laura dipped her head and kissed Jillian, claiming all of her at once. As she slid her fingers inside, she circled her thumb hard against her swollen knot. Laura was driven by the satisfaction of knowing she was responsible for how wet and wanting Jillian was.

She kissed her way down her neck, nibbling as she went. When she reached Jillian's soft breasts, she sucked a tight nipple into her mouth. Jillian's hips bucked against her hand. Laura thrust in response and Jillian cried out. She was close. Laura could feel her begin to tighten around her fingers. Jillian grabbed her ass and dug her fingers in, pulling her closer.

Laura added another finger, filling Jillian and drawing out another more intense cry. She sped up her strokes urging Jillian closer and closer to ecstasy. She could feel her body begin to tense and shudder as Laura drove her to the edge.

"Come for me," Laura said.

"I am," Jillian said as her body convulsed and bucked beneath her.

Laura stroked her until every last ounce of pleasure squeezed from her body and she came for her. Just for her.

CHAPTER SIXTEEN

It took Jillian less than a second to realize where she was when she was startled awake. Wrapped in her arms among a pile of pillows from the couch, was a very beautiful and very naked Laura. However, her expression was tormented and not one of a woman who slept peacefully. Laura's legs jerked against the blanket that Jillian had pulled down from the couch earlier. She mumbled and whimpered in her restlessness, and Jillian stroked her face until her eyes fluttered open.

"Hey. Was I snoring?" Laura's voice was soft and sleepy.

"No, my sweet girl. I think you were having a nightmare." With the way she had been thrashing about Jillian found it hard to believe that she hadn't been chasing demons just moments ago.

"What time is it?" Laura asked, squinting her eyes and looking around for a clock.

"Eleven thirty-ish."

"Oh, Christ," Laura said as she shot straight up and glanced around for her clothes. "I've got to go."

Jillian sat up as well and wrapped her arms around Laura's shoulders. "You don't have to," she said, placing a few soft kisses across Laura's back.

"What if someone sees me?" Laura moaned.

"If you leave now it's an absolute certainty that someone will see you." It was time for shift change, and Laura was guaranteed to run into any number of people on her way home. "Stay with me."

"And in the morning? There will still be people out there." Laura tipped her head back against Jillian's.

"We'll worry about that in the morning." She kissed her shoulder.

"Are you going to make me sleep here on the floor if I say yes?"

"Nope. Believe it or not I have a big girl bed. Wanna see?" Jillian stood up and held out her hand for Laura.

"I do."

Jillian led her down the short hallway to her bedroom. "Do you want something to sleep in?" she asked while secretly hoping she'd say no.

Laura smiled and shook her head. Jillian was wrecked from the day. She wanted nothing more than to stay up until dawn teasing, touching, and pleasing Laura, but she had less than five hours until her alarm. Morning hadn't even arrived yet, and Jillian already wished that she could sleep in.

Laura pulled back the covers and climbed into Jillian's bed. She fluffed up the pillow beneath her head and lay back, rubbing her hand out across the empty space beside her for Jillian to fill. Jillian stood at the edge of the bed and stared at the beautiful vision before her; Laura was stunning even in her post sex, sleep disheveled state.

"Are you coming to bed or what?" Laura asked, pulling up the blankets but leaving the corner folded back for Jillian. As she climbed in, Laura pulled her close and draped herself over Jillian's body. She was soft and warm. Laura wiggled even closer as if trying to melt their bodies into one.

Her center heated. "If you don't stop that we're gonna be up all night," she said.

Laura brushed her finger over Jillian's bare belly. "And what's wrong with that?"

Jillian groaned and set her hand on top of Laura's to halt its movement south. "I have to get up in a few hours, and trust me that's not a vision you want to behold."

Laura whimpered, and Jillian almost gave in, but instead she laid her head on her chest and sighed. They fit so well together, their dips and curves aligned as they held each other, neither content with the slightest space between them. Jillian wanted to be closer, to be inside Laura, body and soul. Wrapped in her arms in this perfect moment, Jillian had never been more connected to anyone.

She fought against sleep as it came for fear that when she woke this would be just a dream. Laura's soft, peaceful breaths on her skin lulled her busy mind. There couldn't have been a more magical ending to a day filled with so much emotion.

Jillian kissed Laura on the head and said, "I love you," before drifting off to sleep.

Laura woke to the feeling of Jillian spooned up behind her with an arm wrapped tight around her waist. She playfully pressed her ass back against Jillian, which elicited a delicious moan into her ear. When Jillian slid her hand between Laura's legs she groaned. She opened up to make room for Jillian's roaming fingers. They found their mark in an instant, and Laura's hips bucked at the first stroke of her clit.

Jillian's fingers moved fast and fierce against the swollen flesh. She was already wet and ready, and she'd not lost an ounce of her desire during the few hours she'd slept in Jillian's arms. If anything, the feeling of having her naked body pressed into Jillian all night had kept her lust humming. Jillian slid her free arm beneath her and squeezed her breast, pinching her nipple between her fingers. Laura hissed. She needed more than just Jillian's fingers on her clit. She wanted her inside. Laura shifted her hips and hooked her leg over Jillian's thigh spreading herself open for her.

Jillian didn't hesitate to accept the invitation as she slipped three fingers inside, filling her fully. Laura cried out as she thrust in and out of her. Jillian's thumb circled her throbbing clit in rhythm with her thrusts, and Laura's hips jerked with each plunge deep inside her. When Jillian bit down on her neck, her body began to tremble. She was on the edge of ecstasy, but she fought against letting go. She wanted this moment, this pleasure, to last forever.

Her body revolted against her mind as she began to tighten around Jillian's hand. She turned onto her back, her leg still draped over Jillian. She wanted her kiss. She wanted to taste her as she came. Laura kissed Jillian's mouth. Their tongues tangled together, and Laura moaned at the overwhelming intensity of her desire. She wanted Jillian to have all of her. To claim her and take her.

Laura's body convulsed; her muscles tightened as she gasped for air and came hard. She shuddered with each stroke as Jillian pulled her over the edge. Laura twisted her fist into the sheets and called out Jillian's name. Every nerve ending tingled through her body as she lay there weak and sated.

"That's one hell of a good morning," Laura said, her chest heaving to catch her breath.

"I've been wanting to do that for the last forty-five minutes. But you looked too peaceful to wake."

Laura was embarrassed. "You've been watching me sleep? You should have been the one sleeping." Now she felt bad that she'd kept her awake.

"I did, sort of."

Laura turned onto her side to face Jillian. "I am so sorry. Was I snoring? Oh my God, did I kick you?" Laura covered her mouth.

Jillian laughed. "No, my love. You didn't do either. At least not once we moved into the bedroom."

"Huh?"

"You don't remember me waking you up because you were flopping around like a fish out there in the living room?"

Laura hadn't the slightest recollection of that. She did remember walking to the bedroom with Jillian and getting into bed with her though. Her embarrassment returned with a vengeance. "I honestly don't remember that." She sat up in bed and pulled the covers up around her.

Jillian sat up as well. She took Laura into her arms and explained what had happened the night before. "You don't recall a dream or anything?" she asked.

"No. Not last night I don't think. I used to have nightmares pretty much every time I fell asleep. Even if it was just a little nap. There was a time that I couldn't close my eyes without some kind of flashback."

It had been ages since she'd had one of those, or so she had thought. Just then Jillian's alarm blared to life, and Laura jumped out of her skin. She groaned when Jillian leaned over to hit the snooze button, refusing to let go of her as she did.

"You can go back to sleep if you want."

Laura loved the idea of snuggling back into bed beneath the covers with her. "If you stay with me."

"Oh, my sweet girl. I'd love nothing more than that. But duty calls."

"Grrrr. Adulting sucks," Laura whined.

"Sometimes, yes." Jillian gave Laura a soft pinch on her chin.

It would be easy to fall back asleep in Jillian's bed with her scent all around, but Laura decided against it. "I'll go back to my room."

It was in her best interest to be in her own room when everyone started to rouse. The last thing she needed was to get caught in her walk of shame across the park. Although, there was nothing about what she'd done that she was even the least bit ashamed of. If anything, she wanted to do it all again, slower, longer, and better. She wanted to kiss her way over Jillian's entire body and lick at her sweet sex. Her mouth watered, and her tingling body shivered.

"What was that? Are you cold?" Jillian asked, rubbing her warm hands briskly over Laura's arms.

"No. Definitely not cold." Laura gave Jillian a coy smile.

"Oh. Don't look at me like that. I've already been in bed…" She glanced over at the clock, "eight minutes longer than I should be."

Laura loved how pained Jillian looked at the idea of having to leave as she clearly wanted to stay. "When can I see you again?"

"Any time you wish, my sweet girl," Jillian said, kissing Laura on her lips. "If we had more time, I could break into my toy box and see what kind of trouble we could get into."

An unexpected shiver wracked her body at the thought of what that box might contain. It wasn't as if Laura's raging fire needed any more fuel, and she was too curious for her own good. Her imagination conjured an image of Jillian standing before her in nothing but a black leather harness. Less tactical than the one she'd worn earlier that day, but much more practical. At least for what Laura had in mind.

The sweetness of Jillian's kiss and the promises of hotter things to come was short-lived when Laura remembered that she was scheduled to begin overnight rounds with her team that night. There would be no way she could sneak over again to be with Jillian. Now she was the one who was pained.

"I've seen you every single day for the last two months that I've been here, and now I have to wait forever to see you again."

"The great thing about being the boss is that I can be anywhere at any time without any rhyme or reason."

"Oh really?" Laura purred.

"Yes, really. But right now, I have to get out of this bed and into the shower."

Laura waggled her eyebrows and smiled, and Jillian shot her down. "No. If you get in there with me, I'll never make it out of this house."

Laura stuck her lip out even though she knew Jillian was a hundred and ten percent right about that. They shared one more kiss before Jillian jumped out of bed and shuffled off to the bathroom. Laura consoled herself by watching Jillian's sexy, naked ass walk away.

CHAPTER SEVENTEEN

Jillian thought about Laura all day to the point of being delightfully distracted and aroused at the idea of seeing her again. She hadn't considered it at the time, but Laura was right about how long and painful the wait would be. Jillian had been slammed with administrative garbage all day and was stuck in her office because of it. Paperwork had always been her least favorite part of her job, now more than ever. At least when she was out in the park or working with her pod, Jillian was a hundred percent more likely to run into someone, preferably Laura.

It wasn't always her intention to seek out Laura during her rounds through the institute. Yet regardless, her feet often found their way to her. Jillian was almost certain that Laura was unaware of just how many times a day she saw her. Sometimes she would catch a glimpse of her across the lagoon and pause just to watch her walk by. But being stuck inside eliminated any opportunity for that. She could feel Laura's absence deep inside her, like she'd walked off with a piece of her soul when she left that morning.

A while later, Jillian glanced at the clock again. The odds of running into Laura now were against her. She would be headed to bed, if not already there, as she adjusted her schedule for the next week on the midnight shift. For a brief and wicked moment, Jillian thought about turning the tables on Laura and showing up at her door unannounced just as she had done the night before. Of course, there were a few too many logistical hurdles to overcome. The most impossible being how to get to her room in the dorm at three o'clock in the afternoon in broad, bustling daylight. Not that she didn't run through a few not so good ideas.

Jillian was running on empty. Her eyes were starting to glaze over, and the idea of just curling up in bed with Laura for a nap sounded almost as good as any of the naughtier activities she could come up with. She set her elbow onto her desk, rested her chin in her palm, and stared out the window into the parking lot at her truck.

The foggy windows had long since cleared from their make out session. It seemed like so long ago that they'd kissed for the first time, yet it hadn't even been twenty-four hours. If she couldn't make love to her or snuggle up with Laura, maybe she could find a way to just kiss her again. Her hands, lips, and heart ached for some way to be with her if even for a moment. Although she didn't think that she had the strength to stop at kissing. Jillian had tasted her passion, and she wanted to taste much more.

The sun had long been set, and Jillian was well beyond being productive in the office. She needed to fall into bed instead of falling asleep at her desk. The air was still and heavy with fog. The paths and trails were pitch-dark amidst the dense shrubbery as Jillian ambled along in the silence of the early morning. This wasn't the first time she'd found herself out for a walk in the moonlit twilight, especially on nights when she was restless and struggled to sleep. As always Jillian found herself at the lagoon with Pepper, Luna, and her boys. She sat at the edge of the pool and listened to the peaceful lapping of the water against the rocks. She crossed her legs and rested her hands on her knees. She closed her eyes and relaxed her shoulders, breathing in the fresh salted air.

Through the quiet, Jillian heard her. She wasn't close, but Laura's voice was like a beacon in the night. Jillian opened her eyes and scanned the darkness. On the beach, two beams of light darted across the surface of the water. As they got closer, Jillian could make out two distinct figures in the moonlight, Laura and BJ. They had paused near the shore before he announced it was time for their break. Neither had noticed Jillian sitting less than fifty feet from where they now stood.

He walked off toward the bathrooms leaving Laura alone. "Tell Brooke I said hi," Laura shouted out to him.

He laughed and said, "I will."

Jillian was afraid to move for fear that she'd scare the daylights out of Laura. But when Laura began to walk away, she became more afraid that she'd missed her chance to get that kiss she'd wanted all day. Before Jillian could call out for her, Laura stopped short at the edge of the pathway.

"Are you just going to let me walk away without saying anything?" Laura said.

"How could you possibly have known that I was sitting here? It's pitch-black out." Jillian stood and hopped into the sand a few feet from where Laura was standing.

"BJ and I both saw you. That's why he made himself scarce." Laura chuckled.

"And here I thought I was being stealthy watching you from the shadows."

"You do that a lot, I've noticed."

Jillian kind of liked the idea that Laura knew when she was being watched. "I must think I'm more enigmatic than I am."

"A little." Laura began to walk away, stepping off the beach and onto the sidewalk that led around the lagoon.

"Where are you going?" Jillian asked, following along behind her.

"I'm working. I'd hate for my boss to find out I was out here in the middle of the night flirting," she said as she kept walking along the dark forested path.

"Well, surely you get a break, right?" Jillian took Laura's hand, stopping her in her tracks.

Laura turned back toward Jillian. "Mmm," she said, looking at her watch. "I suppose it is about lunch time."

"Even better." Jillian pulled Laura off the path, unclipping a rope barrier before leading Laura through and clipping it back behind them. She led her down a trail to a clearing on the edge of the river that wound through the park.

"Where are we?"

"It's the small mammal interaction area. See?" Jillian pointed to the well camouflaged building beyond the thick shrubbery.

This was Jillian's favorite place to be when she couldn't be in the water. It was secluded, peaceful, and except for the swift water crashing over the rocks, it was quiet. Few people knew that this place even existed except for the few small animal handlers and the groups of VIP tours that occasionally came through.

Jillian stared at Laura as she stood near the stream with the moonlight reflecting off the ripples and casting sparks of light across her face. She was mesmerizing. She'd waited all day for this moment and couldn't wait any longer. She pushed Laura back against a large tree and pressed their bodies together. Laura's eyes flashed open when she felt it. Jillian was hard and ready, but this time she was the one with the surprise.

Laura slid her hand between Jillian's legs and cupped her crotch. The base of the strap-on pressed into her and she moaned. Jillian kissed her hard. It was just as good, if not better than she remembered. Neither of them held back. There was no hesitation in their touch as their hands and tongues explored each other. Jillian pressed her thigh between Laura's legs. Her hot core burned through her thin nylon pants.

Laura's fingers were swift as they worked the button and zipper before pushing Jillian's pants over her hips, following them down as she went. Jillian grabbed at her shirt and pulled it over her head. She looked at Laura who was on her knees with her hand wrapped around the shaft of her cock. She stuck out her tongue and licked the tip, and Jillian's knees trembled. She could feel her wet mouth like it was against her very own skin.

She pulled Laura up from the ground. She wanted her naked. She wanted to feel Laura wrap around her. With Laura's help, Jillian stripped her free of her clothing. She cupped one of Laura's breasts in her hand and dipped her head to take a firm nipple into her mouth. Laura wrapped her leg around Jillian's hip and pulled in hard against her. She let out a hiss as she pushed open her legs. Jillian slipped her fingers through Laura's wet folds coating her hand with her smooth liquid before sliding it slowly along the shaft. She guided the tip slowly over her clit, teasing her open farther. When she slid the dildo in, Laura let out a desperate cry.

"Oh fuck," Laura said as Jillian filled her.

Stirred by her need, Jillian thrust into her again and again. Laura stared into her eyes with the sparkle of the moonlight reflected in them. She panted with each thrust, biting her lip to control her building pleasure. Jillian hissed in delighted pain as Laura dug her fingers into her ass. Laura wanted her deeper, harder as she now pulled on the straps for leverage. When Jillian pulled out, Laura begged her not to.

"Come here, baby," Jillian said, leading her to a bench nearby.

Jillian sat and leaned back. She turned Laura around and pulled her down until she was straddling her lap. She lowered herself onto Jillian taking her fully inside. She held on to Laura's hips as she bucked and rocked against her. Laura leaned back against Jillian's bare breasts as she thrust her cock into Laura. She squeezed her nipples hard between her fingers, and Laura growled with need. Jillian was slick with sweat as Laura slid against her chest and her sweet liquid heat spread over her thighs as she rode her.

Laura took Jillian's hand and slipped it between her legs to her swollen clit. As Jillian flicked and circled the peak, Laura matched her rhythm. She rode her fast and hard as Jillian's fingers danced over her delicious flesh. She was close. She wanted Laura to come loud and hard just for her.

"Come for me, baby."

Laura moaned and whimpered as her body began to jerk. "I'm...I'm coming," she said breathlessly. "Oh, shit."

Laura's body convulsed as Jillian stroked, and she went rigid before collapsing against her. Jillian wrapped her arms around Laura's waist and held her tight as she panted. Jillian kissed her slick back and licked the salty taste from her lips.

"You are amazing, my sweet girl," Jillian said, kissing her back again.

A loud knock on the door startled Jillian causing her to fling back in her chair, nearly toppling backward. Her chest heaved and her heart pounded in her throat. "What the hell?"

Katie stood in the doorway looking just as startled as she was. "Hey, it's just me. Sorry, I didn't realize you were asleep."

Jillian rubbed her face with both hands. "Unfortunately, neither did I."

"What are you looking at?" BJ asked, squinting his eyes into the darkness.

"Nothing. I thought I saw something." Although it was more like a hope rather than a thought. Laura hadn't seen hide nor hair of Jillian all day, and it was just about twenty-four hours since they'd been together. She found herself looking at every shadow wishing it were Jillian lurking in the dark just to catch a glimpse of her. Laura didn't want to be the only one longing for their next chance together.

"Okay, you've been acting weird all night. Like you're afraid of the dark or something."

"You know I'm not," Laura said, peering over the wall at the manatees floating lazily below the dark water.

"Well then, what is it, because you've got my nerves all kinds of twitching."

She wanted to burst at the seams and spill her guts all over him. Laura wanted to tell him about her night, and her morning, and how she was turning every corner hoping that she'd run into Jillian. It wasn't like he was oblivious to her attraction, but she wasn't sure how he would react to finding out that she'd slept with their boss. And moreover, every thought in her head was about doing it again.

She looked around, shining her light across the horizon one last time. "If I tell you something do you promise—"

He didn't even let her finish. "I promise."

"You don't have any idea what I was going to say."

"Seriously?" He pointed his light up at his face just so she could see him roll his eyes at her.

Laura didn't even bother with the back story. She leaned in close to BJ. "I slept with Jillian."

"Shut up," he said quietly at first, but then much louder each time afterward. "Shut. The. Fuck. Up. When? Where? I won't ask how."

Laura laughed, and she shushed him. She hadn't said it so quietly just so he could broadcast it anyway. "Last night at her place, and I wouldn't tell you that anyway."

"Okay. Okay. So, you never came home last night?" He wriggled his fingers in front of his grinning lips.

"I did. For a minute and then I went to her place. She didn't even know that I was coming over. I just sort of showed up on her doorstep."

"Aww. Like a horny, lost puppy."

Laura laughed. "Yes, something like that." She was certain that's exactly what it had looked like considering that her hair was still wet and tangled from the shower.

"So?"

"What?" she asked even though she knew very well what he was asking. It was hot, wet, sexy, and she couldn't stop thinking about it, but she wasn't about to say that out loud. "It was…nice."

He cringed. "Nice? That's it? Yikes."

"No. It wasn't nice. I mean it was." Oh my God, what was she thinking when she decided to tell him? She wanted to talk about it. Hell, she wanted to tell the world about it. Sort of. They could have just been a one-time thing, although it didn't feel that way, then or now. Plus, they talked about seeing each other again so there was that. But they were both riding high from the day's events. Laura just didn't feel like some random fling. Yet, she wasn't sure if Jillian did and whether that made the situation better or worse.

"Nice, but not great. Well, sometimes the fantasy is better than reality."

"Oh no. Reality was better. Way better."

A smile spread across his face. "Now, we're talking."

Screw it. It happened. He knew and she wanted to talk about it. "It was unbelievable. I don't even know what came over me. When we got back to the park, we were just so energized." As Laura filled BJ in on the activities of the day, they continued along the path checking in on the sea turtles as they passed.

"Wow. So, you just left her sitting alone in her truck all hot and bothered?"

"No. Well, yeah, I suppose. But she wasn't the only one, and she stopped it not me." She waved her finger at him.

"Not that you listened."

"What? I did. I left."

"But then showed up at her door soaking wet. Pun intended." BJ laughed at her.

"I'm regretting everything about this conversation," she said, rolling her eyes at him.

"All right. All right. I'm done fucking with you. Are you happy?"

Her heart skipped at the thought. "Yes. Very."

CHAPTER EIGHTEEN

Jillian made sure that she would be at the time clock when Laura's shift ended. Several times throughout the night she'd thought about wandering out into the park to find her just to steal a moment together. But she wisely decided against it. After her vivid daydream, she wasn't sure she could trust herself alone in the dark with her.

She made herself busy at the fish house for a few minutes just showing her face and giving things a quick once-over. Jillian was pleased not to find anything that needed resolving that would make her miss the whole reason she was there in the first place.

She heard the growing chatter of people outside making their way to the time clock en masse. Jillian leaned over the wide steel sink to look out the window. When she spotted Laura, her heart surged and her face warmed. She looked exhausted from her first overnight but still so beautiful. At some point in the early morning, it was obvious that she'd stopped trying to tame her hair as its unruly wisps stuck out like a dancing sea anemone. It was too adorable. Jillian greeted everyone with a bright hello. Her enthusiasm was returned with a dozen skeptical glances.

She might have gone overboard with her attempt to seem casual, and nearly everyone knew it. When she saw Laura's eyes light up, none of that mattered. She wished in that moment for everyone around them to disappear. She wanted to take Laura in her arms and kiss her once for each minute they'd been apart. Instead she offered a gentle smile and made small talk with the others until they'd each clocked out.

BJ hugged Laura and mumbled something into her ear. Whatever it was, it got him a swift chop to his gut. He trotted away pleased with himself and left the two of them alone together. Although unlike in her dream, they weren't truly alone. They stood in front of each other for several seconds until Jillian said, "Hi."

Of all the words that swirled in her mind that was all she could say. She'd said far more than that the first time they'd met, yet this seemed safer than anything her heart wanted to say.

"How was your night?" Laura asked.

"Long," she said. "Yours?"

"An eternity."

No kidding, and it was getting worse the longer they stood there trying to find their words. Jillian looked around for anyone who might be watching and then grabbed Laura by the hand. She pulled her into a small dark closet next to them and closed the door. As soon as the latch clicked, Laura threw her arms around Jillian.

"Miss me?" Laura asked.

"You have no idea, my sweet girl." She dipped her head and kissed Laura long and deep. She knew that she missed her, but it wasn't until this moment that she'd realize just how much. It wasn't just her body or her lips that she missed but her very presence. She missed her scent, her voice, and her energy. Everything was so much more alive and vibrant when Laura was near. It was intoxicating and addictive, and if they spent any more time in this closet, it would get dangerous.

"I haven't made out in a closet since…never," Laura said.

"Well, we better get out of here before it turns into more than just making out."

"But now I'm curious," Laura said as she ran a finger lightly inside the waistband of Jillian's pants.

"Oh, no." Jillian grabbed Laura's hand. "Don't get me started."

"You seem to stop me far more often than we start."

"You seem to have the world's worst timing." Jillian opened the door and stepped out of the room before she could change her mind. Laura was laughing at her when she followed her out. "What's so funny?"

"Not funny as much as amusing," Laura said, closing the door behind her.

"And that is?"

"How easy you are to get riled up."

"That's what you do to me," Jillian said.

"Trust me, I'd like to do a lot more than that." Laura winked at her.

The words alone made Jillian's clit jump, but the wink sent a buzz of electricity over every inch of her skin. "You're killing me."

"I'm sorry. I'll stop."

"Don't stop, just pause." Jillian pinched Laura's chin.

"Deal. So, what do you have scheduled for today?" Laura asked as she stepped over to the row of lockers to get her things.

"Actually, the dive team will be in the lagoon today doing some cleaning. Me, Diana, and Nate, I believe. I've been looking forward to it. Besides working with the girls, spending a few hours of quiet time underwater was the next best thing. Would you like—"

Laura waved her hands in front of her. "Oh no. I'm not ready for that."

"No." Jillian grabbed Laura's hands in hers. "That's not what I was gonna ask. I just wanted to know if you'd want to come and hang out?"

"What do you mean hang out?"

Jillian felt silly like a teenager in high school for even asking. If she was going to be underwater the whole time why in the world would she want to just sit around and watch her float around? "Never mind, I just thought maybe..."

"That I'd want to come watch you swim around looking super sexy in your tight rubber suit?"

When she put it like that it was almost worse. "Yeah, kind of."

"I'd love to."

Jillian gathered her gear from the dive room and they headed to the lagoon. Even though they weren't going to be spending this time together, Jillian was content just knowing that she'd be near. When they got to the beach, Diana and Nate were already there and suiting up. Diana shot Jillian an unmistakable look of disgust that didn't go unnoticed by Laura.

Laura paused and said, "Uhm, maybe I should just go."

"It's fine. I promise." Jillian set down her gear and gave Nate a friendly fist bump. When she held it up for Diana all she got was an angry glare.

"What's she doing here?" Diana asked under her breath.

"She had a few hours to kill after her shift, so she came to observe."

"We work in three-man teams. I can't watch the two of you and babysit her."

"She's not a toddler, Diana. And she's not even getting into the water."

"Good thing. Maybe she should just hang out by the lifeguard to be safe," Diana said, nudging her chin toward the kid standing beneath the umbrella.

Jillian was taken aback by Diana's viperous attack. She could be snarky, but this was unusual for her. She glanced back at Laura to see if she'd heard any of it. Thankfully, she seemed unfazed as she sat in one of the lounge chairs nearby. Just in case, Jillian pulled Diana a few more steps away. "What's with the nasty attitude?"

"Don't you think it's a little much to have her follow you around like a stray kitten?"

"I told you, she's here to observe."

"Right. Whatever. As long as she doesn't get in the way and leaves the adults to their business." Diana slid her hand up Jillian's arm and smirked.

Jillian pulled her arm away. "What are you doing? I think you're forgetting your place about now. I'm still your boss, remember?"

"Hers too, remember?" The last word was filled with mockery, and it made Jillian's blood boil. She didn't think that Diana was as concerned about the organization chart as she was jealous.

"Is this going to be a problem for the next few hours? Because we have a job to do."

"No. I'm just looking out for you. That's all."

"Good. And I appreciate that, since that's your job as my friend and our team lead." Jillian made sure to emphasize the word friend.

"Yup, and as your team lead, you're late. Get your ass geared up, and let's go." Diana gave a weak half smile.

Jillian turned away and saw Laura watching them. She was sitting on the edge of the lounge waiting for the okay to relax. She might not have heard the conversation, but she was aware of the tension. Jillian winked and smiled at the concern in Laura's face that turned into a shy and painfully adorable smile. Even better than that was the look on her face when Jillian stripped to her bathing suit so she could get into her wet suit. She laughed when Laura covered her bright red face and looked away.

Laura grabbed one of the guest towels and her things and followed them to the water. "I'm going up there to get a better view," she said, pointing up to the boulders on the edge of the lagoon.

"Perfect," Jillian said before pushing the regulator into her mouth and taking a few practice breaths. Laura climbed up to her perch, and Jillian waded into the crisp water with Nate and Diana.

❖

The water was cool through her thick wet suit, but Jillian was invigorated. That kiss she shared with Laura was the best way to start her day. It was sweet but sexy and full of all the unspoken words from their time apart. The one thing that could have made it better was if it had been hours earlier when she'd rolled over in bed with Laura's body against hers. Jillian just liked having her near. Her smile, her laugh, everything about her just brightened her life. She submerged herself into the cold, clear water content to know that Laura was just feet away and waiting patiently for her to return.

Pepper and the rest of the pod were their usual curious selves. They swarmed and circled the team to check out what was going on. Jillian loved how Pepper would tilt her head back and forth trying to get a good look at who was behind each mask. After a few minutes, Diana sent them away so the team could get on with their work. As cute as they were, their curiosity and size got in the way of getting any work done.

Jillian and Nate swam along the bottom of the first ledge picking up various debris like sticks and leaves and putting them into the mesh bags that hung off their belts. While the dolphins were trained to retrieve foreign objects, they didn't rely on the children to clean their room. Jillian checked her air gauge as they prepared to drop over the ledge to fifteen feet.

She enjoyed being not only in the water but under. The noises of the world replaced with the lulling sounds of life below the surface. Beyond the rhythmic bubbling of her breaths were the playful clicks and whistles of the pods and the splashing of the waves on the rocks above. It was anything but silent, but it was peaceful. A bright red object caught her eye, and Jillian reached out for it. It never ceased to amaze her what random items they found in the lagoons. She inspected the debris and concluded that there was someone on the loose with only nine perfectly manicured fingernails.

Jillian stuffed the nail into her bag and made a few more sweeps over the bottom before checking the glass around the underwater viewing window. She unclipped her squeegee brush and swiped the glass clear of any algae. A little girl in pink ribbons pressed her face against the glass in awe. Jillian waved and blew out a mass of bubbles that made the little girl's mouth drop open in surprise. She gave her a wave before turning away and swimming back toward Diana. They waited there for a few minutes before Nate made his way over.

Each of them checked their gauges, and all gave the okay before she and Nate went to the next level at fifty-five feet. They each inspected their side, following along the bottom as it graded downward into the ninety-foot-deep well. Diana stayed up around twenty feet above them. Suddenly, a loud bang blasted behind her head and a choking gush of air and salt water burst into her mouth as her regulator exploded out. A deafening roar rumbled in her ears as she was enveloped in a blinding mass of bubbles. She was gagging on the salty water in her mouth, but had no air in her lungs to spit it out.

Jillian searched for any sign of Nate or Diana, but she could see nothing beyond the turbulent curtain of air. She checked her gauge and was shocked to see it spiraling toward zero. She tipped to the right and swept for her regulator a couple of times, but it was pinned against the tank. Her backup was also in mass free flow as the air billowed out. Where was Diana? All she could see were shadows and flickering rays of light beyond the wall of air that she was caught in. There was air all around her, but she couldn't breathe it in. Within fifteen seconds, she was completely out of air and anxiety kicked in.

She couldn't wait any longer as the need to breathe grew stronger. Jillian took a panicked kick toward the surface, but a firm grip on her arm stopped her. A regulator was shoved into her mouth pinching her lips against her teeth, and she tasted blood on her tongue. She had nothing in her lungs to blow the mouthpiece clear for her first breath. She pinched her nose closed when her body instinctively tried to inhale. The salt water burned her nostrils, and her eyes teared. She fumbled for the purge button and cleared the regulator.

Jillian was desperate for air, and she inhaled deeply, water, blood, and all. She pressed the regulator into her mouth and coughed, but even with the supply of air she struggled to catch her breath between coughs. Jillian could hear the gurgling of liquid in her lungs as she hacked and heaved desperately trying to clear her airway for a full breath of oxygen. The words "don't panic" were stuck on a loop in her mind, but they meant nothing to her body. The thick taste of blood and salt clung in the back of her throat, and she gagged. Between the coughing and retching, Jillian wanted to scramble to the surface, but Diana held fast and controlled their slow and steady ascent.

Something wasn't right. Laura had been watching the pockets of air gurgle to the surface with a steady cadence. But when a massive boil of air broke the surface, she knew it was nothing good. She stood on top of the rock wall and tried to see what could be happening, but there was no movement she could see beyond the turbulence of air bubbles.

When she saw someone's head pop up she held her breath waiting to see if it was Jillian. When she saw that it was Nate, her heart dropped. He called out for oxygen to the lifeguard standing on the shore. Oh God, had someone's tank exploded? Could that even happen? She looked all around for some way to help, but she didn't know what to do. The lifeguards on the shore gathered and waded into the water as far as they could. Laura ran to the shore and fought against running out into the water with them. She had given up her bird's eye view from the rocks and now she paced through the hot sand holding her breath and counting the seconds.

When two heads popped up at the center of the bubbles, she ran toward the shallows at the edge of the shoreline. She needed to see Jillian, but which one was she? When Diana spit out her mouthpiece and ripped her mask from her face, Laura's heart stopped. The rushing of blood filled her ears, and she heard nothing but mumbled chaos.

Diana called out orders as people crowded around her. Laura ran into the water and pushed her way into the crowd until she saw her. Laura let out a cry of relief when she saw Jillian awake and responsive, although white as a ghost and coughing uncontrollably.

Diana and a lifeguard hooked Jillian's arms over their shoulders and carried her to the shore. They set her on her knees into the sand where she vomited. "Just let me catch my breath." Laura heard Jillian say with a raspy voice, and tears welled up in Laura's eyes. She called out to her.

"Laura," Jillian said as she scanned the crowd for her. When their eyes met, Laura felt ill. She could see the fear in them, and it shattered her heart into a million pieces. Laura didn't know what had happened, but she knew terror when she saw it. She reached out for Jillian's hand, but Diana grabbed her by the wrist. She squeezed it so tight that Laura let out a yelp.

"Find someplace else to be, Miss Carter," Diana said as she let go of Laura's hand with a flick.

"But—"

"Now." The look in Diana's eyes was one of fury, but Laura could still see the fear she tried to hide in the moment.

Laura wanted to argue. She wanted to demand that she had every right to be there with Jillian, but she didn't. She was no one. She kissed two fingers and blew Jillian a small kiss. Laura wasn't sure she'd seen it before she was wedged out of the circle and away from the commotion. No matter what Diana had said, she wasn't going to walk away. She might not be able to help, but she'd be damned if she was going to go farther than she had to.

Laura didn't take her eyes off Jillian as they sat her back and slipped an oxygen mask over her face. Jillian fought them off for a moment but ultimately relented. There were protocols and she of all people knew that. Laura was taken back to her own incident, and the thought that Jillian had experienced anything like she had ripped at her soul. She wouldn't wish those terrifying minutes on her worst enemy, let alone someone she loved.

Laura did love her.

Yet there she was ten feet away from Jillian but unable to be with her. Unable to comfort or console her. She felt like a caged animal as she stood behind a chair and squeezed the bars so tight she thought her fingers would crack and bleed. Laura jumped half out of her skin when BJ set his hand on her shoulder. She spun around and wrapped her arms around him and cried.

"Shhh, sweetie. It's okay," he cooed and rubbed her back. "She's okay."

A golf cart pulled up to the group, and they sat Jillian in the front seat, while Diana climbed in the back with a tight grip on Jillian's shoulder. Laura let BJ go and lunged toward the cart as it pulled away. "Where are they going?" Laura asked. Diana instructed everyone to get back to work while looking right at Laura while she said it.

"I'm sure they're taking her back to the med building to get checked out."

"I don't even know what happened. I was right here the whole time, and nobody would tell me anything. Diana wouldn't let me near her even though she called for me. She called my name, BJ. I should have been allowed to see her." Laura felt like a ghost, and except for when Diana wrenched her by the arm, she'd have thought she was.

"There was nothing you could have done but get in the way," BJ said.

She shot him a look of disgust. "She needed me."

"No, she needed to be checked out by trained professionals. Whatever happened down there was bad enough to enact emergency protocol, and you aren't part of that response team. We are trainees, Laura."

"So we're useless?"

"Technically? Yes."

"You're being an asshole. You know that?" Laura immediately regretted what she'd said and apologized.

"Don't be sorry. It's true, but it's obvious that you aren't thinking clearly right now. You're way too close to the situation in more ways than one. Can't you see that?"

Laura sniffled and wiped her running nose with the hem of her shirt. "Yes, I just need to know that she's okay, BJ."

"All right, sweetie. Let's go see what we can find out." He took her by the hand and followed after the cart.

CHAPTER NINETEEN

Diana supported Jillian by her elbow as she helped her through the front door. She told her about a hundred times that she was fine and didn't need help, but Diana refused to hear it. Jillian had given up trying to convince her and just let her do what she needed to. When they got to her bedroom and Diana tried to undress her, she drew the line.

"Enough, D. I'm not an invalid."

"You need my help."

"You've helped me enough for a lifetime, but I can change my own clothes," Jillian said, gripping at her shirt.

"Okay. But I'm going to make you some hot tea or some soup. Are you hungry? I can make you a sandwich or something while you get into bed."

"I'm not getting in bed." As much as she appreciated Diana for her attentiveness, she was growing agitated with her insistent coddling.

"But you need to rest. What happened to you could have been very bad, and—"

"Stop," Jillian said as she slammed the top drawer of her dresser closed. "Enough, okay?"

Diana looked wounded standing there in the middle of the room. "I'm sorry. I'll let you change," she said before walking out and leaving Jillian alone.

"Shit," Jillian mumbled as she went into the bathroom. She hadn't meant to snap at Diana like that, but she was just overwhelmed, and the adrenaline was beginning to wear off. She stripped out of her clothes and turned on the shower. She set her hands on each side of the sink basin and stared into the mirror until her reflection was nothing more than a dark blur in the foggy glass. It was a strange feeling to watch herself disappear before her own eyes. To be aware of what was happening but unable to stop it. She thought of Laura and how helpless she had been struggling and breathless beneath the water as she felt her life fading away.

Jillian stepped into the hot spray of water and let her silent tears fall. She cried for herself, but also for Laura, because now she truly understood a fear unlike any other. As she stood there, Jillian could feel exhaustion beginning to set in. Her arms and legs grew leaden as the tension eased in her muscles. She pressed her forehead against the cool tile of the wall as it supported her weakening body. Before she collapsed into a heap on the shower floor, Jillian turned off the water and got out.

She dried off quickly, but not well enough to keep her sweats from sticking to her body as she dressed. When she made it out into the living room, Diana had in fact made the hot tea, and she was very much grateful. Jillian sat on the couch and curled her legs beneath her. She laid her head against the soft cushion until Diana came over and handed her the steaming mug of Earl Grey. She tossed the throw over Jillian's lap before sitting on the opposite end of the sofa. Jillian rubbed the soft fabric and remembered when Laura had been wrapped in this very blanket what felt like an eternity ago.

"I'm sorry for mothering you. It's just that you scared me to death, Jillian."

"I know. I was just overwhelmed. I'm sorry I snapped at you."

"All I could think of was that if you—" Diana's voice rattled with emotion. She scooted closer to Jillian set her hand on Jillian's knee.

"It's okay. I understand, and I'll be forever thankful that you were there." She patted Diana's hand until she laced her fingers with Jillian's. Before she could pull away Diana brought her hand to her lips and kissed her fingers. Jillian pulled her hand away.

"I still love you, Jillian."

Jillian swung her legs onto the floor and took a second to make sure she had heard her right. She closed her eyes and tapped her fingers on her forehead before looking over at Diana. She scrunched her face up and scoffed. "What?"

"I do. I love—"

"Stop. What are you talking about? That was years ago, Diana, and we were never in love. You can't still have feelings if you never had them to begin with," she said, turning her head to look at her.

"Maybe we didn't then, but now?"

"No. Not then and not now. Where is this coming from?" Jillian asked.

"Today made me realize that I can't imagine my life without you. I don't think we ever gave us a real chance. But we could."

"Look, Diana. You are one of my dearest friends, but it didn't work then, and it wouldn't work now."

"Because of her?" Diana put a zing on the last word.

This was the last thing Jillian wanted to discuss with Diana. Yet here she was pushing the subject at the worst possible moment. "You know, I'm really exhausted. I think I'm going to go lie down after all."

"Are you sleeping with her? Is that why?"

Her pulse increased. If ever there was a reminder of why things never worked out with Diana, this was it. "Let it go."

"You are," Diana said as she stood up, crossing her arms and hovering over her.

"Yes! We slept together. Is that what you want to hear, for fuck's sake?"

"I knew it. I knew it," Diana repeated, throwing her hands in the air. "Why? Are you trying to destroy everything?"

Jillian took a deep breath and paused for a few seconds before responding. "I will not justify my actions to you, Diana, and I really think you should go."

Diana knelt in front of Jillian. "I get it. She's hot, young, exciting. Even a bit of a challenge, I suppose. But come on, it's just a fling and you need to stop before someone gets hurt. Again."

Jillian leaned back away from her. "Again? She had nothing to do with what happened with my gear."

"No, but that doesn't mean she wasn't in the way. There's a protocol, and her feelings for you just had her in the way."

"I was there, and she was never in the way, if anything, it was me who wanted her closer."

"See what I mean? She's clouding your judgment. The real Jillian would never let some piece of ass jeopardize everything she spent her life trying to achieve. Why can't you see that?" Diana stood back up.

Jillian was a hair's width from losing her shit. Diana didn't know Laura the way she did. No one did, and she refused to let anyone speak about her with such disrespect. "Laura has more passion for this work than you and I combined. She makes me remember all of the reasons why I still do this."

"You're her fucking boss, Jillian!"

Jillian was just about to demand that Diana leave when there was a knock at the door. She fell back into the couch exhausted when Diana went to answer it.

Laura's voice was like a soothing balm on her frazzled nerves. She was what Jillian needed right now. After a few long seconds, Diana still hadn't let her into the house, and she heard

Laura raise her voice. "With all due respect, I need to see her, and I'd appreciate it if you'd please tell her that I'm here."

Diana had finally crossed the line. Jillian pushed off the couch and made her way to the door. She came up behind Diana, and Laura smiled. It was the purest look of love that Jillian had ever seen, and her heart burst open with a flood of adoration. She'd never wanted anything more than she wanted Laura right now.

"Thanks for everything, Diana, but you can go," she said as she took Laura's hand to pull her inside. Out of the corner of her eye, she saw the scorn on Diana's face, but she couldn't have cared less as she closed the door on her.

Once the door was shut, Jillian practically fell into Laura's arms. "You have no idea how glad I am to see you," Jillian said against Laura's neck.

If it was even half as glad as she was, Laura knew exactly how she felt. "Oh, sweetheart. I know. Come sit." Laura walked Jillian to the couch, but she went past that and down toward the bedroom.

"Would you please lie with me for a bit?"

Laura's heart ached at the weak innocence of the question. Jillian was exhausted from the inside out, and Laura knew that feeling. "Forever, if you wish, my heart." She had nowhere to be until midnight, and if Jillian wanted her to lie with her until then she would.

She was so relieved to have Jillian safe and close, but she wanted more. Even with her wrapped in her arms, Laura still felt too far away. She needed to have her skin pressed against her, sharing space and heat. As they stood at the edge of the bed, Laura faced Jillian. Her eyes were heavy and dark circles were forming beneath them. Laura ran her fingers across Jillian's forehead and down the soft skin of her cheek. When Laura turned to the bed to pull back the covers, Jillian stopped her.

Jillian hooked the hem of Laura's shirt with her fingers and pulled it up. Not that she would deny her, but Laura wasn't sure this was the best time for sex. "Baby, wait."

"I need to feel you. Feel your body against mine. That's all."

Laura wanted the same. It wasn't about sex. It was something much more intimate than that. Laura helped Jillian strip out of her sweats and then got into bed before slipping out of her own. The coolness of the crisp sheets was in stark contrast to the smooth warmth of Jillian's skin against hers. She pulled Jillian close and their bodies melded together. Jillian laid her head on Laura's chest and weaved their legs together until there wasn't an inch of space between them. She ran her fingers through Jillian's damp hair listening as her breaths grew slow and steady.

Laura reveled in this moment. She wanted to tuck it away into the deepest and safest corners of her memory so she would never forget it. She was weightless, even under the heaviness of Jillian's body. Had things turned out differently a couple of hours earlier, Laura would never have known this feeling. She had never known the feeling of being so connected with another person that the idea of being without them was unfathomable. She was content to lie in the silence with nothing but the peaceful cadence of Jillian's breaths as she drifted off to sleep as well.

A loud cry startled Laura awake, and she knew in an instant that it was Jillian. She rubbed her back briskly to wake her from the nightmare she was having. "Baby? Love, wake up," Laura said.

Jillian's breaths were short and fast as she tried to catch her breath while Laura held her. "I had no air." Jillian was winded as if she'd just ran a marathon.

"Shh, baby. It's all right, I'm here. You have plenty of air. I promise." They both sat up in bed and Jillian paced her breathing as Laura coached her. After a few breaths, Laura was lightheaded and stopped, as Jillian was more than capable of breathing on her own. She supposed it was a bit of her own anxiety manifesting in this situation. *What a hot mess we are together.*

"I'm okay. Thank you, my sweet girl." Jillian kissed Laura on her bare shoulder before scooting back down beneath the covers. This time Laura spooned close to her. She could hear the rapid beating of her heart still hammering in her chest, and she pressed her palm against it.

"I'm sorry," Laura said.

"For what?" Jillian asked as she circled a lazy finger over her exposed collarbone.

"That I couldn't protect you and keep you safe from this." Jillian was the last person on earth that Laura wanted to be haunted by this demon of fear as she had all these years.

"Sweetheart, there's nothing you could have done. It was an equipment malfunction, and the high-pressure seat failed. It all happened so fast I didn't have much time to think about what was happening. It's still all sort of a blur."

Laura wasn't going to force Jillian to talk about it, but she encouraged her to continue. "Mm-hmm."

"It was so loud. I'm not even sure I could have heard myself think had I tried. I was on autopilot."

Laura thought back to her own accident. "All I did was think once I realized I wasn't going to get myself free. They said it was about two or three minutes, but it felt like hours." Laura hadn't ever really talked about those final moments before she blacked out.

"What did you think about?" Jillian asked.

There was so much about that day that she couldn't remember or had tried to forget. Wrapped in Jillian's protective arms, Laura let herself return to those moments for the first time. She could feel the claw-like grip on her leg, but there was no pain. Her arms floated at her sides suspended in space and time. "I remember feeling at peace. I could feel tiny bubbles from the spring tingling over my skin before they drifted up above me. Some of the bubbles stuck to me as if trying to take me with them to the surface."

Jillian tapped her fingers across Laura's skin like tiny bubbles. "They tried that with me too. All of the air shooting toward the sky and I had to fight myself not to follow it."

"When I saw the water boil up, I didn't even know what to think. I thought a tank exploded or something." She squeezed her arms tighter around Jillian's waist.

"That's certainly what it sounded like. I've never heard a thing like it before. You know that feeling when someone sneaks up behind you? That heart-stopping, ass-clenching sort of shock?"

"When your ears burn and you can feel your stomach lurch into your throat? Yeah."

"It was kind of like that. It's just so hard to describe. So many things happened all at once and then suddenly, I had no air."

Laura shivered at the reality of what Jillian felt in that moment. *Your body wants to breathe and your chest spasms with uncontrollable attempts to inhale. You clench your mouth closed trying to keep in whatever air you have left. Every muscle in your body is fighting against itself in a battle of life-and-death.* She didn't need to say it out loud to know how she'd felt.

"Did you think you were…going to die?" Laura stuttered over the words.

"I don't think I had the time. I think I was just trying to live. Does that make sense?"

"Yes. I'm not sure I thought about it either. It just sort of happened. I went from struggling to live and then just acceptance. I wasn't afraid at the end." Laura had never told anyone that, not even Dr. Shaw. She hadn't been scared of closing her eyes and letting go. It was only after she'd woken up in the hospital that the fear had set in.

"What changed?"

"When I woke up, I was surrounded by people—friends, doctors, nurses, my mom and dad, and all of them were telling me how afraid they were or how frightening it was. Soon I started to accept their fear as my own, I guess. How do you tell your parents that you were okay with dying? Their stories were so much different from how I thought I'd experienced things."

Laura had been afraid. She was trapped beneath the water unable to breathe. She was fighting against her instincts to gasp for air as nature held her in its tight grasp. She was terrified at first, but then she wasn't anymore. She couldn't explain it to herself let alone anyone else, so she never tried. Until now. Jillian kissed the top of her head, and Laura snuggled closer.

"I understand what you mean. Diana sort of did the same thing and her feelings about what happened, while valid, were far more intense than mine. The more she went on the more anxious I felt about it."

The thought Diana was with Jillian during this ordeal still stung. "She wasn't happy that I was standing on your stoop when she answered the door. You should've seen her face. Especially once I told her that I wasn't leaving until I saw you."

Jillian chuckled. "I can imagine."

"Sweetheart, there was nothing that would have stopped me. Just ask BJ." As always, he'd really come through for her and the chaos following the incident.

"That I can also imagine. But I'm glad you came. As soon as I saw your face, I knew everything would be all right," Jillian said.

"I wish I'd been so certain. All of the worst thoughts were rushing through my head."

"But here I am, and no worse for wear. I'll lie around here today and get back at it tomorrow."

"Tomorrow?" Laura pushed onto her elbow and looked at Jillian. "Are you sure?"

"Yeah, Why not?"

"What if—"

Jillian cupped Laura's cheek in her warm hand. "My sweet girl, you know better than anyone that we can't let the what-ifs stop us. Anything in this life worth doing should scare us to death. But being brave isn't about being fearless, it's about recognizing that fear and doing it anyway."

Laura turned over onto her belly and propped herself up on her elbows to look into Jillian's eyes. "Are you afraid of me?"

Jillian leaned in close. Her lips were a breath away from Laura's as she whispered, "Terrified."

CHAPTER TWENTY

The truth was that the one thing about Laura that frightened Jillian was how much she wanted her. And she wanted more than just her body, she wanted her heart. With every touch, and every kiss, Jillian had given pieces of her heart to Laura until it was no longer hers. Laura's eyes sparkled and she stared straight into Jillian's soul. Whatever she would ask for could be hers if she didn't already have it.

"Jillian?"

The sound of her name on Laura's lips made her lightheaded. "Yes, my love."

"Can I kiss you?"

Laura's eyes darkened with desire, and a fire ignited in Jillian's belly. She rolled over pushing Laura onto her back and covered every inch of her body with her own. Laura opened her legs and wrapped them around Jillian's hips. Her smooth, wet heat coated her skin as she pressed up against Jillian. "If you promise never to stop."

"I promise." Laura sealed the vow with a kiss.

Laura ran her hands up Jillian's back. Her fingers traced the muscles along her spine to her neck and into her hair. Jillian closed her eyes as Laura kissed her harder. Her tongue thrust into Jillian's mouth with a deep, wanton passion. A rush of heat flooded between Jillian's legs, and she throbbed with a painful need. Laura's hands worked their way back down to Jillian's ass. She pressed into Laura and groaned as her tight clit rubbed against her. She thrust again and their wet lips slid together. The sensation of their slick heat melding with each other drove Jillian into a wild frenzy.

Laura slid her hand between them. Her finger slipped around Jillian's hard clit and she bucked beneath her. It was too much. She was afraid that a few more strokes like that would send her over the edge too soon.

Jillian took Laura's hand. She brought it up to her mouth and licked herself from the tips of Laura's fingers.

"My turn," Laura said, taking back her hand and sucking on the fingers coated with Jillian's wetness.

Jillian's body shuddered as Laura moaned at the taste of her. The thought of Laura licking and sucking her into her mouth intoxicated her. But she hadn't yet had her fill of this delicious woman under her. She lifted her hips and Laura whimpered. Jillian slid her hand between Laura's legs. She was soaked, and it was all for her. Jillian ran her fingers over Laura's lips, reveling in the silky, hot liquid.

Laura's legs opened wider with each stroke. Jillian spread herself open with a couple of fingers and pressed her swollen center into Laura. Their combined juices were slick as their rigid clits rubbed and slipped against each other. Jillian pushed herself up off Laura and locked her elbows. She wanted to see where the most intimate parts of their body connected. The small tuft of brown was glazed with Laura's wetness.

Laura pulled Jillian back against her. Their bodies interlocked belly to belly, breast to breast. Every dip and curve fit together like a key in the lock. Jillian looked into Laura's eyes. They were glistening with tears, and Jillian froze.

"Baby, what's wrong?" Jillian asked, wiping away the tears that slid down her temples.

Laura opened her mouth to speak, yet no words came out. She squeezed her eyes shut and took a deep breath. Jillian's heart was breaking. What had she done? Did Laura not want this? She moved to roll off onto the bed, but Laura grabbed hold of her. "No," Laura cried out. "I'm just...I..." She took another breath and blew it out slowly. "I love you."

A lump rose up into Jillian's throat. What was left of her own heart was gone. It wholly belonged to Laura. The only thing she had ever hoped for was Laura's heart in return for hers, and with those three little words Jillian knew she had it.

Jillian kissed Laura. She wanted Laura to feel as loved and complete as she did. She would show her every day and, in every way, starting now. Jillian pushed into Laura, and she gasped. Her thrusts began slowly, but as her need for release grew, she increased the pressure and speed. Laura met each of Jillian's moves with her own. The mixed sensation of heat, liquid, and rigid friction were combined into a whirlwind of pleasure as they sped toward ecstasy together.

Jillian ground into Laura harder and faster as their bodies prepared for release. She dipped her head against Laura's neck and inhaled her sensual scent. Her pulse pounded against Jillian's lips. She licked at the salty sweat that formed on her skin, and Laura moaned prompting Jillian to take a nip of her tender flesh.

Laura's body tightened and shuddered beneath her. Her pending climax pulled Jillian along with her. Laura's cries of pleasure took Jillian over the edge with her, and she called out Laura's name as she came. Her pussy throbbed and her muscles shook with the ripples of a long, hard orgasm. Laura panted beneath her, and she pulled Jillian's wet and sated body on top of her. Every piece of them connected in that moment, body, heart, and soul.

❖

Jillian slid off Laura and curled around her side. They lay there in a peaceful and satisfied revelry. Laura was happier than she'd ever remembered feeling. All the joys and hopes she had struggled so long for were right there within her reach. And more than that she had found a love she'd never known she was missing. Even through all her faults and burdens, Jillian saw her.

She knew the real Laura with her scars and blemishes, fears and anxieties, and still wanted her. Jillian believed in her when she wasn't sure she believed in herself. From the very first day she came into her life, she stood beside her.

"Laura?"

There wasn't another name more beautiful than when Jillian said hers. "Yes?" Jillian took her hand to her lips and kissed it. She held it tight against her mouth, and Laura smiled.

"I love you, too."

Laura swallowed around the knot that formed in her throat. Her eyes burned as she fought back tears. Jillian brought Laura's hand to where her heart pounded in her chest. "Do you feel that?" Jillian asked.

Laura could feel the steady and strong pounding of her heart above her breast. "Yes."

"It's yours. Every beat and every pang is for you."

Laura moved her hand and leaned in to kiss that special place on Jillian's chest. If there was one thing she would do until the end of time it would be to keep and protect this precious gift she'd been given. She looked up at Jillian and said, "I'll do everything I can to make sure you never regret giving it to me."

Jillian held her hand over the same place on Laura's chest. "Ditto."

Laura looked at her hand resting a touch away from her beautiful pink nipple. She slid over a couple of inches and brushed her fingertips over it. Even a light touch caused an instant reaction as it rose to attention before her eyes. Her mouth watered for a taste. Laura dipped her head and took the stiff nub in her mouth and sucked it to a more rigid peak.

She pushed Jillian over onto her back and continued to tongue at her nipple. She kissed her way over to the other and played it into an identical erection. Encouraged by the response, Laura worked her way down Jillian's body. She licked along the dips and curves of her belly moving lower to the beautiful apex of Jillian's full thighs. She slid down and nestled between them. Laura gently pushed open her knees and slid her hands up her legs beautifully spread before her. She ran her thumbs up each side of her swollen lips and exposed the rigid bundle of nerves.

Jillian squirmed beneath her gaze. Laura looked up over Jillian's belly to see her watching with a building desire. She stuck out her tongue and licked the length of her sweet folds, and Jillian gasped. She flicked the tip of her tongue over her hard clit, and Jillian raised her hips for more. It seemed that Jillian wanted to be in her mouth almost as much as she wanted to take her.

Laura set her hands on the inside of Jillian's thighs and took her in. Jillian cried out as she sucked and dipped her tongue inside to taste the pure flavor of Jillian's wet heat. Jillian's fingers twisted into Laura's hair and held her head as she lifted herself up against her face. Laura hooked her arms around Jillian's hips and pulled her in. She teased her clit with her tongue and sucked on her lips. Laura pressed her face into Jillian, diving into her silken center as her wetness dripped from Laura's chin.

"Oh, Laura, I love you so much." Jillian's hand slapped against the bed and curled her fists into the sheets. Laura was relentless with her need to bring Jillian to the absolute height of pleasure. She drank her in and feasted on her delicious arousal. Laura slipped her finger inside and stroked along with the quick rhythm of her tongue. Jillian was close. Laura could feel her tighten around her fingers as she cried out.

"Come for me, baby," Laura said.

Panting and breathless, Jillian said, "Yes."

Laura groaned against Jillian and the vibration added another level to the work of her dancing tongue and fingers. Jillian began to convulse as Laura coaxed her ever closer to orgasm. She stroked every drop of pleasure from her as she called out her name. Her body stiffened and legs squeezed around Laura's head before she fell back weak and heaving onto the bed. Laura took a last final lick of the luscious essence, and Jillian's body trembled.

Laura left her fingers inside Jillian until every bit of bliss was drawn from her body. She rested her head against the inside of Jillian's smooth leg and licked the last of her from her fingers.

CHAPTER TWENTY-ONE

Jillian lunged forward to kneel on the edge of the pool and groaned. Her tight muscles reminded her of how she'd spent the previous day in bed with Laura. Not that she needed any help keeping those images in the forefront of her mind. Her thighs burned as she knelt and sat back on her legs. If she and Laura were going to keep up that kind of energy when they were together, Jillian would need to stretch first. Although she was quite enjoying the tender memento of their lovemaking.

Jillian slapped the surface of the water with her palm and waited. The double ripple cut through the water toward her, and she smiled. Jillian waved her hands in excitement when Pepper and Luna popped up in front of her. She gave each of them a scratch and a kiss on their rostrum before tossing them each a small capelin. She scrubbed her fingertips over Pepper and then held her hand up to get her attention. She turned her head just a touch to focus on Jillian's command. Luna rested her head on the edge of the pool and waited.

Jillian gave a quick hand signal for her flukes and Pepper presented them. She ran her hands over her cool skin checking for any bump or bruise that wasn't there the day before. She reached back for a specimen cup but misjudged where she'd set them. She knocked them over and sent them rolling off behind her. Luna nodded her head as if chuckling at Jillian's clumsiness.

"No comments from the peanut gallery. Thank you."

"If she answers you, I'm gonna freak the fuck out," Laura said from behind her.

"Hey, love. Could you—" Before she even finished her question Laura set one of the cups into her hand. "Thanks, babe." Jillian pressed against Pepper's bladder and collected the urine that pooled on her belly.

"Is she okay?" Laura asked.

"Yeah, just doing weekly diagnostics." Jillian screwed the top onto the jar and tapped Pepper on the fluke and blew her whistle. Pepper flicked her tail and shot off away from them. "Do you want to get the chuff sample from her while I collect Luna's urine?"

Jillian loved how excited Laura got whenever she had the chance to try something new. Even if it was collecting dolphin snot. "Really?" she asked, kneeling beside Jillian.

Jillian called Pepper back and Laura squeaked with joy when she popped up out of the water in front of her as Jillian handed her a petri dish that contained a slip of paper to collect the sample. "You're going to give her the chuff command and hold that about an inch above her blowhole. Simple as that."

"Okay." Laura smiled ear to ear, and she blew out an excited breath.

Jillian laughed at just how damn cute she was. She demonstrated the command on Luna by tapping two fingers lightly on the top of her melon, and Luna chuffed. A puff of air, water, and whatever else sprayed out and floated away on the light breeze. "It's basically a cough. And we'll run some tests and make sure that we've got a clear respiratory system."

Laura held the dish out over Pepper's head. She gave two quick taps on her melon, and just like that, Pepper chuffed, and Laura giggled. "Good job, honey." Jillian took the dish, covered it, and set it on the tray beside her. She was surprised to see a pair of bare legs standing next to her when she turned around. Jillian looked up to see that it was Katie hovering over them. "Hey. What's up?"

"Hey, guys. I was sent out here to find you both for Liz," Katie said, ringing her hands together.

"Me?" Laura asked.

"Yes," she said.

Jillian said, "Okay. Let me finish here and I'll be right there." Jillian hadn't talked to Liz, the institute director, about the incident yesterday so she didn't think anything about the request.

"Is there anyone who can finish it for you?" Katie asked.

"Why?" Jillian asked as she stood and tossed a few treats to each of her girls.

"I can't say, Jillian. Liz is in the boardroom with Beck from HR, and Mr. and Mrs. Allen from the board of directors. You really need to come with me." Katie's face was washed of color.

"Is this about what happened yesterday?" Laura asked as she stood as well. Katie didn't answer; she only shrugged.

"Well, let me get someone to take care of this and we'll be there."

"I'll wait," Katie said.

Something was wrong. Katie's face was solemn, and there wasn't a hint of color in it. It was clear that she was sent to retrieve them and wasn't going to return empty-handed. Jillian called to one of her assistants working with the rest of the pod. "Shannon, can you collect the urinalysis for Luna?"

"Sure," she said, taking the cup from Jillian.

Jillian and Laura followed along behind Katie toward the administrative building. The day had just begun, and she had a feeling that it was about to take a header right into a wall. Once they got there, it took Katie a brief moment to announce their arrival before she sent Jillian down the hall and had Laura take a seat in the empty lobby.

Though she hadn't said it, Laura was uncomfortable. Jillian could tell as much by looking at her. She knocked on the door to the boardroom, and Mrs. Chapman called out for her to enter. Even though Katie had told her who was in the room it hadn't prepared her for the intense energy that bombarded her when she entered. She greeted everyone with a smile and hello before taking the one empty seat at the table. The air in the room was thick and warm. Jillian assumed they'd been in there a while although it wasn't even nine a.m.

Mrs. Allen, the board president, thanked her for coming. Jillian laughed to herself knowing that they most definitely hadn't given her a choice. "How are you feeling?" she asked.

"I'm doing great, thanks." That was true, except for the apprehension she was feeling now. Though she kept that to herself.

"I know that Liz filled us in on the incident from yesterday, and I'm very relieved that it wasn't worse."

"You and me both." Jillian chuckled.

"It's important that we ensure not only the safety of our animals in our care, but our staff. We are a family after all." Jillian was beginning to think this whole show was for nothing more than a cover-your-ass meeting.

"I wholeheartedly agree. And I'm thankful for Nate's and Diana's and everyone's exceptional response to the situation," Jillian said sincerely.

"As are we," Mr. Allen added.

Jillian made a move to push herself from the table assuming that they'd checked all the boxes to absolve themselves of any liability. She understood an accident like this could ruin them. "Everything is good," Jillian said.

"Not exactly," Liz said, motioning for Jillian to keep her seat.

"What do you mean?" Jillian leaned forward and rested her arms on the table, clasping her hands together in front of her.

Beck opened a folder in front of him and flipped through a few pages before asking, "How well do you know the trainees in your program?"

Jillian thought about it for a moment. Except for Laura and BJ, she knew little more than what was in their admissions packets. "I suppose I know them just well enough to know they belong here. Less than most of my staff, I suppose. I don't usually get involved once they've been accepted into the program."

"Are you aware of any physical or mental issues disclosed during the medical evaluation and release?"

"Yes." That was part of the admissions process, of course she was. "What are you getting at, Beck?" This HR legalese nonsense was annoying.

"It's been brought to our attention that one of the trainees in the program has a disorder that was not disclosed during the application process."

Jillian's heart leapt into her throat and threatened to choke her. How the hell would he know that? "I see," she said.

"Did you know that Laura Carter has PTSD?" Liz asked point-blank.

Jillian brought her clasped hands to her mouth and blew out an audible exhale from her nose. "Yes, but—"

Beck cut her off. "Was a special exception made for her in order for her to stay in the program?"

"No."

"So, you didn't establish an extracurricular training schedule for Miss Carter in order to keep her with the institute?"

"Yes."

"Which is it? Yes or no?"

Jillian couldn't get more than one word between their rapid-fire question. "No and yes. You asked two different questions." Her temper was beginning to flare, and she rubbed her hands on her thighs. "No, there was no special exception. Unless that's what you're calling the supplemental sessions I created to help her. But I didn't change her schedule, and it didn't impact her existing classes at all. Laura, err…Ms. Carter maintained the same course and work schedule as the other trainees."

She sat silently in the room as everyone else shuffled around papers and scribbled down Lord only knows what. Jillian rubbed her forehead, pinching the skin across her brow. She tried to make eye contact with Liz, but she looked anywhere except at Jillian. It was obvious that this meeting had nothing to do with the accident and everything to do with Laura. She just didn't know why.

"How has her disorder affected her performance?" Beck asked.

"It's not an issue anymore. She's moved mountains to overcome this, and in my opinion it's the least remarkable thing about her."

There was no way in hell she would ever say that Laura didn't deserve to be there. And if that's what they were fishing for they were going to be there a while. Jillian would fight every accusation or suggestion that she recommended sending Laura away.

"At any point has Miss Carter been in danger or put anyone else in danger while at the institute?" Mrs. Allen asked.

"Absolutely not."

"Are you defending her and your decision to help her based on your intimate relationship with Miss Carter?" Mr. Allen added.

Jillian's stomach somersaulted, and the blood rushed to her head making her dizzy. She clenched her jaw so hard she thought her teeth might crack. "I don't know where you heard any such thing, but I suggest you think twice about whatever it is you plan to say next."

"Are you denying that you and Miss Carter are involved?" Beck asked.

"Whatever involvement I have with Laura is personal and in no way conflicts or interferes with my professional decisions as this institute's educational director." Jillian pumped her fists slowly beneath the table.

"Jillian, surely you can understand that from where we sit it appears that your romantic relationship with Miss Carter may be clouding your judgment and giving the impression of favoritism," Liz said.

"Are you kidding me?" Jillian stood up. "I was dating Diana for over a year and it was never an issue. Liz, that's not how I am, and you know that."

"Perception is reality, Miss Marshall," Beck said.

"I understand that, *Beck*." The zing of sarcasm Jillian had added to his name was stronger than she'd intended.

"He's right. You're her boss, Jillian. Diana wasn't your subordinate at the time and certainly not a trainee in your program. Do you think there's a possibility that Miss Carter may have put herself into your path for her advantage?"

Jillian was on the edge of rage. It was a feeling she'd never experienced before. While Laura had made mistakes, this one was hers alone, and there wasn't a chance in hell she'd allow Laura to carry any of the blame. She took several deep breaths as she gripped the back of the chair with stark, white knuckles. "Absolutely not," she said through gritted teeth.

"Jillian, please sit," Liz said. Her knees were quivering beneath her, so she did. Jillian crossed her arms over her chest but remained silent.

It was Beck who delivered the final blow. "Jillian, as of now we are placing you on administrative leave for the next two weeks while we conclude this inquiry and determine our next course of action."

Jillian heard very little of whatever was said next. Her ears were pulsing with the sound of the blood racing through her veins, and her head drummed along with the beat. "…No animals… Revoke access… Off limits…" Few other words broke through. What she did make out through the haze was that she could stay in the house until a final determination was made, but until then she could have no contact with any staff, trainees, or animals within the park. She was silent as she left the room.

❖

Jillian's voice reverberated out into the lobby, and Katie refused to look up from whatever had her laser focused attention on her desk. Laura's leg vibrated as she clenched the arms of her chair. It took all her senses to remain seated and not rush out of the room to find Jillian. Something had her in a wrath, and Laura could not only hear it, she could feel it. When she heard a door open, she jumped up from her seat.

Laura's heart squeezed when she saw Jillian appear in the doorway behind Katie. Her face was red, and her lips were clamped tight. Laura lunged for her, and Jillian stopped short without looking up from the floor. When Laura reached to take her hand, Jillian pulled it away as if afraid of being burned.

"Baby? What's wrong?" Laura asked.

"Laura, they'll see you now," Katie called out to her.

"They're calling you, Laura," Jillian said.

"Okay. They can wait a second. What happened?" Laura tried once again to touch Jillian, but she stepped back away from her. The distance she had just put between them was more than physical, and the string between their hearts pulled tight.

When Jillian looked up at Laura, the wind was knocked from her chest. There was so much pain and sadness in her eyes it tore into Laura's core.

"Laura?" Katie called again.

"Give me a minute, please," Laura said.

"Go, Laura."

"No. Not until you tell me what happened."

The scarlet blood rushed up from her neck and she snapped. "They found out about us." It was almost a growl.

"So."

"And they suspended me, Laura. I'm banned from you, the park, and the pod. All of it."

Laura's heart shattered so hard she almost heard it. She felt like she'd been kicked in the guts. "What? They can't do that."

"Well, they did," Jillian said.

Katie stepped over to them and pleaded with Laura. "Laura, please. You need to go, now."

Laura looked from Jillian to Katie and back again. "Jillian?" Jillian's eyes filled with tears, and Laura waited for her to say something, anything, but she said nothing. The tears streamed down Jillian's cheeks before she bowed her head and walked away.

She wanted to call to her, chase after her, but Katie's hand on her arm held her fast. Jillian walked away, and her heart pressed into dust. A wave of sickness washed over her. She was weak and trembling as Katie led her to the boardroom without another word. When they reached the door, Laura just stood there, frozen between hell and the unknown.

It was Katie who knocked on the door and then led her into the room. Besides Mrs. Chapman she recognized no one, yet they all seemed to know who she was. She sat in the empty chair. She could still feel the warmth from when Jillian had sat there minutes earlier. It was a stark contrast to the icy chill she felt throughout the rest of her body and all that remained of Jillian when she walked away from her.

The group introduced themselves, and Laura feigned a smile in response. They asked her how she was feeling and if she was enjoying her time at the institute. The forced niceties were annoying.

"Can I just ask why I'm here?" Jillian was hurt and alone, and Laura was sitting here in this room instead of comforting her. They needed to get to the point.

"We'll get right to the point then," Beck said. "Did you falsify your admission application when you failed to disclose any medical issues that could impact your—"

Laura cut him off. "Yes. You already know this, obviously."

"Are you aware that knowingly excluding this information violates TMRI policy?" he asked.

She leaned back in her seat and crossed her legs, resting her clasped hands on her knee. "Yes. It was a conscious decision that I made to not include it with my application. Had I done so I never would have been considered fairly based upon my qualifications."

"That's not how we operate here at TMRI, Ms. Carter," Mr. Allen said.

"You're joking, right?" she asked.

"We make it our mission not to discriminate based on many factors, including disability," he added without acknowledging her disrespect.

Laura scoffed. She had no intention of believing they would have admitted anyone with an outright fear of water. Even Jillian told her as much. "Okay, if you say so."

"How are you coping with that and your training?" Liz asked.

"Fine, now. Jillian and I have been using our combined experience in psychology and behavior to—"

"Yes. Your supplemental training sessions," Beck said.

"Exactly. Is that why you fired her? Because of these lessons?" Laura cocked her head at him.

He didn't answer her instead he asked, "Are you in a romantic relationship with Ms. Marshall?"

"Why? What does that have to do with this?"

"Do you feel that you were obligated to accept her advances in order to keep your position at the institute?"

Laura laughed out loud. Were they for real? This whole damn thing was a joke. "Let me get this straight. You are accusing Jillian of using her position to sleep with me? The woman who's dedicated every minute of her life to this place. The woman who risked her own safety to protect these animals? That woman? You're accusing her of sacrificing her career and everything she loves to get into my pants? You can't be serious." Laura was on the verge of hysterical laughter, and she rubbed her face. These assholes had no idea who Jillian was.

"So, the two of you are not in a relationship?" Mr. Allen asked.

She leaned forward on the table. "You don't get it, do you? She would die for these animals regardless of who she was sleeping with. And she would never put me, or anyone else above them. Including herself." Laura ached for Jillian. To have her whole life's work ripped away from her because of something she would never do. They couldn't do this to her. Laura refused to let them. It would kill Jillian to be separated from her pod, her family. She would break her own heart before she allowed them to break Jillian's.

"Expel me."

"Excuse me?" Beck asked.

"Expel me. Kick me out of the program. I shouldn't be here; I lied on my application, and I'm a danger to myself and others. Give Jillian her job back, and I will leave." Laura choked back the tears. She coughed away the thick phlegm that stuck in her throat.

"Due to your disability it's not so easy as that. Someone needs to be held accountable for this, and as the director that responsibility falls on Ms. Marshall," Beck stated.

"That's bullshit, and you know it. What if I quit? Then I accept full responsibility, and she stays."

"It doesn't work that way, Laura," Liz said.

"So, you're forcing me to stay?" Laura asked.

"No, of course not. However, it won't change the terms of her suspension or affect the ultimate outcome," Liz said.

"Correct," Beck said. "And if and when Ms. Marshall returns there can be no *we*. The institute cannot condone a personal relationship between a member of management and a trainee. The perception, the liabilities, the consequences are unacceptable."

Laura slammed back in her chair as if she'd been punched. They were forbidding them from being together. They were being forced to choose between their careers and love where there could be no true winner. Hard as it would be, Laura knew she could survive two weeks without Jillian, as she knew that on the fourteenth day she could hold her in her arms. But to spend the next six months living and working together without ever being able to touch or kiss would be a torture worse than death. How was she supposed to stop loving her? To stop wanting her? Had Jillian accepted these terms so easily? Was that why she couldn't look her in the eye?

"So that's it." Laura's voice cracked and a sharp, searing pain burned in her chest.

"You'll continue in the program as you've been. Although, it's obvious that any arrangements you had with Jillian will stop immediately."

"Uh-huh." Laura's hands were folded in her lap as she stared blankly at the glassy surface of the table. She wanted to run, but where would she go? The one place of refuge she could think of was Jillian's strong embrace, and now it was forbidden.

"Laura?" She heard her name through muffled ears and looked around, uncertain of who had called her. "That will be all, unless you have anything else you wish to add."

Nothing Laura had said or would say mattered. So even if she'd had anything more, she didn't have the energy to waste. Laura walked away.

CHAPTER TWENTY-TWO

Jillian was oblivious of time. She'd walked the path from the admin building to her house more than a thousand times before, yet with each step she took, the distance between her and her sanctuary grew. The pained look on Laura's face when she had pulled away from her was burned into her mind. No matter how hard she tried she couldn't rub her eyes enough to make it disappear. Her head pounded with every heavy footstep she took, and her arms felt cumbersome as they hung at her sides.

In an instant, she'd lost everything. She'd been forced to choose between a love she'd always had and the one she had just found. Except it hadn't been a choice. If she wanted to keep her job, she was no longer allowed to see Laura. For so long Jillian had spent her life living the dream she'd made for herself. She'd done everything just as she should. She sacrificed her social life, her family, and her friends to devote herself to this career. Jillian regretted nothing. She'd started at the bottom and busted her ass for eighteen years to get where she was today.

It should've been a no-brainer. She should've been thankful that the board had just suspended her. She should be glad that they made the decision to choose her career over Laura. It was the smart move, the safe move. It was probably the exact one she'd have made on her own as little as six months ago. Yet she felt none of those things. Because as she stood there at her front door, she realized that she had nothing. Not even the house she lived in was hers. She was in limbo.

Jillian unlocked the door and stepped inside. She looked around at the life she'd made for herself. It looked like hers with its mismatched farmhouse décor, and it smelled like hers with the scent of jasmine and fresh linen. Yet, she felt uneasy with the surroundings. Like it could all be gone on a breeze like a wisp of smoke.

She closed the door behind her and slid to the floor. The weight of reality felt like it would crush her bones. Jillian leaned back against the door, wrapped her arms around her knees, and sobbed. She was alone and lost without the comfort of the water, her pod, or Laura. How was she supposed to survive without everything she needed to live? It was like trying to breathe but getting no air. Something that she now knew all too well. There was a small part of her, in the darkest corner of her brain, that wished she had died in that accident the day before. It would've been swift and painless compared to the squeezing agony in her chest that threatened to compress the life from her body as slowly as possible.

As Jillian cried, she thought about Laura and what she must think. Had she thought that Jillian had used her? If she hadn't before, did she believe that now that the board had undoubtedly implied it just as they had with her? And what about the truth of her PTSD? Laura knew the effect that information would have on her eligibility at the institute. Jillian knew as well, which is why she'd kept it a secret when she'd found out. The board would have every right to pull Laura's enrollment and send her away. She too would lose everything she'd fought so long for.

How could Jillian have been so nearsighted? Not even when Diana had warned her of the potential consequences, did she ever have a second thought about Laura or helping her. Now, here she was sitting on the cold tile in her foyer without any of the things she held most dear. She hadn't just risked her own career, she had risked Laura's too. Just as Laura feared, she would once again be forced to start over, and this time it was Jillian's fault.

What have I done?

❖

As soon as the door slammed shut, Laura stripped out of her work clothes. She thought for a second about taking a shower but crawled into her bed instead. The cool sheets felt even colder on her overheated skin. She turned over to face the wall and pulled the blankets up over her head. Laura buried her face into the soft pillow and let the tears come. A knock on the door made her growl. "Go away," she yelled from beneath the covers.

The second knock was louder and more persistent. She tried to ignore whoever it was hoping they would give up and leave. The third knock sent her over the edge. Laura threw back the covers, kicking her legs free of the tangled sheets. She stomped over to the door and flung it open. "What?"

BJ stood on the other side in the hallway with his mouth agape. "Do you want a robe or something?"

Laura looked down at herself. There she was standing in the doorway in nothing but a pink bra and blue cotton panties. But she couldn't care less. "BJ, I'm not in the mood. Please, just leave." Even if she tried there was no hiding her pain.

She tried to close the door, but he pushed his hand against it. "What happened?" The look on his face was of true concern, but she couldn't talk about it.

"Please. I love you, but I can't handle this right now." She wrapped her arms around her bare torso. The last thing she wanted was his wise words.

"Come on. I promise I won't speak unless spoken to."

He took her hand and stepped into the room, closing the door behind him. He led her back to her bed and sat her down while he picked up the mangled pile of bedding from the floor. BJ flapped out the sheets and told her to lie down before tucking her beneath them. He kicked off his shoes and lay down next to her. She curled up into his side, and he stroked her hair. As he promised, he kept his opinions to himself.

She cried into his shirt, soaking it with tears and snot, but he just held her close. She sniffed and tried to wipe away the evidence, but it was a hopeless attempt. "I'm sorry."

"Seriously? That's nothing compared to what was on this shirt last week." He leaned over to her nightstand, picked out several tissues from the box, and handed them to her.

As she wiped her stuffy nose she said, "They know about us."

"Who's they?"

"Who isn't? The board, Director Chapman, human resources. Probably everyone at the park by now," she said.

"I swear, I didn't say a thing. Not even to Brooke."

"It's fine. It doesn't matter."

It didn't matter how they found out, but whoever had told them had done so with the intent of destroying one or both of them. There was one person at the institute who clearly had too much time on their hands while everyone else was minding their own business. Whatever the reason behind it, Diana had succeeded. Laura explained how her morning had played out and how it had gone from heaven to hell in a matter of minutes. She had been living her best life, caring for the animals she loved next to the woman who had stolen her heart.

"Are they going to fire her?" he asked.

"They better not. That would be the worst mistake they could ever make."

"That's for sure," he said.

"I just need to figure out what I'm going to do. She may be back in a couple weeks, but she'll still be the director, and I'll still be a trainee." That knot in her throat felt like a ball of rusty nails. He kissed her on the top of her head just like Jillian had done, and her heart twisted. "You should have seen her face, BJ. And she wouldn't even look me in the eye." Laura almost would have preferred an actual slap in the face than have Jillian pull away from her like she did.

"You can't know what she was thinking. No matter how close you are, you aren't a mind reader."

"Don't. Don't feed me your creepy wisdom like you're a fucking ancient wizard in a teenager's body."

"Uhm, sorry?"

"You said you wouldn't, BJ."

"And you didn't honestly believe me, did you?" He took one of her tissues and wiped away the tears that had pooled in the corner of her eye. "What I'm saying is that you don't know what happened or what she's feeling. She may be as brokenhearted as you are."

The thought of Jillian hurting as much as she was made Laura feel ill. She sat up, ready to lunge for the trash can if she became sick. Laura tried to speak through the outburst of violent sobs. "And I...can't even be...there for her."

"Bullshit. Do you want to see her?"

Of course, she did. Why would he even ask her that? "Yes, but—"

"Then get dressed and let's go," he said, jumping up out of bed.

"If someone sees us together, she could lose her job, BJ." Laura was talking rationally, but she had also gotten out of bed and rushed to pull on a pair of jeans.

"Don't worry about that."

Laura stuck her arms into her T-shirt as she chased after him. She had no idea what she was doing, she just knew that she had to see Jillian. Instead of taking the path through the park that she knew, he led her out into the parking lot.

"Where are we going?"

"Don't ask questions."

At the edge of the parking lot was an eight-foot chain link fence with a spiral of barbed wire running across the top. She followed him along the fence behind several maintenance buildings toward a thick bamboo grove. Once through the foliage, they reached the edge of the property where it touched the shore line. The emerald waters of the Bay lapped gently at the narrow strip of sand between them and the water.

"It's beautiful here, but what are we doing?"

BJ set his hands on her shoulder and turned her to the left and pointed up the coast about fifty yards. Through the vegetation, set back from the water was Jillian's house. Laura's stomach leapt into her throat. Her sense of direction was so turned around, and she wanted to know how on earth BJ knew about this back road to the house, but more than that she wanted to see Jillian.

"Go on," he said and nudged her forward.

Laura hesitated. "What if Diana's there now like she was that last time?"

He took her hand and led her to the corner of the house and had her wait while he knocked on the door. Several long seconds ticked by without an answer, and Laura's heart sank. This was all so high school, and she began to feel embarrassed that she'd let him drag her through the bushes like this. He turned to her and shrugged, and she was waving him back when the door opened. She couldn't hear what was said or even see if it was Jillian who'd come to the door. He stepped off the porch toward her and her heart hammered in her chest.

"She's alone and honestly looks worse than you do." He kissed her cheek and gave her another light push toward the still open door before disappearing the way they had come.

Jillian was standing just inside the doorway looking as wrecked and weary as Laura felt. She was afraid to reach out for her in case she once again pulled away. "You shouldn't be here, Laura." Her eyes were puffy and bloodshot from crying.

"I know. Can I please come in before someone sees me?"

Jillian stepped back and let her in. "They suspended me. For two weeks. I can't see you or the girls. I can't even go into the park that's ten steps away from my front door."

"I know." When Laura took a single step toward her Jillian didn't move away.

"Then what are you doing here? We could both lose everything."

She took another step and said, "It wouldn't be the first time."

"It would be for me, Laura. This is all I've ever known. I just can't take these risks like you can."

Laura hadn't considered their love a risk. "But you told me that anything worth doing—"

Jillian cut her off. "This isn't a game or some wild adventure. This is my life. I have people and animals that rely on me. I can't just throw all of that away and start over at the beginning."

"But you can throw us away?" If Laura had thought her heart couldn't be broken any more, she was wrong, because Jillian had just shattered it. "Don't you love me?"

"This isn't about love. We got caught up in the excitement, the emotions. Neither of us thought this through."

"That's what love is, Jillian. That's how it begins, not why it should end." She reached for Jillian hoping she didn't pull away this time. When she didn't, Laura wrapped her arms around her waist.

Jillian shuddered as Laura held on tight. Even if she had wanted her to let go Laura wasn't going to.

Jillian rested her head on Laura's and held her. "I'm so sorry for this mess we're in, my sweet girl. I just don't know any other way around it."

"I'll withdraw. They won't expel me, I asked. But I will leave the program and we can be together."

"You what?" Jillian pulled back from Laura and looked at her. "Why would you do that?"

Laura wiped away the wetness on Jillian's cheeks with her thumbs and held her face gently in her hands. "Because I love you."

Jillian squeezed her eyes shut and tears dripped from her lashes. When she opened them, they were pained and distant. "No, Laura. You've come too far. I can't. I won't let you do that, not because of me."

"So, what then? We go on working and living side by side and pretend none of this ever happened? That we never happened?" This time it was Laura who backed away.

"We have to."

"And then what? Six months from now you'll still be the director and I'll...I'll just be that girl you fucked once. Is that it?" Laura could barely speak and breathe at the same time. Her head was throbbing, and her empty stomach threatened to revolt.

"Please, Laura, this is killing me."

"It's fine. I get it. I'm not worth it. I'm just not worth the risk." Through a cloudy haze of tears, Laura fled Jillian's house. She ran down the porch and through the bushes toward the fence the way BJ had brought her. Her face and limbs stung as thin branches whipped across her skin. When she reached the fence line where it stretched out into the water, she dropped to her knees and vomited.

CHAPTER TWENTY-THREE

Laura had spent the rest of the day in bed. She didn't eat. She drank very little, and she called in sick for her shift that night. BJ had come by to check on her, and she'd sent him away. Unlike the time before, he didn't continued to knock until she relented and let him in. Somewhere around two a.m. she'd roused enough energy for a quick shower.

Thankfully, at that time of morning the chances of running into anyone was less than slim. She was glad for the moments that she was asleep because she was free from the melancholy that consumed her while she was awake. During every waking minute she replayed Jillian's rejection. In the end she simply wasn't worth the risk. Jillian had chosen the safety and stability of the life she had instead of taking a chance on the promise of something more.

She wasn't sure how she could blame her. Who didn't want the comfort and security that Jillian had? Laura knew it was what she wanted as well; she just wanted it with Jillian. Laura wished for nothing more than to crawl back under the covers and stay there until the pain went away, but she couldn't.

The silence of her room was deafening, and she would go mad trying to hush the voices in her head.

Laura got dressed, pulled her hair back into a messy knot, and headed to the fish house. She took the long way around to avoid any chance of running into Jillian, even though it was next to impossible as she wasn't allowed in the park. She took her time shuffling along past the turtles and otters and stopped for a bit to watch the trainers feed the sea lions. Their playful antics and loud barking put a tiny smile on her face. A small group of young pups wrestled in the waves while the older lions were more focused on the leggy squid they were getting for breakfast.

"Laura, don't just stand there, grab a bucket," one of the trainers shouted from the rail. She didn't have to be told twice. She picked up a heavy steel pail and joined in the feeding frenzy.

It was an instant mood booster, and for a second her heart felt a little lighter. She grabbed a large slimy squid from her bucket and threw it out to the large bull, Leroy. It caught a spin, like an alien helicopter and wrapped around his face and mouth. Laura and everyone else laughed as he whipped his head around to shake it off and gobble it down. It was a short-lived joy when she heard Diana holler out her name. It almost reminded her of the way her mother had shouted at her when she'd done something wrong. Laura set the bucket down and turned around.

"Too sick to make rounds, I see."

"I'm feeling better now. I was just getting out for some air."

"We don't get to pick and choose the tasks that we do around here, Laura. Regardless of how you're used to doing things."

Laura supposed she should've expected the snark. "I know that."

It was clear that Diana didn't want to hear anything Laura had to say. "You shouldn't even be here, Ms. Carter. It's because of you that Jillian isn't. Thanks to your lies and secrets."

Diana could have easily slapped her in the face and had the same effect. The sting of fresh tears burned her tired eyes, but she wouldn't give her that power. "Do you think I don't know that? Do you think I haven't spent every second of the last twenty-four hours blaming myself for all of this?"

"Then why are you still here, and she isn't?" There was a grumble in Diana's voice that almost made Laura step back, but she stood her ground.

"I asked them to expel me instead, and they refused. And I should ask you the same questions since we wouldn't even be having this discussion if you knew how to mind your own damn business."

"I suggest you change your tone, Laura," Diana snarled.

"Or what? They'll expel me? Suspend me? I already told you, I tried that."

"Then quit. Quit before someone else gets hurt."

"I haven't hurt anyone except myself. And I'm certainly not going to quit because you tell me to." Sure, she had thought about it. Truthfully, she was still thinking about it. But she'd be damned if she was going to give anyone, most of all, Diana that satisfaction.

"Give it time."

"If we're done here, I'm going to finish helping with breakfast." Laura turned her back to Diana and reached for the bucket. As she hooked her two middle fingers around the handle, Diana snatched it away from her. Ice and gelatin cubes sloshed out onto the concrete along with a fishy soup mixture. Laura stood there in shock with the tips of her fingers stinging where the nails had bent back. She clenched them into a fist and squeezed against the pulsing pain.

"I don't want you anywhere near the animal enclosures unless it's during your rounds. No feedings, no encounters, no animal interactions whatsoever. Those are privileges, not rights, and you no longer have either."

It seemed that Diana had just put Laura on the fast track out of the program. "So, what am I supposed to do when I'm not working?" Laura asked.

"You can spend all your time in the fish house scrubbing scales off the walls for all I care. Until Jillian gets back, I'm the boss around here, and I suggest you make yourself invisible."

"So it was a power play? And here I thought you did all this out of raging jealousy." For someone so furious about Jillian's suspension she sure was quick to step into her shoes.

Diana's face was scarlet, and her eyes burned with ferocity, but Laura stood her ground. She knew that she had gotten in a good blow. Although it was Diana who got the last word when she tipped over the bucket and dumped the entire cold, gelatinous stench onto the ground and Laura's sneakers along with it.

"I need you to clean that up," she said as she dropped the pail with a loud, metal clang and walked away.

As Laura stooped to scrape up the ice and muttered, "Bitch." She hadn't said it discreetly, though Diana hadn't given her any indication that she'd heard her. Next time she'd be sure that she made it clearer.

What bothered Laura most wasn't that her shoes had been soaked through with fish guts, but that Diana had intentionally deprived these animals of their meal. Her jealousy and madness had her so consumed that she had wasted an entire bucket of food. Laura had to wonder what someone like Jillian had ever seen in a woman like Diana.

Laura pushed the mess into the bucket as best she could with her hand. Her fingers were still throbbing where her nails had been torn away from the bed. She was a little disappointed that she wasn't a violent person because she would have loved to have broken Diana's damn nose, sore fingers or not. She took the wasted seafood back to the fish house and threw it out. After vaguely letting them know what happened, she picked out a replacement bucket from the cooler. Laura thought twice about going back to the team at the sea lion exhibit, but then decided she didn't give two shits if Diana saw her or not. The only reason she had to do it was because of her anyway.

It was almost shift change when she returned to the fish house and waited for BJ and Brooke to clock out. As they were a team, she felt it was necessary to warn them in case Diana decided to include them in her vengeance plan. It was one thing to punish Laura, it was another to punish the others just because they were friends. As soon as she saw them, it was obvious they already knew something.

"Don't tell me she already got to you." Laura rolled her eyes.

"Yeah," Brooke said.

"Oh, for the love of God. Who pissed in her cereal?" Laura asked.

"You did, apparently," BJ said.

"We've never said more than a couple of words to each other before Jillian's accident. Suddenly, I'm some enemy to be crushed."

"There isn't a person out there who believes this is anything other than jealousy," he said.

"I know I haven't made all of the best decisions in life, but what the hell?" Laura scratched her fingers into her hair.

"I don't think this has anything to do with you. Not personally anyway," Brooke said.

They wandered back behind the office and meandered along the high-walled corridor that led to a small alcove near the lagoon. They sat on a bench and looked out across the water. Laura enjoyed seeing their world from this side. Even on the busiest days at the park there was always somewhere behind the scenes that you could catch a few quiet minutes. It was one of the many things she would miss if she had to make the hard choice. "She wants me gone. She even told me as much, if you can believe it," Laura said.

"Who cares what she wants? You've busted your ass to prove yourself here. Probably more than any of us," Brooke said, leaning over across BJ and patting her on the arm.

"Because I had help, and it's not fair to you."

"We all have our shit, Laura. And whether anyone knows it or not, you aren't the only person Jillian has gone out of her way to help in some way or another," BJ said.

The idea that Jillian's heart was so big that she would help anyone or anything in need was bittersweet. It was that very thing, her heart, that led them here. "Well then, the real difference is that I'm the one she's sleeping with."

"Yeah, that one's all you. For sure," BJ said, and they laughed.

"Not anymore." Laura told him what had happened when he left her with Jillian as well as she could without breaking down.

"I'm so sorry, Laura," Brooke said.

"Me too. But you can't blame her for being afraid. Eighteen years is a long time. I know how much she cares about you, but you're so new in her life compared to everything else," BJ added.

"I suppose, but it just feels like she gave up so easily. I never even had a chance. She pushed me away." The stinging in her eyes began, and she blinked hard to make it stop. "How…how am I…"

BJ wrapped his arm around her shoulder and pulled her close. "Are you hungry? I'm hungry. Wanna go get some breakfast?"

Laura nodded her head. "Can I change my shoes first?"

"No, you can throw them in the dumpster, and we'll go buy you new ones," Brooke said.

"Yeah, they're already putting me off my eggs," BJ said, holding his nose.

"I'd put them under the driver's seat in Diana's car if I knew what she drove." Laura laughed.

Brooke raised her hand. "I do."

It was well before dawn when Jillian found herself searching for solace after being banned even from her quiet haven on the edge of the park's lagoon. She got in her truck, rolled the windows down, and drove. She headed west toward the Gulf of Mexico until she found herself alone on a white sand beach. She lay in the soft, cool sand for hours listening to the water crash onto the shore. She stayed there until the sun began to rise and the ocean breeze started to warm.

Instinctively, Jillian found herself back at the institute sitting in her truck without the desire to move or a need to go. She sat behind the wheel and picked at a loose string on the fabric cover.

The air was still through the lot, and without the wind she could hear the park begin to awaken. Even the wild seabirds helped to announce the day as they flocked in for their free meals. Jillian felt an unfamiliar sense of worthlessness as her world continued without her.

As she stepped out of the truck to escape to the quiet of her home, she heard it. It was a lighthearted giggle that floated to her like a wisp of sweet lavender. Jillian hopped back into the truck and slumped in the seat so she wouldn't be seen, but she still caught a glimpse of Laura.

Laura sauntered out into the parking lot with Brooke and BJ on either side of her. Laura had her head resting awkwardly on his shoulders as he did what he could to support her. With her window rolled up she couldn't hear what it was they were saying, but when Laura lifted her head and shot a glance toward Jillian's truck, she imagined what it was. She was ninety percent certain that they couldn't see her sitting behind the tinted glass, but she would have sworn that Laura had looked her right in the eyes.

For a moment, as Laura looked at her, the weight of the world had lifted. When she turned away, the tidal wave of reality came rushing back. Had that been what Laura had felt when Jillian had sent her away? She had never meant to hurt her; that wasn't why she had pulled back when she reached out for comfort. She had wanted to protect her. She didn't want Laura to lose all the progress she'd made over the last few weeks, and to think that she had nearly thrown it all away for Jillian was too much for her to handle.

Once they had loaded into Laura's car and drove away, Jillian was free to move, and yet she didn't. Her mind wandered back to the night they'd sat in this very spot and kissed for the first time. It was a kiss so sweet, so passionate, that neither of them had been strong enough to resist. Jillian wondered where they would be now if they'd not fallen victim to their desires. Given the chance to do it again would she still surrender to the hunger they had for each other? Could she have turned her away that night when she arrived on her doorstep literally wet and wanton?

The truth was Jillian wouldn't have changed a thing, even now. She had never been so consumed with attraction; time and consequence had not diminished the fervor. But why was she so afraid? Why had she given up so easily on someone who just wanted to love her? Laura wanted nothing in return except the promise of her own heart. As much as it seemed like she was losing everything, Jillian could find another job, another home in another city. She'd never find someone who would love her as purely as Laura did. How was she supposed to know if the chance was worth taking?

It seemed that now was an appropriate time for her own words about fear to come back to haunt her. Jillian was dripping with sweat when she finally got out of the truck. The temperature had already begun to rise on what was going to be a beautiful Florida day. Although despite the potential the day held, Jillian felt less than hopeful.

CHAPTER TWENTY-FOUR

Laura wanted nothing more than to call in sick and stay in bed like she had the day before. As much as she struggled to participate in life, she couldn't spend any more time alone in her mind. Of course, BJ wasn't going to just let her squirrel away in her room to wallow; it was as thoughtful as it was annoying. Laura would show up, but there was no guarantee that she would put in much effort beyond what she needed for walking.

She was mad at herself. Laura was no stranger to failure or setbacks, but there was something different about a broken heart. It had no logic or reason; it couldn't be smothered or ignored. Laura was mad that in spite of everything she had overcome it was Jillian's change of heart that seemed impossible to accept. She had felt a love so pure that she couldn't imagine a life without it. Laura was mad that it had become what she wanted over everything else she'd worked for.

"I wish I was mad at her. Or something. It would make it easier if I hated her," she said to BJ as they left for another midnight shift. Unfortunately, with Diana in charge this would probably be just one of many more to come.

"I suppose. However, you don't."

"I don't. I hardly even blame her, let alone hate her." Laura couldn't help but steal a glance down the dark path toward Jillian's house when they passed. She'd done the same that morning when they passed by her truck in the parking lot. Laura supposed she couldn't be lucky enough to see her more than once in the same day. BJ clocked in and pulled down the charts, handing half of them to Laura. They went through the day's reports and logs looking for anything they needed to keep an eye out for.

"Do you have Pepper's chart?" BJ asked, putting the others back on the shelf.

"I do, why? She flipped to the page and handed him the clipboard.

"I overheard Kelsea tell Diana about some possible hyporexia. I guess she's not eating her full meals."

"Pepper? That's not like her. What did Diana say?" Laura couldn't help but think that she didn't give a rat's ass about who ate what considering her wasteful display that morning.

"Nothing, really. Just told her to put it in the chart, so I was curious."

Laura looked over his shoulder and read through the numbers with him. "Looks like she didn't really interact much today either. Oh, and yeah look, she's under by two pounds for today and one yesterday."

"That's gotta put her pretty low on fluids. Why wouldn't Diana have followed up on this?" Laura asked.

"Maybe she did and just didn't write it down?"

He put the charts back with the rest and they went into the park. There was no question where they were headed first, though neither of them said it. Laura was worried that something could be wrong with Pepper. In the three months they had been there, the pod matriarch had never been one to turn her head from food. When she and Jillian had worked with her a few mornings earlier, nothing had seemed out of order, although Laura was there for just a few minutes before they were called away.

"Did you happen to see any results for the lab work Jillian ordered the other day?"

"No, but they don't put those on their day charts. Jillian, or rather Diana, would have those," he said.

That's what she was afraid of. If those tests had come back with something abnormal Jillian would have been all over it. Laura had a sinking feeling that Diana wasn't quite as attentive in her new role. Before they even reached the lagoon, they could hear it. It was a distinctive sound that Laura had heard Pepper make. The chuffing sound wasn't just an occasional clearing cough, it was more of a frequent blow with an audible whistle. It was a sound Laura could only compare to a human's wheeze.

When they reached the water, the sound had stopped. Laura and BJ scanned their flashlights across the surface of the water. In the dark of night, it was difficult to pick out one particular dolphin from the bunch. Several minutes went by without a sound or sight of her.

Laura had BJ climb up onto the observation platform while she scaled up onto the boulders opposite him. Her heart was thumping in her chest as her anxiety increased with every second Pepper didn't surface. While they were counting the other members, a loud exhale huffed in the shallows. Something was very wrong. Laura shouted for BJ and they both ran toward the beach.

"She's separated herself into the shallows."

"You don't think she's trying to beach herself, do you?"

The rest of the pod was anxious and distressed as they circled around making laps between Pepper and the deep water. While they made a scene with loud vocalizations, Pepper swam lethargically, surfacing no more than once every six minutes or so.

"She's having trouble coming up for air. Where'd she go?" Laura called out to him when she didn't come up for another breath.

"I don't know. Wait," he said as he ran up to the rocks and shined his light down.

Laura's heart was racing. "Where is she, BJ?"

"I'm looking." The seconds continued to tick by, and she begged Pepper to surface. "There," he shouted.

Illuminated by the flashlight was a dark gray mass beneath the surface. Laura ran into the cold water as far as she could and dove in. The shock of the frigid water zipped through her body. She could just see the rays of light from BJ's flashlight through the water. Her eyes burned from the salt, so Laura closed them and kicked her legs, propelling herself blindly toward Pepper. She hoped.

Laura opened her eyes, and thankfully, she'd made it to her. She put her hands beneath Pepper's head and pushed her upward to the surface.

When they both broke through Laura gasped and called out to BJ. "Go get help. Call Dr. Sharpe and Diana." Laura's teeth chattered from the shock of the cold.

BJ set off at a run and disappeared. Laura hooked her arm around Pepper and guided her toward the shore where the water was waist deep. She looked into Pepper's beautiful eyes and spoke softly to her as she shivered. Laura stroked her smooth skin as she held her head above the surface. Laura hadn't given her a single command, and yet she made no move to swim away. Laura tried to blink away the stinging in her eyes instead of wiping at them because she refused to take her hands away from Pepper.

"Look at Luna. She's worried about you, pretty girl. It'll be okay." Pepper took a breath through her blowhole, and Laura rested her ear against her side listening for anything that didn't sound right. Not that there was anything right about holding up a dolphin too weak to swim.

"If Jillian were here, she'd know what to do, wouldn't she? Though if she were here this wouldn't be happening would it?" Laura continued to talk to Pepper about whatever came to mind. She hummed a few songs and tried not to focus on how long it had been since BJ left.

❖

Even if Jillian hadn't already been awake, the banging on her front door could have roused the dead. There wasn't a soul alive who would pound like that if it wasn't an emergency. Her startled heart was hammering out of her chest when she opened the door. BJ stood on her porch white-faced and gasping for air. The sight of him in such a state made her stomach twist on itself. *Please God, don't let it be Laura.*

"It's Pepper," he said, his words breathy and forced. "And Laura. She's in the water." Her fears went from bad to worse. Jillian had a thousand questions but wasted no time on the details as they ran through the darkness and into the park.

"Where is she?" Jillian asked, frustrated by his pace when she could get anywhere in the park twice as fast blindfolded.

"The shallows."

She sprinted ahead of him; if she lost him, she didn't care. She needed to find Laura now. Why was she in the water? Why had he left her there? The worst images flashed into Jillian's head as she ran. Jillian pushed them from her mind as she raced toward the unknown. She stumbled in the soft sand when she reached the beach. Just off shore she could see a faint light floating in the water, and she called out Laura's name, her voice cracking with desperation.

"Jillian?"

A wave of relief rushed through her when Laura returned her call, but she didn't slow down. Jillian ran out into the water fighting to reach her. Her relief turned to fear again when she saw Pepper, lifeless in Laura's arms.

"What's wrong? Did you call Dr. Sharpe? How long has she been like this?" Jillian fired questions at Laura.

BJ waded into the water beside them. "Dr. Sharpe's on her way."

Jillian cupped her hands beneath Pepper's head and kissed her rostrum. She looked into each half-lidded eye and spoke to her. "What's going on, baby girl?" Pepper chuffed a wheezy cough.

"That's bad, isn't it?" Laura asked.

"It's not good," Jillian said. "BJ, can you get the triage case from the—"

He was already on it before she finished asking. Laura scooped water up over Pepper's skin where she'd been holding her up out of the water.

BJ returned with the box and several trainers, vet technicians, and Dr. Sharpe who rushed in with him. They all went right to work in a silent orchestration. Dr. Sharpe threw a hundred questions at Jillian that for the first time she couldn't answer. She'd been away less than forty-eight hours, and she couldn't have been more removed than if she'd never spent a day with these animals.

All she could do was hold Pepper and comfort her while they attempted to diagnose her. "We need to prep the medi-tank and move her," Jillian said to no one in particular.

"Agreed." Dr. Sharpe removed the ear tips and hung the stethoscope around her neck. "We need a complete blood panel, ultrasound, and histopathology. When was the last lung screen performed?"

Now that, Jillian could answer. "Two days ago."

"Results?"

And just like that, her knowledge was inadequate. "I don't know." Despite the cool water, Jillian's temperature was flaring. She should have fought harder when they handed down her sentence of suspension. She didn't, and now her dear Pepper was suffering. "BJ, Kelsea, prep the tank. Alex, pull the sling and hit the floods. We need more light in here." Everyone hesitated for a moment at Jillian's commands. "Now," she yelled, and they scattered like minnows.

They guided Pepper into the sling and lifted her up and out of the water. The team worked swiftly despite the five-hundred-pound weight they carried on their shoulders. The floor of the tank was raised to the surface when they stepped onto the platform. Once she was safely set onto the perforated deck, water began to bubble up through the holes as it sank back down and refilled with water. Having regained a spark of energy, Pepper kicked herself to the surface for a breath. However, it was clear she hadn't the strength to continue to support herself.

Jillian and Laura wasted no time scooping their arms beneath her from either side and walking with her. They only stopped when Dr. Sharpe was ready to continue with her exam. The infrared thermometer registered a low-grade fever while a listen to her lungs hinted at possible fluid. Jillian's stomach dropped when Dr. Sharpe called for the ultrasound machine to check for the possibility of pneumonia. While it was a common illness in all dolphins, wild or captive, without treatment it was almost always fatal.

While they prepped for the ultrasound, Dr. Sharpe asked if anyone had the results from the diagnostics and no one answered.

"Hello?" Jillian asked anyone who was listening.

"Diana has them," Laura said quietly. It was the first time she'd spoken to Jillian since she arrived at the scene. Her voice was sweet and soothing in the chaos surrounding them.

"Thank you. Can someone call Diana and—"

"No one else needs to call me. I'm right here," Diana said as she strode up to the wall of the tank. "And the two of you definitely shouldn't be."

"I don't care who should or shouldn't. I know who was and who wasn't. Now someone get me the damn results I've asked for." Dr. Sharpe's face flashed red beneath the bright floodlights.

Pepper's eyes were wide as she stared into Jillian's. "Shhh, baby," she cooed and stroked her.

Diana sent someone off for the results, before ordering both Jillian and Laura from the water again. They looked at each other and said nothing nor did they make a move to comply with her command.

"Her labs were fine. Her appetite is off, but it's most likely just from recent staff changes," Diana said. While it was possible that Pepper was upset about Jillian's absence, that didn't explain any of the other symptoms. Had Jillian been out of the water with Diana she would have argued that point vehemently. However, right now she had much more important issues at hand. Dr. Sharpe was ready for testing, so Jillian asked Pepper to present herself by rolling over to her side with Laura's help. She ran the probe over her chest, squinting at the black-and-white images on the screen, and Jillian held her breath. It didn't take long for Dr. Sharpe to confirm that it was pneumonia, although everyone knew they'd have to wait for the lab work for an official diagnosis.

Jillian released Pepper from the maneuver, and she knew it was bad when she didn't even ask for a reward. "How long before we can start her on a treatment plan?" Jillian asked.

"Immediately after we confirm pathology. She'll need twenty-four seven support with monitoring until she regains her strength."

"I'm not going anywhere," Jillian said.

"Me neither," Laura added.

Jillian would stay with Pepper for as long as she needed or until she couldn't stand anymore. Of course, she knew in reality she couldn't stay in the water more than a couple of hours at a time. But while things were still critical there wouldn't be a force strong enough to drag her more than twenty feet from this pool. And with Laura by her side there wasn't anywhere else she wanted to be.

After what seemed like a lifetime, Dr. Sharpe's team returned with the lab confirmation and an expansive range of medications for immediate administration. It would be a long night and an even longer road ahead of them, but Jillian was hopeful that they were on the right track. Jillian had been so occupied with the issue at hand she hadn't realized that Diana was no longer standing over them. She looked around, but there was no sight of her.

"She left when we refused to get out. She's probably looking for a bucket of fish to dump on our heads."

"What?"

"Nothing," Laura said without any elaboration.

Jillian noticed that she was shivering uncontrollably in her sopping wet T-shirt and half dried hair, and her lips were tinted a light shade of blue. "Maybe you should go get warmed up."

"I'm okay," Laura said as she shivered.

"You're no use to me, err, uh…Pepper if you get hypothermia." Dr. Sharpe discounted the hypothermia, but she did suggest that they both change into their wet suits if they planned on taking the first shift. Jillian and Laura both reluctantly followed the doctor's orders as she and her team took over and began administering the extensive first round of antibiotic injections.

Jillian kissed Pepper on the head and promised that she'd be back soon. They walked to the locker room without saying a word to each other. Every time Jillian tried to speak, her tongue tied. What could she say? Should she tell Laura that she missed her like a piece of her own soul had died? Should she apologize for all the words she had and hadn't said? Jillian wanted to reach out and take her hand, pull her into her arms. She wanted to tell her how relieved she was that she was okay. Her body and soul ached to feel Laura against her and to know that she was safe and protected. But her actions tonight proved that Laura no longer needed Jillian's protection.

"I'm proud of you, Laura. What you did tonight was both selfless and fearless. You saved her life."

"I couldn't have done it without you," Laura said.

"And yet you did."

Chapter Twenty-five

Laura and Jillian exchanged no more than a few courtesies while they worked alongside the team of techs supporting Pepper through the night. They traded off every hour and never spent more than a few brief minutes together when they did. For Laura, every one of those exchanges soothed the ache in her chest only to tear open the wound once Jillian stepped away. There was a painful battle within her heart.

The words, *I'm so proud of you*, echoed in her mind all night. Laura felt stronger, taller almost.

Despite the situation they were in, she felt so much of the tension she'd carried for years lift off her shoulders. She knew she couldn't have done it without Jillian, and she would forever be grateful. She had sacrificed so much, and Laura didn't even know how she would ever be able to repay her.

For six long hours, she took every opportunity there was to watch Jillian. To have been so loved by her even for a short time had been a gift. And while the heaviness in her heart would surely last a lifetime, Laura would always be thankful for how Jillian had changed her life.

When the sun began to rise and daylight pushed away the twilight sky, she slipped into the pool one more time. As she crouched into the chilly water and hooked her arms beneath Pepper, she looked at Jillian. Her eyes were heavy and ringed by dark circles, and Laura offered an understanding smile. Their arms pressed against each other beneath Pepper, yet neither of them shied away. She gripped her hand around Jillian's forearm and held it for a moment. She looked into Jillian's eyes, and for several moments they held on to each other until Jillian pulled away. Her hand slid down the length of Laura's arm and squeezed her hand before she backed away and climbed out of the pool. The cool water turned frigid as the chill of Jillian's loss penetrated her bones.

Laura had long ago run out of things to say to Pepper and had instead begun to sing to her an eclectic mix of her favorite songs. She rested her forehead against Pepper's side and sang the first song that came to mind. Brandi Carlisle's "The Story" was as much for Jillian as it was for Pepper. It was true. She crossed lines and broke the rules with Jillian, but she would always believe that they were made for each other even though it seemed they weren't meant to be together.

Laura was lost in her solemn thoughts when Pepper flicked her tail and swam out of her arms. "Hey. Hey!" Laura called out to Pepper and then to everyone outside the tank. Kaylea jumped into the water with Laura as Pepper made nearly a full lap on her own for the first time since Laura had dove into the lagoon after her. When Nate slapped the surface of the water Pepper responded. She swam over and set her head on the wall of the tank in front of him. Laura felt the weight of the world lift from her shoulders when Pepper accepted the small capelin Nate tossed into her mouth. She wished with all her heart that Jillian had been there to see it.

Dr. Sharpe arrived with her team within minutes and discharged Laura from the remainder of her shift. Laura wanted to stay, but the adrenaline that had kept her going all night was running out. Her job here was done. Laura kissed Pepper on her head and said, "Be a good girl, now."

Laura cleared her throat and choked back the tears that were always on the edge of falling. She didn't look back as she pulled herself up out of the pool and walked away. She bypassed the lockers and stayed in her wet suit as she made her way across the park. There was something more important that she needed to do.

The admin office felt like a freezer when the cold air hit her warm suit. Katie immediately asked about Pepper, obviously having heard all about it when she arrived for work.

"She's stable. Is Director Chapman in?"

"Yes, she's been here a while. One sec." Katie called back to Liz and then sent Laura into her office.

Laura paused for a moment and took a deep breath. She gave a quick rap on the door before going in. Liz motioned for her to have a seat, but Laura looked at the cloth chair and then down at herself before saying, "Oh, no. I'm soaked."

"You wouldn't be the first. Go ahead," Liz said, waving off the concern. Laura hesitated for just a second before sitting at the edge of the seat. "I'm glad you stopped by. I wanted to thank you for everything you did for Pepper. It was very brave, and I'm proud of you. So is Dr. Sharpe, who I had a very long and insightful conversation with this morning, by the way."

"Thank you, ma'am. While Dr. Sharpe may be, I'm sure Diana isn't quite as impressed."

"That's irrelevant at this point."

"Eh, not really," Laura said but didn't elaborate. She wasn't here to complain about Diana.

However, Liz didn't let the comment slip by that easy and demanded to know what had been happening. Laura told her about everything Diana had done and said, as well as her suspicion about why she'd filed the complaint against her and Jillian. Liz didn't say anything; she just listened and jotted down the occasional note onto the pad in front of her. Despite not having intended to discuss this, Laura was relieved at getting it off her chest. When she was finished filling Liz in about Diana, she said, "Unfortunately, that's not why I came to see you."

Liz leaned back against her chair and sighed. "You're dropping out."

"Yes, and while I know you said that it wouldn't change your decision about Jillian, I think it should." Liz tried to interrupt but Laura kept on. "She's the most valuable resource you have here. You should have seen her last night. Sure, she broke the rules, but not for herself, not even for me." She leaned forward and tapped her finger sharply on the desk with just about every other word. She'd forgotten that she was wet when she sat back into her seat and took a deep breath.

"And you're willing to give up on your training just to save someone her job?"

"She isn't just someone to me, Mrs. Chapman," Laura said.

"I can see that."

"I cannot make her choose between me and everything she loves. I'd rather just walk away and know that she is where she belongs."

"And you?"

Laura stood up, and her pulse pounded through her body. "Nothing is worth doing if it doesn't scare you to death."

Liz stood as well. "It takes a fearless heart to give up your life for love. Good luck, Laura." Liz shook Laura's hand.

How she'd managed not to shed a tear as she gave up her dream, Laura didn't know. She had cried so many times these last few days that she thought maybe there were no more tears left. Yet when her face hit the warm morning air they poured from her like a spring. She ran across the parking lot toward the dorms praying that her unstable legs would carry her the whole way.

Despite heaving sobs, Laura told herself that everything would be okay. She knew that Pepper was in the best hands, BJ could hold his own, and Jillian was better off without her. And whether she ever worked with dolphins again, she had done what she had set out to do; she'd overcome her greatest fear.

Laura unzipped her wet suit and peeled it off. She held it up in front of her and ran her thumb across the institute logo before throwing the water-logged suit at the door with a loud slap. She wiped the salt water that it had sprayed across her face and then slumped onto the floor with it. "No," she said, slamming her fists onto the bed and pulling herself right back up.

Laura grounded herself and straightened up to stand tall. She wasn't a failure. A quitter, maybe, but she hadn't failed, and she didn't regret her decision. Laura would have given Jillian her very last breath if she needed it because she loved her. This was nothing in comparison.

It didn't take her long to pack up her things. She never spent enough time in her room to get comfortable. A dirty laundry basket, a few totes, and a suitcase sat by the door. She folded her uniforms and piled them on the naked mattress. She thought for a moment about not saying good-bye to BJ but knew that it would break his heart, and there was already enough of those around there. Laura carried her things out to the living room and stacked them against the wall before heading to his room.

Laura knocked once and he called out, "One sec."

She could hear the frantic shuffling and when he answered the door with his hair and shirt awry, Laura's mouth dropped open. What she came to say suddenly flew from her mind.

"Hey. Hi. Hey, 'sup?" he said while keeping a firm grip on the half-opened door.

She couldn't just come back later, and she needed to know if it was Brooke's hands that had done that to his hair. Yet the burden of what she had to say sat heavy over the moment. "I'm sorry to interrupt, but I...came to say good-bye." Laura tried to smile.

"What?" He flung the door open and it slammed against the wall. "What the fuck are you talking about?"

"I withdrew." Brooke appeared in the doorway looking as disheveled as he did, and this time, Laura did smile.

"I don't understand."

"I just spent the last eight hours with Jillian, and we didn't say more than two words to each other. I can't do that, BJ, and I would never forgive myself if anything happened to these animals because she wasn't here to save them."

"But you can't just leave," he said.

"I have to. It hurts too much. This is better for everyone."

"Laura," he said as he threw his arms around her.

She swallowed hard round the knot in her throat and patted him on the back a few times. "Keep in touch, okay? And let me know how Pepper is doing." She pulled away and gave him one more tap on the shoulder. Laura looked at Brooke and smiled. "I'm happy about this." She pointed back and forth between them before Brooke lunged in for a hug.

"Do you need help with anything?" Brooke asked.

"Nope, you kids get back to studying or whatever you're calling it these days." Laura kissed two fingers and pressed them to BJ's chest before she walked away.

As worried as she was for Pepper, Jillian was on the verge of uselessness. Her arms and legs could've weighed a hundred pounds each, and she dragged her feet along the path toward home. She was both physically and emotionally exhausted having been awake over twenty-four hours. She had barely enough energy to close the door behind her before slumping onto the couch with a hollow thump.

Her skin was stiff and dry with a layer of salty residue. She longed for a shower, yet fought for enough energy to push herself off the sofa. She motivated herself with the comfort of the clean sheets on her soft bed and rolled onto her feet in one motion. Jillian slogged to the bathroom stripping off her salt encrusted suit along the way.

The spray was intense as she clicked over the showerhead to the deep massage setting. The lukewarm water was near to scalding after being in the cold water of the lagoon all night. The one time she'd been warm was during those few brief moments when Laura had held her hand. As she stared into Laura's weary eyes, she told her how much she loved her, missed her, and how much she longed to make these seconds last forever. Jillian just hadn't spoken the words aloud. It would have done nothing except further break their hearts and inflict more pain, and Laura didn't deserve that. Especially not now that her greatest battle had been won.

Jillian knew that for as long as she lived, she would never again feel more pride than she had for Laura. When she saw her, chest deep in the lagoon without fear or panic, she knew that she'd made it. Every dream that Laura had since she was five years old had come true, in spite of every obstacle placed before her.

She'd fought her way there and never let anyone tell her that she couldn't. Jillian had never been even half as determined. She'd always gone with the flow and taken the smooth road. She supposed that was how she'd gotten where she was today. She hadn't sought out to advance into the director's position; she wasn't really sure how she'd gotten there. How could she be so afraid to lose something she wasn't even sure she'd ever wanted?

Jillian washed her body and let the suds swirl down the drain as she rinsed it all away. Her eyes drooped and her body swayed as she moved closer to full collapse. Before she risked falling into a heap on the shower floor, she turned off the water, wrapped herself in a dry towel, and stumbled into bed.

Jillian had no idea how long she'd been asleep when the persistent ringing of her phone woke her up. "Yeah?" Her voice was groggy.

"Jillian?" Katie asked.

She cleared her dry throat and tried again. "Hey. What's up?" Jillian rolled her eyes when Katie told her that Liz would like to see her as soon as possible. She supposed she should have expected it, but it still grated at her already tired and frazzled nerves.

Jillian took her time getting motivated and putting on her clothes before heading off to hear her fate. As soon as she arrived, Katie didn't hesitate to call back to Liz's office. Jillian was surprised when Liz came out to meet her in the lobby.

"Walk with me," Liz said, cocking her head toward the door Jillian had just come in.

Jillian's stomach tumbled and twisted as Liz led her out of the admin building. "Is Pepper all right? Laura?" Jillian couldn't help but think she was taking her out to pasture to shoot her or something.

"Pepper is doing well. Had a full breakfast this morning after you left."

"I'm sorry I missed it," she said. Jillian was sorry, but she also felt a bit lightheaded with relief and let out a huge exhale. While Pepper's condition was still serious, a good appetite was an excellent sign.

"I'm sorry you did, too." Liz sat on a wooden bench in a garden clearing and patted the empty space beside her.

"I understand that you had no choice the other day. I apologize if I said anything out of line."

"Are you kidding? If I were you, I'd probably have thrown chairs." Liz laughed.

"There may've been an inkling of that."

"So, some things have come to light this morning and we… we let Diana go."

Jillian blinked slowly trying to understand, but she thought she'd just misheard. "I'm sorry. What?"

Liz said she preferred not to go into detail, but it had to do with her treatment of trainees and what led to the lack of action and Pepper's unchecked illness. "But that's not why I wanted to see you, well, not entirely anyway. The board of directors and I want you to come back."

Part of her wanted to scream "Yes. Absolutely. Whatever you want." But another quieter part of her stammered with the answer. What did she want? Truly? They sat in silence as Jillian struggled to make sense of the warring feelings inside her, but the choice was clear even if she didn't know it. "I'll come back on one condition."

"Okay. Which is?" It seemed Liz hadn't expected any answer besides "Yes."

"I resign as director of education. No more office or paperwork, just Jillian Marshall, marine mammal trainer." Jillian blew out a loud breath.

"You worked so hard to become a director, why would you give it up?" Liz asked.

"Have I? I never wanted this, it just happened. I liked being a trainer and spending my time in the water. I hate being in the office." Jillian could hardly believe that she'd said it out loud, but it was just spilling out of her.

"Are you doing this for Laura?" Liz asked.

It was a two-fold answer. "Not for her. Because of her." Laura had shown Jillian everything she loved but in a whole new light. "But now we can be together with no conflict, no misperceptions."

Liz touched Jillian's knee. "Jillian, she's gone."

Every breath was knocked from her lungs, and she shook her head. Jillian's world hazed over, and her skin tingled with a million painful pins. "What?" No wonder Liz had brought her outside, even in the wide-open space, Jillian's world closed in on her.

"She withdrew from the institute this morning. And demanded that once she left, we take you back. I never even had the chance to tell her that it was already in the works."

"And you just let her go?"

"I don't have the power to stop her, Jillian."

Jillian jumped up from her seat. "You could have called me or tried harder. Flattened her fucking tires, for fuck's sake, Liz."

"This is right about the time when you would start throwing chairs."

"If you hadn't brought me out into the fucking wilderness I probably would be." Jillian waved her arms like the crazy person Liz thought she was now.

"It's interesting to see the passion this woman brings out in you. Scary, but interesting." Liz laughed.

Jillian paced around not sure whether she should stay or go. "When did she...Where?"

"I don't know. I was too busy firing your ex-girlfriend to worry about your current one." Liz laughed louder this time.

"I need to go." Jillian stepped away and then stepped back again.

"I know. Go bring her back, will you?"

"Really?" Jillian asked.

"Yes. And I'll start looking for some gullible sap to replace you."

Jillian sprinted toward the dorms. Knowing Laura, she was long gone by now, but she had to start somewhere. Although she had expected as much, her heart twisted when she saw Laura's door standing wide-open to a spotless room and her clothes piled neatly on the bed. She leaned against the cold steel of the doorframe to help keep her balance. Her mind flashed back to the many times she'd stood here waiting for Laura to answer. She rested her head on the wall and sighed.

"She left about an hour ago I guess," BJ said from behind her.

Jillian continued to stare into the empty space. "You wouldn't happen to know where?"

"No. Sorry. But it seems to me that she's only got one more thing to do in order to put this all behind her."

"And what's that?" she asked, turning around to face him.

"She may have overcome her fears here, but how will they translate in the real world?" he said.

The butterflies in her belly set flight and she asked, "Do you think?"

"There's one way to find out isn't there?" BJ smiled.

A burst of energy jolted through her, and she dashed out the door. She had no time to waste.

CHAPTER TWENTY-SIX

The breeze was gentle through the old cypress trees, and the air tasted crisp without a hint of salt. It was an obvious difference, as the last three months were filled with the briny wind and water. Laura sat on the weathered boardwalk and dangled her feet over the clear water of Crystal Spring. Overhead hung the remnants of the rope swing long ago put out of use. The frayed ends were barely distinguishable from the thick Spanish moss that draped from the branches above her.

They told her it was in this very spot where they fought for her life and held their own breath as they waited for hers. Laura hadn't been back here since that day, and it had been a weird journey littered with potholes and failure since. Yet here she was finally able to bring herself to this place without panic or fear. It was as beautiful as she'd always tried to remember it, and the terror and darkness that always tainted her memories were gone. While her pulse raced a little, she was filled with gratitude for being there and wished she could share this moment with Jillian. As without her, this wouldn't be possible.

Laura closed her eyes and imagined Jillian beside her, loving and being loved in this special moment. The wind shifted and Laura heard the quiet tapping of footsteps behind her. She opened her eyes as someone sat beside her. She closed her eyes tightly once again and prayed that her one wish had come true.

"Seems a shame not to share a moment like this with someone who loves you."

Laura squeezed her eyes even tighter and sunk her face into her hands. When Jillian wrapped her arm around her, she fell into her and broke down. She couldn't speak though she wanted to. Each time she tried her words were choked with sobs.

"It's okay, love," Jillian said as she lifted Laura's head with two gentle fingers beneath her chin.

Laura blinked away the blurry haze of tears and stared into Jillian's eyes. "You shouldn't be here."

"There's no other place on earth I should be, my sweet girl. This is where I belong."

"What about Pepper? And your job? You can't lose your job." Laura tried to control her heaving gasps as she spoke.

"Turns out this amazing woman did exactly what I told her not to just to get my job back."

"It worked?" Laura smiled through the tears.

"It did, and I had to personally track her down to thank her and tell her that I'd only accept it if she agreed to come back with me."

"Oh, Jillian, I can't. Last night was too hard. I couldn't do that every day and pretend that I wasn't ripping my heart out."

"No problem. I resigned as director. I'm just a lowly old dolphin trainer now. Free to love and make love to anyone I want."

"Why would you do that?" Laura was certain Jillian had lost her damn mind.

"You're not the only one of us crazy enough to quit their job just because they're in love."

"Yes, I am." Laura knew Jillian didn't have a crazy bone in her body, but it was one of the reasons she loved her so much. She kept her sane.

"Okay, you are. I did it for you, but I also did it for me." Jillian explained why she had done it, and it was one of the best decisions Laura thought she could ever make.

Laura turned to Jillian and took her beautiful face in her hands. "I love you, more than you could ever know."

"And I love you, my sweet girl. Forever."

Laura kissed Jillian for every minute they'd been apart and every word they had yet to say. She pulled Jillian to her feet and held her hands. "Will you do just one more thing for me?" Laura asked.

"Anything," Jillian said.

Laura led her to the open platform that jutted out over the edge of the spring. They stood side by side and looked out at the turquoise water. Jillian looked at Laura and her eyebrows pinched together. She glanced between Laura and the water and back again. Laura smiled as her heart raced. Her whole body was vibrating as she bounced on the balls of her feet.

"Are you sure?" Jillian asked.

"As sure as I'm in love with you." Jillian kissed Laura quickly before they ran off the edge of the dock and leapt into the water together.

THE END

About the Author

Tina Michele is a Florida girl living on the banks of the Indian River Lagoon in the biggest small town on the Space Coast. She enjoys all the benefits of living in the Sunshine State. During the day, she pretends to do what they pay her for but really spends most of that time daydreaming and plotting some wild adventure. She graduated from the University of Central Florida with her BA in interdisciplinary studies—the most liberal of the liberal arts degrees—majoring in fine art and writing with a minor in women's studies. To say she is motivated by her Right brain is a major understatement. Afflicted with self-diagnosed Sagittarian Attention Deficit Disorder, she spends a lot of time starting projects that she might, possibly, one day, probably finish. When she isn't writing, playing, drawing, painting, or creating something of some sort, she feeds and waters the three dogs that are permanently tethered to her hindquarters.

Books Available from Bold Strokes Books

A Moment in Time by Lisa Moreau. A longstanding family feud separates two women who unexpectedly fall in love at an antique clock shop in a small Louisiana town. (978-1-63555-419-9)

Aspen in Moonlight by Kelly Wacker. When art historian Melissa Warren meets Sula Johansen, director of a local bear conservancy, she discovers that love can come in unexpected and unusual forms. (978-1-63555-470-0)

Back to September by Melissa Brayden. Small bookshop owner Hannah Shepard and famous romance novelist Parker Bristow maneuver the landscape of their two very different worlds to find out if love can win out in the end. (978-1-63555-576-9)

Changing Course by Brey Willows. When the woman of your dreams falls from the sky, you'd better be ready to catch her. (978-1-63555-335-2)

Cost of Honor by Radclyffe. First Daughter Blair Powell and Homeland Security Director Cameron Roberts face adversity when their enemies stop at nothing to prevent President Andrew Powell's reelection. (978-1-63555-582-0)

Fearless by Tina Michele. Determined to overcome her debilitating fear through exposure therapy, Laura Carter all but fails before she's even begun until dolphin trainer Jillian Marshall dedicates herself to helping Laura defeat the nightmares of her past. (978-1-63555-495-3)

Not Dead Enough by J.M. Redmann. A woman who may or may not be dead drags Micky Knight into a messy con game. (978-1-63555-543-1)

Not Since You by Fiona Riley. When Charlotte boards her honeymoon cruise single and comes face-to-face with Lexi, the high school love she left behind, she questions every decision she has ever made. (978-1-63555-474-8)

Not Your Average Love Spell by Barbara Ann Wright. Four women struggle with who to love and who to hate while fighting to rid a kingdom of an evil invading force. (978-1-63555-327-7)

Tennessee Whiskey by Donna K. Ford. Dane Foster wants to put her life on pause and ask for a redo, a chance for something that matters. Emma Reynolds is that chance. (978-1-63555-556-1)

30 Dates in 30 Days by Elle Spencer. A busy lawyer tries to find love the fast way—thirty dates in thirty days. (978-1-63555-498-4)

Finding Sky by Cass Sellars. Skylar Addison's search for a career intersects with her new boss's search for butterflies, but Skylar can't forgive Jess's intrusion into her life. (978-1-63555-521-9)

Hammers, Strings, and Beautiful Things by Morgan Lee Miller. While on tour with the biggest pop star in the world, rising musician Blair Bennett falls in love for the first time while coping with loss and depression. (978-1-63555-538-7)

Heart of a Killer by Yolanda Wallace. Contract killer Santana Masters's only interest is her next assignment—until a chance meeting with a beautiful stranger tempts her to change her ways. (978-1-63555-547-9)

Leading the Witness by Carsen Taite. When defense attorney Catherine Landauer reluctantly becomes the key witness in prosecutor Starr Rio's latest criminal trial, their hearts, careers, and lives may be at risk. (978-1-63555-512-7)

No Experience Required by Kimberly Cooper Griffin. Izzy Treadway has resigned herself to a life without romance because of her bipolar illness but wonders what she's gotten herself into when she agrees to write a book about love. (978-1-63555-561-5)

One Walk in Winter by Georgia Beers. Olivia Santini and Hayley Boyd Markham might be rivals at work, but they discover that lonely hearts often find company in the most unexpected of places. (978-1-63555-541-7)

The Inn at Netherfield Green by Aurora Rey. Advertising executive Lauren Montgomery and gin distiller Camden Crawley don't agree on anything except saving the Rose & Crown, the old English pub that's brought them together. (978-1-63555-445-8)

Top of Her Game by M. Ullrich. When it comes to life on the field and matters of the heart, losing isn't an option for pro athletes Kenzie Shaw and Sutton Flores. (978-1-63555-500-4)

Vanished by Eden Darry. A storm is coming, and Ellery and Loveday must find the chosen one or humanity won't survive it. (978-1-63555-437-3)

All She Wants by Larkin Rose. Marci Jones and Tessa Dalton get more than they bargained for when their plans for a one-night stand turn into an opportunity for love. (978-1-63555-476-2)

Beautiful Accidents by Erin Zak. Stevie Adams and Bernadette Thompson discover that sometimes the best things in life happen purely by accident. (978-1-63555-497-7)

Before Now by Joy Argento. Can Delany and Jade overcome the betrayal that spans the centuries to reignite a love that can't be broken? (978-1-63555-525-7)

Breathe by Cari Hunter. Paramedic Jemima Pardon's chronic bad luck seems to be improving when she meets police officer Rosie Jones. But they face a battle to survive before they can find love. (978-1-63555-523-3)

Double-Crossed by Ali Vali. Hired thief and killer Reed Gable finds something in her scope that will change her life forever when she gets a contract to end casino accountant Brinley Myers's life. (978-1-63555-302-4)

False Horizons by CJ Birch. Jordan and Ash struggle with different views on the alien agenda and must find their way back to each other before they're swallowed up by a centuries-old war. (978-1-63555-519-6)

Legacy by Charlotte Greene. When five women hike to a remote cabin deep inside a national park, unsettling events suggest that they should have stayed home. (978-1-63555-490-8)

Royal Street Reveillon by Greg Herren. Someone is killing the stars of a reality show, and it's up to Scotty Bradley and the boys to find out who. (978-1-63555-545-5)

Somewhere Along the Way by Kathleen Knowles. When Maxine Cooper moves to San Francisco during the summer of 1981, she learns that wherever you run, you cannot escape yourself. (978-1-63555-383-3)

Blood of the Pack by Jenny Frame. When Alpha of the Scottish pack Kenrick Wulver visits the Wolfgangs, she falls for Zaria Lupa, a wolf on the run. (978-1-63555-431-1)

Cause of Death by Sheri Lewis Wohl. Medical student Vi Akiak and K9 Search and Rescue officer Kate Renard must work together to find a killer before they end up the next targets. In the race for survival, they discover that love may be the biggest risk of all. (978-1-63555-441-0)

Chasing Sunset by Missouri Vaun. Hijinks and mishaps ensue as Iris and Finn set off on a road trip adventure, chasing the sunset, and falling in love along the way. (978-1-63555-454-0)

Double Down by MB Austin. When an unlikely friendship with Spanish pop star Erlea turns deeper, Celeste, in-house physician for the hotel hosting Erlea's show, has a choice to make—run or double down on love. (978-1-63555-423-6)

Party of Three by Sandy Lowe. Three friends are in for a wild night at billionaire heiress Eleanor McGregor's twenty-fifth birthday party. Love, lust, and doing the right thing, even when it hurts, turn the evening into one that will change their lives forever. (978-1-63555-246-1)

Sit. Stay. Love. by Karis Walsh. City girl Alana Brendt and country vet Tegan Evans both know they don't belong together. Only problem is, they're falling in love. (978-1-63555-439-7)

Where the Lies Hide by Renee Roman. As P.I. Camdyn Stark gets closer to solving the case, will her dark secrets and the lies she's buried jeopardize her future with the quietly beautiful Sarah Peters? (978-1-63555-371-0)

Beautiful Dreamer by Melissa Brayden. With love on the line, can Devyn Winters find it in her heart to stay in the small town of Dreamer's Bay, the one place she swore she'd never remain? (978-1-63555-305-5)

Create a Life to Love by Erin Zak. When sixteen-year-old Beth shows up at her birth mother's door, three lives will change forever. (978-1-63555-425-0)

Deadeye by Meredith Doench. Stranded while hunting the serial predator Deadeye, Special Agent Luce Hansen fights for survival while her lover, forensic pathologist Harper Bennett, hunts for clues to Hansen's disappearance along the killer's trail. (978-1-63555-253-9)

Death Takes a Bow by David S. Pederson. Alan Keys takes part in a local stage production, but when the leading man is murdered, his partner Detective Heath Barrington is thrust into the limelight to find the killer. (978-1-63555-472-4)

Endangered by Michelle Larkin. Shapeshifters Officer Aspen Wolfe and Dr. Tora Madigan fight their growing attraction as they work together to destroy a secret government agency that exterminates their kind. (978-1-63555-377-2)

Incognito by VK Powell. The only thing Evan Spears is focused on is capturing a fleeing murder suspect until wild card Frankie Strong is added to her team and causes chaos on and off the job. (978-1-63555-389-5)

Insult to Injury by Gun Brooke. After losing everything, Gail Owen withdraws to her old farmhouse and finds a destitute young woman, Romi Shepherd, living in a secret room. (978-1-63555-323-9)

Just One Moment by Dena Blake. If you were given the chance to have the love of your life back, could you ignore everything that went wrong and start over again? (978-1-63555-387-1)

Scene of the Crime by MJ Williamz. Cullen Matthews finds herself caught between the woman she thinks she loves but can no longer trust and a beautiful detective she can't stop thinking about who will stop at nothing to find the truth. (978-1-63555-405-2)